NOTHING LIVES HERE

A Novel
by
Ian Mathieu

Copyright © 2024 Ian Mathieu
S.P. Press

All rights reserved.

This book is a work of fiction. Names, characters, places, and events are a product of the author's imagination or used fictitiously. Any resemblance to actual persons, living or dead, places or events is entirely coincidental.

ISBN 979-8-9918205-1-6
eBook ISBN 979-8-9918205-0-9

Cover art & design by Ian Mathieu

First paperback edition

For My Wife,
Without you this wouldn't have been possible.

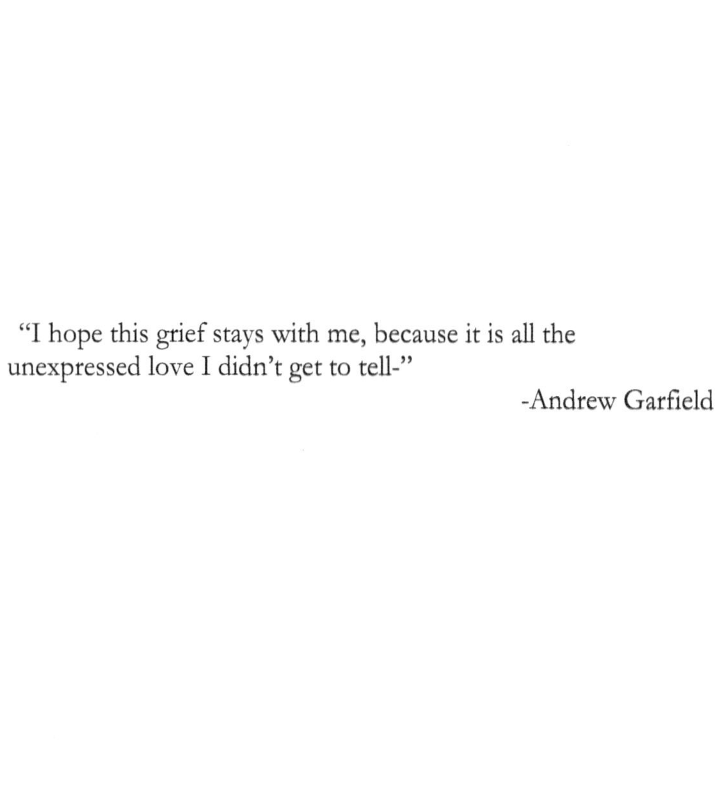

"I hope this grief stays with me, because it is all the unexpressed love I didn't get to tell-"

-Andrew Garfield

PART I

Nothing lives here
Not even me
I am beneath the waves
Observing but never knowing
Wishing but never doing
Searching but never finding

Nothing lives here
I see the light overhead
I see the trees scraping the sky
Begging to be set free
I see the people doing the same

Nothing lives here
Except for dreams
Except for hope
That we'll find what we're looking for
In time even that will leave
Nothing lives here
Not even me

Nothing lives here
You can see it in the stillness of the water
Feel it in your memories
When you drive towards the horizon

Nothing lives here
Except for the ones we leave behind
Nothing but memories to keep them close

Nothing lives here
But in my darkest moments
I return in my dream

Rising Water

My mother died on a Wednesday.

That's not where the story begins.

The story begins before I was born. Before my father and mother met at a diner on the edge of town. Before my parents were born in the same hospital, thirteen days apart, unaware the other existed. Somewhere in the darkness of time. Before God forced the world into existence and made man live together in depravity.

I don't know where the story started, but I know how it ends. Blood, tears, and a storm like no other.

To understand what happened, you need to understand where I grew up.

Clareborne, North Dakota was a nice enough place. Nestled along the northern shore of Devil's Lake, on the southern edge of Ramsey County.

Lots of people live in small towns, but mine seemed especially small. Maybe because I always hoped I would move on to something bigger. Maybe it was the way you felt when you looked out over the fields. Nothing but grass and wind all the way to the horizon.

Most of the roads in Clareborne weren't even paved. The houses were small and worn down. Dust kicked up from the roads and covered everything in a layer of grit.

Every new day brought more of the same. Wake up, absorb the bleak emptiness, wish you were somewhere else. Rinse. Repeat.

For everything it lacked, Clareborne wasn't without its charms. The town was beautiful, in its own way. When the leaves changed in the fall, the foliage would set fire to the lake. Brilliant shades of orange and red reflected on the rippling surface. Spring gave birth to new life. Birds and flowers of a thousand colors emerged from their winter sleep. The summer skies were the most beautiful on the planet. A billion stars shined down over the water. In the winter, the world went quiet. The lake froze over. Animals slept in their dens. Birds flew south. The town rested in tranquil silence.

Life seemed simple where I grew up. The type of place where you recognized every face on the street. People went to church on Sundays. High school kids said their prayers at night, then snuck out and got drunk in Ruger Park. Teenagers made out in cars and tried to run when the police showed up- as if the cops didn't know them by name.

People were nice to each other, for the most part. They waved when they passed you in the street. Had cookouts and invited the whole block. Took in your trash cans on Wednesday morning if they noticed you left them on the curb. Started rumors about their neighbors. Whispered about them when they weren't around.

Normal, small-town stuff.

You knew every story someone had to tell before you even met them. Knew their secrets. All the worst things they've done. The part in the back of their minds where perversion is free to roam in the shadows. Keeping a secret was hard, especially in Clareborne.

Devil's Lake started rising back in '93. I hadn't been born yet, but I heard the story so much I might as well have been. Everyone thought that would be the end of it. The water would go down and things would go back to normal. They weren't so lucky. People around here don't get lucky. The rain kept coming- which was inevitable- but some people, blinded by optimism, thought things wouldn't get worse.

The lake shot up twenty feet in less than a decade, and there's no end in sight. You'd think the town was small enough, but every year the rain comes, and every year the lake rises a little more. Each time, our small town gets a little smaller.

When the water kept coming people had a decision to make. Leave and start over in a new place with new people or adapt to the changes God brought to them.

When I was young, I thought about God all the time. I guess most people did, considering all the churches we had around. The only thing there were more of than churches were liquor stores. I always thought that was strange, but at the same time, it seemed to fit. If God didn't solve your problems, then at least you could forget them for a while.

Not everyone was religious, but most people were- or at least said they were. My dad was one of the few who wasn't. He used to be, but he lost his faith. It's not that my dad didn't believe in God. I know he did. He just disagreed with the way God was running things. After my mother died, he stopped going to church, stopped doing a lot of things.

I never minded the lake rising. I was a kid then. I didn't understand how it was hurting people. I always thought it was beautiful. Nature fighting back. Reclaiming its territory. Bringing the world back to its domain. Unapologetic and free.

There was a house out in the middle of the lake. No one lived there anymore on account of the first floor being underwater. It was like something out of a fairy tale. I would make up stories about the little girl who lived there. Trapped inside her castle. Defending it from the monsters who prowled the lake.

A spot along the shore near my grandpa's had a perfect view of that house. He used to take me there so we could look at it when my dad was at work. Which was a lot, seeing as he was the Sheriff.

When dad was around, he'd tell me about his cases. Not the bloody or scary ones, but the ones he thought I'd like. We used to call them his adventures. I always wanted to have adventures of my own.

My adventure didn't start the way I planned. The day I left, everything happened so fast. I never got to tell my dad I wasn't mad at him. That I understood the pain he was going through.

That I forgave him. I would have told him- if it wasn't for the circumstances.

I wasn't sure if I wanted to go at all. I didn't want to leave him all alone. I didn't want him to feel lost and abandoned, the way I did after my mother died.

In the end, I wanted to stay. To watch out for him. Sometimes life doesn't work out the way we want it to. Sometimes God has other plans.

The Tree

Sheriff Roy Hill's truck rattled to a stop on the edge of the field. His head pounded. He wasn't hungover. He hadn't been hungover in quite some time, but it was only six-thirty in the morning, and his temples throbbed. He grabbed a handful of Tylenol from the glove box and swallowed them dry. The pills never helped, but he took them anyway.

The truck door creaked closed on half-frozen hinges. Wind stung his face as he took in his surroundings. A patchwork of snow and dry yellow grass spread towards the horizon until it touched the cloudless, grey sky. The road was jagged and uneven. Imperfections sculpted into place by the nighttime freeze.

The call came in about an hour before. He was still asleep when Jane rang him from the station. Jim Crawford spotted something strange out in his field on the way into town. Jane said he sounded really shaken up on the phone. Jim was so shocked he could barely tell her what was wrong.

Sheriff Hill walked towards a nearby squad car. Officer Parker sat inside. He looked nervous in the way he always did. On edge, like a kid who broke a vase and was waiting in his room for his mother to come home and find out.

"Where is she, Toby?" asked Sheriff Hill.

Officer Parker jumped at the sudden noise. He looked up at the Sheriff, surprised to see him there.

"By the tree. Out in the field." Toby's voice trembled. "Jane's already out there."

"Alone?"

"No. Hannah's with her."

"Why aren't you?"

"I was but- I- I couldn't look at it anymore."

Sheriff Hill nodded. He understood. Not everyone had the misfortune of being used to this kind of thing. *'Used to'* was an odd way to put it. You never got used to it. You became numb. It still bothered you, but as the years went by you got calluses. The feeling didn't overwhelm you as much.

***

The tree twisted from the ground, knotted and bare. Not a single leaf clung to the branches. A gnarled hand that reached towards the heavens with a thousand boney fingers.

Jane and Hannah were beneath the tree. Jane paced as she stared at the sky through the branches. Hannah crouched by the trunk. She examined the body of the girl that sat against it.

"How are we today, ladies?" asked Sheriff Hill as he walked up.

"Morning, Sheriff." Jane tried her best not to look uncomfortable.

"Any news?"

"Nothing yet. No ID or personal items."

Sheriff Hill looked at the body. Her features were familiar. She was tall, a few inches shy of six feet. High cheek bones painted with freckles. Long blonde hair hung down far past her waste. She was young. Couldn't have been older than sixteen. For a moment he thought it was his daughter sitting beneath that tree. His heart stopped. He saw her face everywhere he looked. But this girl wasn't Georgia. Georgia wasn't around anymore. She was somewhere a long way from here. Living her life as far from Devil's Lake as she could get.

The dead girl's legs were tucked under her, giving the impression she knelt on the frost-hardened grass. Her hair was sprawled across the ground beneath her. She was pale, except on her left side where the skin transitioned to crimson and purple. Her soft green eyes were open. Pale, like the rest of her. Clouded over so nothing reflected inside.

She stared out over the field, not focused on anything in particular. The eyes would have been the worst part if it weren't for her hands. Laid gently in her lap, fingers linked together. Sitting down to pray. Only resting. Ready to stand any minute and go about her business.

"Did anyone find her shoes?" asked the Sheriff.

"No," said Jane.

He looked from the girl to Jane. Even with her dark complexion, he could see the green tinge of her skin. She was one of the fortunate ones. Not yet numbed by the past.

"Officer Barlowe," said the Sheriff. "Could you go back to the car and help Toby, please?"

"Yes, Sir," Jane glanced down at the base of the tree. "Thank you, Sir." Jane walked back across the field towards the squad cars.

Hannah stood and turned towards Roy. He caught the smell of strawberries as her dark hair mingled with the winter wind.

"Hey, Roy" said Hannah, with not quite a smile. "It's been a while."

"Yeah, it has. Sorry it had to be under these circumstances." The Sheriff's eyes drifted to the grass as he rubbed his fingers across the three-day stubble on his chin. "So, what do we have?"

"White female, between fifteen and twenty. Dead at least eight hours. It's been below zero since last night so it's hard to narrow it down."

"Overdose?"

They had become more and more common over the years. Especially with younger folks. Seems like people would rather run from their troubles than try to face them. He knew the feeling.

"Could be," said Hannah. "She's got the track marks of a long-time user, but there's no paraphernalia."

"Could be the cold killed her."

"Maybe, but whatever it was, it didn't happen here."

"How do you mean?"

"Lividity is only present on the left side of the body. She was laying on her side for a while after she died. Probably while she was being moved. No sign of frostbite in her feet so she didn't walk out here. If she did, someone took her shoes after the fact. It's hard to tell anything else. Her clothes are frozen on her body. I won't have specifics until after the autopsy. But whether this was an accident or something else. She didn't get out here herself."

I Heard She Was Murdered

The Red Top Diner served the best coffee in town- which wasn't saying much. Sheriff Hill sat in the corner booth. Jane sat across from him, smack in the middle of the stereotypical picture window straight out of an Edward Hopper painting.
Roy enjoyed his usual. Two eggs, wheat toast with lots of butter, a side of bacon, and black coffee.

He had a lot of memories at the Red Top. The checkered pattern of dirty, white-and-red tile reminded him of simpler times.

He'd been sitting in this very booth by the window when he saw Linda for the first time. Not the "first time" first time. He'd seen her around. On the street, and in the halls at school. She sat in the front row of his chemistry class in junior year of high school. Their paths had crossed, the way everyone's paths cross in a small town, but that day, sitting alone in a run-down diner was the first time he really *saw* her. Red button-down shirt, white apron, and a ribbon holding her hair back in a messy ponytail. She smelled like kitchen grease and maple syrup, and it took his breath away.

He'd been sitting at the counter when he asked her out for the first time. He acted confident, like he was hot shit with his leather jacket and slicked hair. He was amazed when she said yes.

That was before the world had gone crazy. Before everything he cared for was taken away. When he wanted to forget the things that rattled around inside his head. He still wanted to forget those things, but he chose to live with the pain. The way he saw it, he deserved it.

Back then he came to the diner every morning to have a chance to talk to her. Now he came here because it was the only place in town where people didn't bring her up when they talked to him.

"You gonna finish that bacon?" Jane eyed his plate as she shoved a forkful of pancake into her mouth.

He slid his plate to her.

"So, any ideas how that girl could have gotten out there?" Jane spoke through mouthfuls of sopping pancakes and crisp bacon.

"Maybe. Guess it depends."

"Depends on what?"

"Whether or not you can talk without your mouth full."

Jane chewed the rest of her bite and swallowed. "Sorry."

Sheriff Hill took a long sip of coffee. He didn't want to talk about the girl. She reminded him too much of Georgia. Too much of her mother. Too much of what he didn't have anymore. But if he wanted to solve this case then it would be all he talked about for the foreseeable future. "The way I see it there are two options. She got high, stumbled around in the dark not knowing up from sideways until she finally collapsed out there beneath that tree. Or she OD'd at her place- maybe a friend's place. Whoever she was with panicked, drove her out there to the middle of nowhere and dumped her."

"But Hannah said she couldn't have walked there. She didn't have any shoes on. She'd have had frostbite. Hell, it was so cold that night she'd probably would've had frostbite with her shoes on."

"Right. So that leaves us with option two."

Jane nodded. Disagreement was clear on her face. "Do you really believe that?"

He didn't. He'd have preferred a simple answer. An overdose. An accident. A mistake. An explanation that could wrap up the case and put it behind them. He hoped the feeling he got at the crime scene was wrong, the cold trickle down his spine, the bitter taste that coated his tongue.

Jane had instincts that far surpassed his own. They were what made her such a good detective. If she had the same feeling he had then he couldn't deny it anymore. "You think it's something more than that?"

"I don't know. I guess to me it just doesn't seem so- simple."

"Elaborate."

"I don't know. Something about it wasn't right. Everything just seemed- off."

"Off? In what way?"

"I mean weird. Like, if she OD'd like you said, and they wanted to get rid of her body. Why leave her out in the field like that? Go another half mile you can hide her in the woods. A few more miles you can put her in the river."

"But they didn't do either of those things."

"No, they didn't."

"What does that tell us?"

"Could mean they wanted us to find her."

He saw the gears turning in Jane's head. Trying to put together a puzzle to which they only had a few pieces and no picture to go on. An impossible task. "Could mean nothing. What else was there."

"You said she was dumped out in the field. That she might have collapsed out there. But that's not right. She wasn't just thrown beneath the tree. She was placed there. Posed. I mean she looked like she was at prayer for fuck's sake. That's not something you do if you're a tweaker trying to get rid of a body. It's too organized. Too specific."

Roy drained the last of his coffee. "Whoever left her there managed to stay calm long enough to pose her in plain sight of the road. Which means he didn't care if someone saw him. Or that making sure she was posed like that was more important to him than not getting caught."

Jane deflated. "A lot of theories. But theories mean nothing if they're all we have. No one even knows who she is."

"Someone knows her. And they know who she knows, and they know who they think did it. And I guarantee if someone thinks it, they will say it out loud to someone else."

"I've got an ex like that," said Jane. "So that's what we're going to do? Sit around and hope someone tells us who killed her?"

"We don't need them to tell us who killed her. We just need them to tell us something about her. No use trying to fit together the puzzle if were missing most of the pieces. We just need to talk to someone who knows something. Or at least thinks they know something. Rumors can be powerful things. Especially if you find someone who knows enough of them."

Jane took a sip of her coffee, staring at someone approaching over Sheriff Hill's shoulder. "Speak of the devil."

"Morning, officers. Anyone want a warm-up?"

"Sure, Dottie." The Sheriff inhaled the aroma of nutty, slightly burnt coffee as Dottie emptied the last dregs of the pot into his cup.

"Any for you, sweetheart? I'll make up another pot."

"I'm fine, thanks," said Jane.

Dottie lingered at the side of the table for a bit too long, fussing at her dyed red beehive of hair and rearranging the straws she kept in the pocket of her apron.

"Something we can help you with, Dottie?" asked Sheriff Hill.

"Me? No, I don't think so." Dottie placed a curled finger over her lip as if deep in thought. "Well, now that you mention it-" Dottie slid into the booth beside Jane, making herself at home. "-I was wondering if there was any news about that girl."

"What girl?" asked Sheriff Hill.

"The one Jimmy found out in that field. He ain't been the same since. Nightmares and what not. Rebecca says he can't sleep through the night. Makes you curious what someone could have done to her to have Big Jim all worked up like that." Dottie's voice was one of casual conversation, but her eyes burned with curiosity. Everyone around here had to know everything about everyone.

"No one did anything. Just an accident."

"An accident, huh?" Dottie laced her fingers together and leaned across the table towards Sheriff Hill. "That's not what people are saying."

"What are they saying?" asked the Sheriff.

"Well, people say lots of things." Dottie examined her cherry red nail polish, pretended she wasn't dying to share what she knew. "But I don't give credence to rumors."

"I'm sure you don't. But I admit, I'm interested to hear what you've heard about her."

Dottie sat up straight, an over ambitious school kid who wanted to prove to their teacher they had all the answers. "Well. Some people say she was on drugs- you know what the kids are like these days- and maybe she was, but God tells us not to judge others, so I just mind my own business."

"Clearly," mumbled Jane.

Dottie gave her a sidelong glance but continued her rambling. "No one seems to know who the girl is. No word of anyone missing or anything like that, and the Lord knows if there was someone missing the people around here would know all about it. You know what it's like, no one can seem to just mind their own business nowadays." Dottie glanced at Jane, awaiting another snarky comment. None came. "Some people think she's from out of town, got lost somehow and wandered out in the cold. But if you want to know what I think-" Dottie leaned in closer. She looked around the room as if she cared at all about being overheard. "I heard she was murdered."

"Murdered?" said Sheriff Hill. "Don't you think that's a bit farfetched?"

"That's just what I heard."

"And who'd you hear it from?"

"Elaine. Told me Earl heard it from Ed at the bait shop. Said she was frozen to the bone. Clothes all iced up. Face discolored like someone might of did something to her."

A look passed between Sheriff Hill and Jane. A wordless acknowledgment of a problem. Someone on the force was sharing information that hadn't been in the papers.

"Elaine also said she dated Paul McCartney," said Jane.

"Well, it's not just her. The whole towns heard it. You know how people talk."

"They've got nothing to worry about. The girl she just-" Roy lowered his voice so only Dottie and Jane could hear. "She overdosed. That's it. Happens all the time."

"God help us." Dottie looked to the ceiling and made a cross over her heart. "Don't matter how it happened. You know they're gonna believe whatever they believe. And right now, they think someone killed that girl."

"That's ridiculous," said Roy. "That kind of thing doesn't happen here."

"Doesn't happen?" Dottie let out an exasperated breath. "Then how do you explain that business in Edmonton last fall?"

"That was different."

Roy could tell Dottie wanted to argue but something in his eyes must have made her reconsider.

"Well, maybe," said Dottie. "Doesn't change the fact people are scared. Doors have started locking at night. Jim and Becky won't even let Sarah walk home from school. Jim's been leaving work early every day to pick her up and I don't blame him. Seeing that girl like that. He probably sees little Sarah under that tree every time he thinks about it. She must have been so scared. All alone out in the cold in the middle of nowhere. Anything could have happened to her. I can't even imagine how her parents feel. To lose a daughter like that. Here one minute and gone the next."

Roy stood and took his wallet from his back pocket. "There's nothing to worry about." Roy laid a twenty on the table. "And tell Elaine to stop spreading rumors. It's not helping anybody."

<u>Henry</u>

Roy spent most of the job on the road. Solitary drives traveling from town to town, case to case. The drives were all the same, straight roads cut through never-ending flatness. That about summed up Ramsey County, thirteen hundred square miles of flat. Vacant grass fields checkered with occasional houses and trees that failed to break up the monotony.

The drives weren't all bad. They got him away from home. Away from his father, whose constant ignorance of Georgia's absence ensured Roy could never forget it. Away from the lake, sitting in silent judgement of all the people it destroyed. He even considered some of those days' good ones, when he was able to put distance between himself and here.

Today wasn't a good day.

The rain started on the way back from the station. He rolled down the window despite the chill. Cold air blew over him, relieving some of the pressure behind his eyes. His head still throbbed- it always did- but for now, it was bearable.

The lake blurred by outside the passenger window. A sheet of ice reaching towards the horizon. The lake would be frozen for at least another month. Maybe longer, given how cold this winter had been.

He often caught himself looking out over the water. His stomach tightening as the tide rippled across the surface, calm and uncaring. The sun reflected on the waves. Arrogant. Sitting beneath the sky, knowing nothing could stop it. The way it said, *"Look what I can take. Look what I can take without even trying."*

That's what the lake did. It took and took, until there was nothing left. Winter was the only time he could stand it. When the water froze and the lake couldn't do anything to stop it. Trapped in its own skin. A cage of its own making.

Something about the layer of ice calmed him. Like the world was fighting back, saying, *"We're not gonna let you take anything else."*

In a couple months, spring would come, and the ice would thaw. For now, it had to wait like everyone else. Stop whatever it was doing and wait for a spring day when it was warmer, and the sun was shining.

The brakes whined as the Sheriff pulled into the driveway. He turned the key and listened to the engine fade. He'd been searching through missing persons reports for three days, trying to ID the Jane Doe. He hadn't had any luck.

She might live out of state. If she was from North Dakota, no one reported her missing. It was a common thing with users. They'd leave home, and their parents -secretly glad they didn't have to deal with them anymore- never looked.

Living with an addict isn't easy. They lie and break promises. Swear they'll try harder. They don't. They mean to- most of the time- but they don't. It takes a toll on people. Sometimes it's harder on the family than it is on the person. That didn't change the fact a little girl was dead, and nobody was looking for her.

Since the body appeared, everyone in town asked him what happened. He told them all the same thing. *"It was an accident.",* *"She overdosed."* Now the rumors about murder had started and it was hard to tell them anything different. Accident or not, people will only believe what they want to believe.

The truth was, he didn't know what happened. They wouldn't until after Hannah performed the autopsy. Due to the nature of living in a frozen wasteland, an autopsy had proved complicated. The night the body found its way under the tree had been cold. Cold enough for a body left outside for an extended period to freeze. Before an autopsy could determine the cause of death,

Jane Doe needed to thaw. That could take a lot longer than someone might think.

Roy got out of his truck and walked towards the house. The screen door hung open at the end of the driveway, slapping against the wall whenever the wind came.

"Dad?" called Sheriff Hill. "Dad, you here?"

He waited for a response. Silence answered.

He walked down the hallway to his father's room. His steps were measured and calm, they needed to be. If he rushed, he would be admitting something might be wrong.

He opened the door to his father's room.

Empty.

Kitchen, living room, basement.

Empty.

His stomach clenched. This wasn't happening. *Not again.*

"Dad? Dad, where are you?" He ran back outside. Praying to himself as he rounded the gate into the backyard. Begging whoever was listening that the feeling in his stomach was wrong.

He looked towards the water and started to breathe again.

His father stood on the shore. The remnants of his snow-white hair waved in the winter breeze. Roy walked up to him, calmly, so as not to worry him.

"Dad, why are you outside by yourself? Where's your nurse?"

His father stared out at the lake. The groan of the ice echoed beneath the surface.

"She's in the water," said his father.

"What do you mean?" The panic he had reigned in moments before bubbled back to the surface.

"Georgia. She's in the water. She's got that coat on. The red one her mother liked."

Roy let out his breath, the tension in his chest replaced by fluttering emptiness.

His father's memory had been getting worse since the diagnosis. Dementia. The doctor said it was in the early stages, but he'd declined over the last few months. He could still take care of himself- for the most part. Roy hired a nurse to help him in case he got confused. He forgot things from time to time. Not the big things. He remembered his birthday and his anniversary. He remembered mom passing on. His parents and his sisters. Linda dying.

His father remembered a lot of things, but something about Georgia didn't stick. He knew everything about her, but he could never seem to get hold of the fact she wasn't around anymore. He didn't want to remember that part. If he couldn't remember her leaving, she'd always be around.

His father's memory wasn't the only thing affected. He still talked the same and walked the same, but deep down something was different. From day to day, moment to moment you never knew who you'd be interacting with when you talked to him: A sick old man. A middle-aged man with a teenager at home. A newlywed with a son on the way.

"How was she?" asked Roy. Letting his father stay for a while in a world where Georgia was still here.

"I don't know. We didn't get to talk. She seemed sad, though. Something was bothering her. I wanted to say hello but-something in her eyes told me she needed to be alone for a while."

His father turned towards him. A look of realization crossed his face. Noticing his son, he smiled. "Roy? How are you? You come by to paint the barn?"

Roy pressed his fingertips into his eyes, anything to relieve the pounding pressure behind them. "Not today, dad. Just came to see how you're doing."

"Well hell, I'm alright. How's Georgia? She still writing poetry? I'd love to read some more of it. Say, why don't you call her? Have her stop by. I'll throw some steaks on. We'll have a couple beers."

"Not tonight. I got a new case. I'm tired."

"Well alright. I get it. Work. Believe me." Henry stopped to gather his thoughts. "How 'bout you come by this weekend then? We can start fixing up the barn."

"I can't this weekend, Dad. I got a case. Maybe we can start next month."

"Well, that's alright, don't worry. Probably for the best anyway. Rain keeps up this whole place will be underwater by next spring.

I just hate to see it so run down. That was your favorite place when you were a kid. Remember?"

The barn held a special place in Roy's heart when he was young. He would hide away in there. An escape from the noise of the real world. When he got older, he would sneak in girls or bottles of liquor. Spend the night wishing he was somewhere else.

When Georgia discovered the barn, it became her safe space. She would play farmer and organize all the junk his father had piled up over the years. That barn was their oasis. A fond memory shared between father and daughter. Now it was a ruin. A memory of times dead and gone. "Yeah, Dad. I remember."

"I bet you do. Couldn't get you to come out of there if I tried. You used to say *'I have to protect my castle. There's a monster on the lake.'*" His father laughed as he reminisced. "You remember when I caught you in there with that girl? What was her name? Pretty little thing. Black hair. Used to wear your leather jacket all around town." His father's lips curled into a smile.

Roy started to smile too. The expression foreign to his face.

"Hannah," said Roy. "Her name was Hannah."

"Hannah!" said his father. "That's right. How is she? You still see her?"

"Yeah, every once in a while, for work. She's doin' alright. I think." Roy thought of Hannah, of the time they used to spend together. Days blowing off school and nights drinking under the stars, hopelessly in love the way kids in high school were.

High school was long gone now, the memories smudged by the passing of time and the worries of life. Before a few days ago, he hadn't seen Hannah in almost eight months.

"Just for work?" asked his father.

"Yeah, Dad. Just for work. I don't have time for anything else. I don't have the energy."

"You should make the time. Everyone needs someone."

"I got you, Dad."

"*Hah.* I'm hardly company. Besides that's not what I mean. I mean someone special. Someone who makes you want to get up in the morning. Makes you want to be a better person. Your mother was that for me. Best woman there ever was." His father still smiled, but a sadness crept into his eyes. "Losing your person is hard. Especially when you don't get as much time with them as you expected."

Roy looked out over the lake. A cold stretch of unrelenting ice stared back. "How did you do it after mom died? How did you get yourself through it?"

His father was silent for a long while. "I think of the good times. The laughs. The love. We had a lot of good years. I knew if I just sat there and missed her, I'd go crazy. And I know- I know that with Linda gone, it feels like there's no point going on. And I know you think you owe it to her to be alone, but you don't. You deserve someone to spend your life with and Georgia deserves a mother."

Anger slipped into Roy's voice. "Georgia has a mother."

His father hung his head, a sigh left his lips, soft and tired. "I'm sorry, Roy. I didn't mean anything like that."

A weight pressed on Roy's chest. Memories flooded his head. Rain and thunder. A shower running in an empty room. Georgia sitting up in bed, wondering what was wrong with her mom. The pictures came to him all at once, chiseled themselves inside his skull. This was the pain of remembering. The pain he deserved.

"I know dad. It's just been a long day."

His father regarded the lake as he sauntered closer to the shore. "You know, our family's been here a long time. Your grandfather used to sit right there on the back porch and tell me about the lake. Its history. He said the Dakota people called it Spirit Lake. Said they would see mirages across the water. Echoes of their lost loved ones. When your grandma died, your grandpa told me she was still here with us. Out there in the lake. Waiting for us in the mist. Down below the water where no one could hurt her."

Roy's father stepped out onto an outcropping of rock that hung over the frozen lake. The place Georgia and her mother used to sit together whenever they would visit. "You wouldn't know it now, but at one time, this lake was all but gone. Drought back in the thirties. Dried everything up until the water damn near disappeared. I used to walk out on the lakebed for miles, searching for my mother, but I never found her out there. The water was gone. She had nowhere to stay anymore. Nothing left to protect her. Now look at it." He thrust his arms out to the sides to detail the grandeur of the lake. "You can barely see one shore from the other."

Roy studied the lake, scanning the surface with weary eyes. He listened to the groan of the ice. Pictured the people he loved, trapped under the surface in stygian darkness. "I see them too. Mom. Grandpa. Linda." *Georgia.* He thought it but couldn't say it. He couldn't bring himself to burden his father with reality. "I miss them. I miss them so much."

His father nodded in understanding. "I have a question for you."

"What's that?"

"I'm not sure if it's a good time to ask this but- Who are you?"

Roy's heart sank to his feet. "What?"

His father gawked at him with unblinking eyes. The stare lasted too long before his father relented. "I'm just messing with you, Roy."

"That's not funny."

"Just trying to lighten the mood. You never did have a sense of humor. You get that from your grandmother."

They looked over the lake, laughing together as the sun disappeared behind the trees. An insatiable beast who took until there was nothing left.

<u>Happiness</u>

My next-door neighbor growing up was Mrs. Andrews. She was my freshman-year English teacher. She's the one who got me interested in poetry. She let me borrow some of her books: William Blake, Phyllis Wheatley, Dickinson. Her copy of Leaves of Grass is still on a shelf at my dad's house. When I look back, Mrs. Andrews was one of the people who affected me the most.

Mrs. Andrews always told me I could be great. The parts of me I thought were broken were the parts that made me unique. Some of the best poets ever were troubled beyond belief. Broken, but beautiful. When it comes to what's good and what's bad, it's all about perspective.

She made me believe I could be something. I wasn't sure what that something was, but I knew it was a whole lot better than nothing. I hadn't believed in myself since before my mother died, maybe not ever. I guess I didn't really think about it before then.

Mrs. Andrews showed me kindness at a time when I thought nothing good was left in the world. How could there be? In a world without my mother's laugh. A world where my father didn't smile- didn't even move unless it was to reach for a bottle. Everything good in my life rotted away the second my mother's heart stopped beating.

Mrs. Andrews showed me the beauty I'd refused to see. The poetry in the shaking of the trees. The dance of leaves on the wind. The impossible perfection in the chaos of the rain.

A couple years after I left school, Mrs. Andrew's husband died. A brain hemorrhage, right at the kitchen table while he ate his oatmeal. She drank herself to death two weeks after his funeral. Whenever someone brought her up that's the part they remembered. Not the kids she helped or the good she did.

I had another neighbor named Henry Samuels. He lived two houses down on the corner of Brook Street. We called him Uncle Henry. He would sit out on his porch and tell stories. He wasn't telling them to anybody in particular. He sat outside in his rocking chair all day and rambled to whoever wanted to listen. He gave all the kids change for ice cream when the truck came around. He kept it all in a big empty can of Campbell's baked beans. He once told us he forced a truck full of people off a cliff in Korea, during the war. He said it was him or them, and their screams still haunted him. A few days later when Sarah Crawford asked him about it, he said killing those men made him feel alive.

There's good and bad in everyone. For some reason even an ocean of good couldn't cover up a drop of bad. When you lived around here, bad clung to you every step you took. Like the town itself wasn't content until it drained the happiness from you.

I always thought I didn't deserve to be happy. Maybe it was trauma. Maybe it was my mother dying when I was young. Maybe it's because she died the way she did. I don't know. I used to think about it whenever I had a free moment. Which was a lot considering my dad was always working and I didn't have many friends.

For a long time, my grandpa was my only real friend. He was always sweet to me. I used to write poetry and he was the only one I would let read it. I knew he'd never judge me.

Grandpa showed me a place in the woods. A little pebble-covered beach hidden away from everything else. You could sit on the rocks with your feet in the water and see the parts of town where no one lived anymore. The places the lake swallowed up. Flooded churches and sunken farm equipment. Houses with broken windows. Missing doors filled with shadows. They looked like the faces of the demons they talked about at church. That sunken house sat right in the middle of all of it. My castle on the sea, calling to me on the wind. Beckoning me towards it like sirens on the rocks.

Grandpa always took me camping in the summertime. We would pack up the car with a tent and sleeping bags. We filled an old blue Coleman cooler with hot dogs and all the ingredients for s'mores. He'd drive us to the little path on the edge of town that led down to our secret beach. He'd always pretend he didn't know how to set up the tent and ask me to help him. We spent those nights laughing and looking up at the stars.

After Grandpa fell asleep, I would stay up. I watched the fire through the open flap of the tent. The way the flames flickered and snapped, casting warm orange light across everything. The logs popped. Sparks floated towards the night sky to dance with the stars. I watched the fire until the last flame disappeared into a whisp of grey smoke, and the dull red glow of the coals faded into the night.

Grandpa would wake up before sunrise and cook us eggs on a big sheet of metal he put over the fire. They were always better than the eggs at home, filled with the taste of smoke and nature.

After breakfast we would go to morning mass at St. Peters. The pastor stood in front of the pews and talked to the congregation. He wore black robes, and a white collar around his neck. I often found myself pulling on my own collar, feeling restrained and suffocated.

The pastor spoke about sin and how the only way to be forgiven for our sins was by the grace of almighty God. If we didn't accept God into our hearts and know his love, then we would never know redemption in the eyes of the Lord.

Had God forgiven my mother? Would he forgive me for the anger I held towards her? Why would God put my mother through something like that? Why would he put me and Dad through it?

I tried asking a few people at the church about it. They all said the same thing: *"God has a reason for all things,"* or *"The Lord works in mysterious ways."*

I didn't know if God had forgiven my mother, but I knew I hadn't forgiven Him for the way He tore apart my family.

I spent most of my time at mine and Grandpa's spot. That little stretch of beach was the only place I wanted to be. When I couldn't go there in person, I visited in my head. When I had a bad day or things got hard at home. My safe place. Somewhere I could rest and no one could find me.

I stopped going to school sometime in junior year. I couldn't see the point. No one let me forget I was the girl with the dead mother and drunk father. No one was ever home to make me go anyway. Even when Dad was home, he wasn't there.

I did have a few other friends besides Grandpa. The one I spent the most time with was Tommy. He used to hang around at the Red Top Diner. My mother worked there before she passed. He seemed to be there every time I went. He would look around the room like a lost puppy dog. Something about him pulled me in.

Tommy was handsome enough, in a scruffy, hometown kind of way. A shy smile and sad blue eyes. Eyes you could see yourself drowning in. I think what I liked about him at first was he was a stranger. He had stories to tell. Secrets no one knew. It's hard to be interested in someone when you know everything they've ever done before you go on your first date.

The more Tommy and I talked, the more I liked him. He seemed so strange to me, a book with hidden pages I longed to read. The idea of someone with secrets was foreign to me. The curiosity to learn about him itched beneath my skin.

I showed him the spot on the lake, so he would have somewhere to go when he needed time for himself. We used to go there together. That was the spot where he kissed me for the first time, and where we saw each other for the last time.

After I left, Tommy still stopped by our spot all the time. I think it was his way of visiting me, even though I wasn't there anymore. He never wanted to be home. His father beat on him and his mother. I felt bad for him. I know my dad had his problems, but he never laid a hand on me or my mother. My father was a good man. Troubled. The way we all are. But good.

I was too young to understand back then. I thought my dad hated me for what happened to my mother. He didn't. He was too scared to face his troubles. So, he ran. Just like me.

<u>Who Was She?</u>

The posters were all over town. You couldn't go to your neighbors to borrow a cup of sugar without seeing her face.

A week had passed since the body was found. The rumors and theorizing led them nowhere. Everyone thought they knew who the girl under the tree was, thought they knew a guy who knew a guy who knew her father or brother or uncle. No one did, and no one came forward to claim her. Seven days since a little girl died and no one cared enough to ask where she was.

Eight days after Jane Doe's death something promising came along. Nothing positive. Someone who might have seen her north of town near Sweetwater a couple days before the body was found.

Roy knew the place. He'd been called out to it on several occasions. The house was owned by a young man named Leroy Kent. He'd just finished his latest stint in prison for possession with intent. He'd been out for three months now.

Roy and Jane sat in silence as they headed towards the address. The only sound was the rumble of the engine and the wind that whistled through the crack in the window.

"I'm sorry about the other day." Jane looked out the passenger window. "At the crime scene."

Roy's gaze shifted from the road to Jane. He scratched at his ever-growing stubble, unsure how to respond to the sudden proclamation. "Nothing to apologize for. It's not easy looking at things like that."

"No, it's not that. I just felt like I knew her, when I looked at her, even though I didn't. It was her eyes. The way they stared at everything and nothing at the same time. They just-"

Jane's eyes stayed glued to the horizon. The cab of the truck oozed with tangible stillness.

"I know what you mean," said Roy. "Happens to everyone." The weight of the girl's eyes pressed on his chest. Green, like Georgia's. Those eyes were everywhere, whether he was awake or dreaming. He swallowed down the lump of hard sinew in his throat. He wanted to tell Jane he understood. To bring her some sort of comfort. But he couldn't. "Like I said, it's not easy. You got nothing to apologize for."

Roy pretended not to notice when Jane wiped away a tear. She turned from the window and looked at him, quick to change the subject. "So, any plans for Christmas?"

"It'll just be me and my father. Nothing too extravagant. Just dinner probably. How about you?"

"Not sure. My mom's been leaving me voicemails. She really wants me to spend it with her."

"That could be nice."

"Maybe. We just- It's been a while since we've seen each other. We're not on the best of terms."

"I get that. Family can be tough. I'm not the best person to speak on things like this, but I think you should go. If it doesn't work out, you're always welcome to join me and my old man."

"Thanks, Sheriff. I appreciate it." Jane looked back out the window as they pulled up to their destination.

The house was far past being rundown. To say it should have been condemned was an understatement. Moss covered the few shingles that still clung to the roof. Every window had at least one smashed pane. The frame rotted beneath a layer of peeled paint.

Roy and Jane stood on the crumbling concrete steps, waiting for someone to answer the door.

Inside the house, someone stumbled. The door creaked open. A tall, rawboned young man answered. He opened the door as far as the chain lock would allow. He peered at the officers with bloodshot eyes. From the small amount of his face they could see, it was apparent he wasn't well. Lurid yellow skin and hollow eyes. His face covered with the scabs and pits of a long-time user.

"Hello?" said the man.

"Leroy," said Sheriff Hill. "You're just the man I was hoping to see. Is anyone else home today?"

Leroy shook his head. Unaware of what was happening around him.

"Well, I'm here to ask about a friend of yours," said Sheriff Hill. Jane pulled out a picture of the girl and handed it to Roy.

Leroy didn't bother to look before responding. "Never seen her. No friend of mine."

"You sure?" asked Sheriff Hill. "She's never been here? Maybe she stopped by once or twice to pick something up? Why don't you have a closer look?" Sheriff Hill moved closer to the door, the picture out in front of him.

Leroy gave the picture a fleeting glance. "I never seen her."

"Well, maybe your friends have seen her. Could I speak to one of them please?"

"No one else is here, Sheriff. Like I said before."

"Well, do you mind if we come in and check? Just to make sure?"

"You got a warrant, Sheriff?"

Sheriff Hill chuckled softly to himself. "Sure, Leroy. I could get a warrant, but I have a feeling if I look around, I'll find some probable cause."

"I got nothing to do with her."

"But you do know her?"

Leroy's eyes darted back and forth, refusing to look at Roy or Jane.

Sheriff Hill rested his hand on his revolver. "I just need to know her name."

"I told you I don't know her."

"And I believe you, Leroy. I do. The thing is, I got a call at the station saying she was here a couple weeks ago. Now, I'm sure you don't know her, but I think one of your friends might. I wouldn't want you to get in any trouble for something someone else might have done. So, if you could please open the door and let us have a look around, then I would know you really have nothing to do with her."

Leroy stared at Sheriff Hill through pinprick pupils. He gave a weak nod and slid the chain from the lock. "Okay, you can come in, but like I said, nobody else is here."

Sheriff Hill motioned to Jane to draw her weapon. They stepped through the threshold into the house. The furniture was broken and torn. Graffiti covered the walls and cabinets. Carpets and tile alike were stained with God knows what. The scent of filth and rotting food filled the air.

"So, Leroy," said Sheriff Hill. "When did your friends move out?"

"Ain't got no friends here. Just me."

A loud thud sounded overhead. Dust and dead insects rained down onto them. Sheriff Hill looked at the ceiling. Footsteps creaked across the upstairs floor.

"I thought you were alone." said Sheriff Hill.

"I am," said Leroy. "Just me here, like I said."

"Stay with him, Jane." Sheriff Hill drew his weapon and flashlight from his belt and moved through the house towards the stairs. He cleared every room before he moved on.

He reached the bottom of the stairs and looked towards the upper floor, weapon aimed. "This is the Ramsey County Sheriff's Office. If anyone's upstairs, make yourself known."

The only response was the creaking stillness of the house. Step by step, Roy ascended. After each one, he listened for any signs of movement. When he reached the top, he found himself in a long narrow hallway. Five doors lined the length of the hall. Two on each side and one at the far end that faced towards him.

Every door he passed revealed an unkempt room. Each one piled with more garbage than the last. Empty bottles and crumpled fast-food bags covered the floor. Rows of dirty mattresses and sleeping bags lined the walls. Each one the unfortunate sleeping place of a kid who lost their way. Someone's life dwindled down to a needle and a dirty blanket.

A muffled shuffling came from the door at the end of the hall. He pointed his gun towards it and moved with measured steps. "Police. Come out with your hands in the air."

The hinges screamed as he pushed the door open. The smell hit him like a wall. A pungent smell of filth and rust. He clamped his hand over the bottom half of his face, trying his hardest to hold his breath.

It was too dark to see. Everything appeared as vague forms amidst the shadows. He flipped the light switch several times. Nothing changed. He moved to the window sweeping the darkness as he went. He pulled open the torn, moth-eaten curtains. Daylight streaked in through the grime on the window. The room was quiet. The air thick with dust. Empty, except for that smell.

Something droned amidst the shadows in the corner. A sporadic, high-pitched cacophony. Faint at first, but louder as he moved towards the bed across the room.

The bed had been stripped of its sheets. A large brown stain covered most of the bottom half of the mattress. In the dim light, the stain appeared to be moving. Shadows scurried across its surface. When he reached it, he realized the stain wasn't moving, but the flies that covered it were.

The smell. The flies. He knew what was waiting for him. The beam of his flashlight traced the path of the insects across the floor to a closet in the back corner. Flies stumbled and fought, trying their hardest to push through the slats on the bottom of the door.

Roy holstered his weapon and pulled on a pair of latex gloves from his belt. He slid the closet open.

Flies swarmed around him. He batted at them until they resettled on a pile of dirty rags on the floor. The sheets from the bed, caked in gritty brown blood. He gagged at the smell as he moved the pile carefully with his foot. Each movement sent a new torrent of flies into the air.

At the bottom of the pile, he found what he was looking for. A small brown purse. Inside he found a half empty pack of cigarettes, a condom, and a worn-out leather wallet. He took the wallet and forced the zipper open. He flipped through various cards and crumpled fast food receipts before finding what he wanted. A North Dakota state ID. The girl in the photo was pale. Freckles covered her cheeks and nose beneath a curtain of long blonde hair. He found her.

BAKER
MARGARET MAY
1267 REGINA COURT
ANDERS, ND 58328

Roy continued searching the closet. His light passed over patch work clothes and old shoe boxes. Flies and maggots writhed on every surface. The beam of light crawled over the shadows.

His heart jumped into his throat. A pair of wide bloodshot eyes stared out at him over a row of dusty torn coats.

Sheriff Hill backed away. He kept the light shining on whoever hid inside the closet. His hand rested on the grip of his gun. "Ramsey County Sheriff's Office. I need you to come out slowly with your hands in the air."

Unblinking eyes continued their stare.

"I'm looking for Margaret," said Sheriff Hill. "Margaret Baker. Have you seen her?"

The eyes flicked down to the blood-soaked sheets on the floor, filled with a deep contemplation.

The man charged from the closet. Sheriff Hill noticed the gun just before the man's shoulder plowed into his chest.

Sheriff Hill pulled his own gun as he slammed against the wall. The house trembled under the impact. Drywall and rotted wood crumbled onto them. They struggled back and forth, each trying to gain the upper hand.

A single gunshot boomed. The fight was over as quickly as it started.

<u>Strangers</u>

Then

The diner wasn't perfect. There were smudges on the glass and knicks in the mugs, but compared to his parents' house it was the Taj Mahal. No need to brush off a quarter inch of dust and a few packs worth of cigarette butts to have a place to eat. The ceiling wasn't yellowed by smoke. The air smelled like syrup and burnt toast instead of old beer and cheap whiskey.

Tommy took a seat in the back corner near a window. The table was spotted with rings from decades of spilled coffee. The paper placemat was filled with ads for local businesses.

Ed's Bait Shop - Nightcrawlers and live bait.
J.L. Lawn Car - Mowing, edging, trimming and more.
Crawford Family Farm - Freshest Egg's on Devil's Lake

He picked up the menu and looked it over, front and back. So many options. The choice of food at home was between roach-infested Corn Flakes and roach-infested Rice Chex. He decided on the short stack pancakes: extra butter and drowning in syrup.

He looked out the window as he waited for his breakfast. Cars drove by, blowing around newspapers and old chip bags that made their way into the street.

Things moved faster than they did back home. Tommy wasn't used to this many people. He lived in a small town no one had ever heard of with a population just shy of two dozen. His parents' house was only an hour away, but with the lake between here and there, it might as well have been a different planet.

Here he was a stranger. He liked it that way. Back home, everyone knew him by name. They knew his father too. They also knew about his father's temper and the way he treated his wife and son. If it bothered anyone, they never said anything.

Since graduating last year, he didn't have school to keep him away from home. He worked odd jobs around the county until he managed to save up enough money for a rust-box car. Before he got the car, he was limited to places within walking distance. The only thing within walking distance of his parents' house was grass or the lake. The choice between the two was basically the same. A static view of flat, empty nothingness. Now he was free. For the most part.

He still needed to go home at night. It was too cold this time of year to sleep in his car. Sometimes he could save up enough for a few nights at a motel but the more time he spent away from home, the worse it got when he came back.

His father considered himself a God-fearing man. Tommy never knew his father to fear anything. If he feared God, then He must have been terrifying.

When you lived under his father's roof, you lived by the good book. If you didn't, you'd be forced to repent in whatever way he saw fit. Your repentance was usually based on how much he had to drink that day.

Tommy looked around the diner. He observed all the strange faces. Faces he didn't recognize. What were their stories? Where were they from? How did they end up here?

He made up stories for them.

The old man by the window was alone because he snuck out every morning to get some time away from his wife. He wore a hat so he could hide himself in case she drove by.

The redhead waitress behind the counter was a new mother. She wanted to be a lawyer but got pregnant in college. The guy was a no-good deadbeat who wanted nothing to do with her or her child. Now she slaves away in her apron to get enough money for diapers.

These people could be anyone. So could he. A clean slate. When he was around here, he didn't need to be himself anymore.

Tommy was halfway through his pancakes when the bell chimed over the front door. A new customer come to join the ranks of the other strangers.

Who could it be? A burned-out father on his last legs, wondering if he should take off and start over? A young woman with a secret? Hoping her parents wouldn't find out what she really got up to when she snuck out at night?

He looked up from his meal to view the new contender. Something shifted inside him. A strange feeling in his stomach he'd never felt before. She was beautiful. Long blonde hair and green eyes. A radiance in the simplicity of her smile.

Her beauty wasn't the only thing that gave him pause. There was something about her. Something words couldn't describe. He sensed a connection. A pulse from somewhere in the universe pulled her to him.

She walked up to the register, started chatting with the redheaded waitress.

The waitress handed her a knotted plastic bag full of Styrofoam containers.

She paid for her food then turned and walked out.

He watched her walk past his window. His eyes followed her across the road and down the street until she turned out of sight at the intersection. He needed to meet her. Learn who she was. See if she felt the same pull.

I Didn't Know

Now

Dim light bled through the interrogation room. Leroy sat beneath the single flickering bulb, chewing on filthy cracked fingernails. His yellow skin was like something out of *The Wizard of Oz*.

Jane sat across from Leroy. The drugs had done a number on him. She had seen a lot of this over the last few years. As far as the county was concerned, drinking and getting high were the only things to do around here. The kids getting booked for possession had gotten younger and younger.

Most of the calls that came into the station were drug related. Whether it was dealing or overdoses, addiction was a big problem in the county. Countless people had been affected, and it was spreading. A disease unprejudiced in who it infected. Didn't matter if you were a drifter or a governor. Once it got its claws in you, it tore you up until you were the lowest form of yourself.

Between the drug-induced paranoia and Leroy's general distrust of the police, it took a bit of prodding to get him to tell Jane what he knew.

The recent uptick in drug culture had given Jane experience with this kind of suspect.

Leroy was a few quarters short of a dollar on a good day and today wasn't a good day.

Jane was in the room for less than ten minutes before he started to talk.

"She ran away." Leroy's voice shook. A soft tremor made his words quiver when they left his mouth. "She was having problems with her folks. She was lookin' to score."

"Did you help her with that?" asked Jane.

Leroy went quiet. His eyes drifted away from her as he picked the scabs on his cheeks. They peeled off, leaving his face pocked with drops of blood.

"Leroy, I don't care about the drugs," said Jane.

"You don't?"

"No. I care about finding out what happened to Margaret."

"I told the Sheriff already. I don't know nothing."

"Leroy, your friend is on a table in the ER with a hole in his chest. He attacked the Sheriff. Why would he do that if he didn't do anything wrong? Your friend? Omar? Did he do something to her?"

"No." Leroy focused on the dirt caked beneath his fingernails. Blue-green crescents he scrapped at with his thumb nail.

"Did you?"

"It ain't like that," shouted Leroy. He looked up from his hands, finally giving her his full attention.

"Leroy, we found her ID in your closet. Along with a lot of blood. I want to help you, but I can't if you're not honest with me."

Leroy's foot jackhammered under the table. He gnawed at his lower lip. Buttonhole eyes drifted across the ceiling, searching for some semblance of a clear thought.

This was pointless. Whether it was the drugs or withdrawal, Leroy wouldn't be any help in this condition.

"Okay, Leroy. If that's how you wanna play this." She stood and started for the door.

"I didn't know," whimpered Leroy. "I didn't know when I gave her the drugs. I didn't know."

***

Roy followed Hannah into the morgue, sickly blue light flooded the room. A metal table sat in the center. Some lifeless form laid on top of it covered in a white sheet. A cruel imitation of a ghost.

Hannah pulled the sheet down, revealing the pale skin and empty eyes of what used to be Margaret May Baker.

It wasn't Margaret anymore. This person, this- thing, couldn't be what it once was. Stripped and laid out on a cold metal slab. Cut open and examined like some experiment. That's not how you treated a person.

The thing that was once a young girl stared up at Roy with blank, blaming eyes. Green eyes, like the ones that watched him in his dreams and plagued his nightmares, casting judgement for letting the light inside of them fade away.

She used to be Margaret. A friend. A student. A daughter. Someone with her entire life ahead of her. Now, Margaret was a memory, and this was the shell she left behind. A body without a soul to give it purpose.

"So. Was it an OD?" asked Sheriff Hill.

The look in Hannah's eyes confirmed what Roy already knew. "The toxicology report shows trace amounts of opiates in her system, but-"

"But you wouldn't call me down here for an overdose."

"Right. That's why I needed you here as soon as possible. Her brain tissue shows signs of cerebral hypoxia. There's a large amount of inflammation in the larynx. That in combination with fluid in the lungs points to drowning. Several of her ribs are fractured and she has bruising consistent with CPR."

Hannah pulled the sheet down further. A line of sutures ran from groin to her sternum before branching out to each shoulder. Beneath the stitches she was painted with bruises. A patchwork of purple and blue swirls faded to yellow and green as they spread out to engulf her chest.

"They attempted to resuscitate her," continued Hannah. "Possibly several times. They were unsuccessful- obviously."

Roy's legs turned to jelly. The floor dropped out beneath him. His knees wobbled and his mind went blank.

His fingers searched for a pulse. Hands on cold wet skin.

One. Two. Three.

The crack of breaking ribs.

One. Two. Three.

Leaning down. Forcing air into waterlogged lungs.

One. Two. Three.

Hoping for a cough or a blink. Anything to show some sign of life.

One. Two. Three.

Pressing down.

One. Two. Three.

Pounding.

One. Two. Three.

Screaming.

One. Two. Three.

Losing everything.

One. Two. Three.

Roy counted his breaths. He pushed the panic back down inside, forcing the memories back into the dark.

It didn't make sense. How could someone go through that? Try with everything they had to bring a person back, and then dump them in a field like garbage?

"Roy." Hannah looked at him, sadness in her eyes. "There's something else."

***

"It was everywhere," said Leroy. "I ain't never seen so much blood. We tried to stop it- Me and Omar- but it just kept coming."

"Why was she bleeding?" asked Jane. "Was she hurt?"

Leroy shook his head, tears welled in his eyes. "She- she was- I didn't know when I gave it to her. I never would've if I'd knew."

"What didn't you know Leroy?"

Jane heard the click of a the bolt and the door opened behind her.

Sheriff Hill stepped into the room. He offered no introductions or explanations. He was rigid. Shoulders raised and nostrils flared. His expression carved from molten stone.

She'd never seen the Sheriff like this before. He kept a hard exterior, but he was always kind. Distant, but kind. Anger didn't seem to come naturally to him.

Sheriff Hill leaned down uncomfortably close to Leroy's face. He stared him down with unblinking eyes. "She was pregnant. Wasn't she, Leroy?"

Leroy trembled under the Sheriff's gaze as his head bobbed up and down. Tears fell to the table, splashing across the pictures of Margaret.

"So, what happened?" asked Sheriff Hill. "You shot her up? Gave her a little too much?"

"No."

"She OD'd. You panicked. Dropped her in a field like garbage?"

"No."

"Did you know she was pregnant when you killed her?"

"What? Killed? No."

"Omar then? He killed her and you covered for him?"

"We didn't kill nobody."

"Then what happened to her, Leroy?"

"I- I don- I don't know. I don't know what happened to her. I don't know."

"We found her purse in your house. Her blood was everywhere. And you don't know anything about that? Is that what you're saying?"

"I only just met her a few weeks ago. I didn't know nothin' about her."

"Well, what changed last week? How did you go from not knowing her to having her blood all over your bedroom?"

"I don't know. Omar knew her. She was down on her luck, needed a place to stay for a while. Omar said she was trying to get away from someone. Some guy, but I never knew who it was. I don't know nothing about her."

Sheriff Hill stepped away from Leroy. He pressed his knuckles against his temples and took a long slow breath. His voice was calm, but Jane could sense the way he boiled beneath the surface.

"I'm done playing games, Leroy," said Sheriff Hill. "I know you were with her. I know you lied to me about knowing her, and I know I found her things in your house. Your friend is in the hospital right now bleeding to death. Odds are he doesn't make it. If you're protecting him, there's no need. He won't make it to see prison. So, when I look at you and say, 'tell me what happened to her.' Then you fucking tell me what happened to her."

"Her baby," cried Leroy. "Her little girl. It died. It died inside her." He spewed the words before the sheriff could finish berating him, as though the truth was waiting on the tip of his tongue, too horrible to be spoken aloud.

Silence washed over the room. The Sheriff's face loosened. His fists unclenched.

"I didn't know she was- I never would've given it to her- I never would've if I knew."

"Why didn't you call someone, Leroy?" asked Jane.

"She told us not to. Made us swear. Said to bring her to the hospital and not to tell nobody. So, we dropped her off and tried to clean the mess."

"Did she die on the way?" asked Sheriff Hill.

"No," said Leroy. "We dropped her off. I walked her inside. I didn't even know she was-" A pained sob tore from Leroy's throat. "Oh god. I'm sorry. Oh god, I'm so sorry. I'm so sorry."

What Do Birds Sing About?

My family spent a lot of time together when I was young. My mother, my dad and I would all hop into the truck and drive up to Grandpa's house. We visited him almost every weekend.

My mother said Grandpa was lonely because Grandma was up in heaven. She said it was hard to be alone after having spent so many years with a person. You notice their absence in everything. The places you used to go and the words they used to say. The way they laughed at your jokes when no one else did. You missed having someone who understood you when the world was working against you. The older I got, the more I understood that feeling.

The thing I miss most about my mother is her smile. She could warm a room with a smirk. She always seemed happy. She loved to laugh and dance and tell jokes. She loved music and old books, long walks in the rain and summer nights under the stars. She had so much love in her heart. It's hard to believe one day all that love got up and disappeared.

My mother and I always sat by the shore in Grandpa's backyard. We made our seat on a shelf of rock that jutted out over the water. We hung our feet from the edge and let them dangle above the surface.

We watched the sunrise bring the lake to life with shimmers of golden light. The warmth it brought woke the world from sleep.

The cold wind became a warm spring breeze. Birds took flight from their nests. Their whistling songs echoed over the water.

"What do birds sing about?" I asked my mother.

"I don't know," she said. "Probably the same things people sing about. Love and life and the way they feel."

That never seemed right to me. A bird with all the freedom in the world who could set off on adventure to anywhere at a moment's notice. Why would they sing about the same dull things people did?

"I bet they sing about adventure," I said.

"Oh, really? What sort of adventures do you think they sing about?"

"All kinds. Why be a bird if you don't go on thousands of adventures? With a flap of their wings, they can be anywhere they want. Why would they stay in one place instead of seeing everything there is to see?"

My mother gave me a knowing look. My answer was exactly what she expected. My mother knew me that way. She understood the piece of me that longed to be free, even when I was too young to know what freedom really meant.

"Adventure's important, my love," she said." But birds have responsibilities too, you know. They have nests to tend to and children to look after. They have families and friends. They have other people to think about. A lot of times deciding to leave is harder than deciding to stay."

Behind me, dad called for my mother. She got up to see what he needed and told me she'd be right back.

Something stirred near my feet. The water rippled out in small uneven rings. I moved to the edge of the outcropping to get a closer look. I was greeted by a collection of boring round rocks beneath the surface. I hung my body over the ledge to get a better look. I inched closer to the water as I searched for what caused the sudden ripples. Amidst the jumble of plain brown and black stones hid something else, a northern leopard frog. Small, dark brown oval spots covered the frog's body. I reached down to try and grab it, my fingers just long enough to breach the surface of the water. The frog waited below in the silent stillness, just inches from my outstretched hand. I risked getting closer. My entire body swung from the rock ledge above.

I came to as my dad pulled me out of the water and brought me onto shore. My mother's voice, frantic with worry, "What were you thinking? You could have drowned!"

Dad, Grandpa, and my mother all looked down at me, fear clear on their faces, the worst-case scenario played out in their heads. I sat up slowly and held out my hands in front of me. I opened them to reveal the small, spotted frog.

Dad looked down at the frog and then up at me. Shock and confusion etched into his stare. A smile cracked his lips, and he laughed.

Grandpa joined him.

My mother looked down at the three of us in disbelief. The laughter broke through her stern exterior and a smile peeked from the corners of her lips.

She wrapped me in her coat to keep me warm. My grandfather took the old, worn-down polaroid he always carried and snapped a picture of us. He let me shake it to make the picture appear.

I hung the picture on the fridge when I got home. I looked at it every day before I left for the bus stop.

Dad took it down after my mother died. The smile on her face was more than he could stomach.

Memories

OPEN.

The neon sign blinked on and off with a cold, electric buzz. The smell of stale beer and fresh cigarettes drifted on the wind.

Roy sat on a hard wooden bench across the street, transfixed by the light. It begged him closer, like a moth to an electric trap.

Groups of people walked down the sidewalk below half dead strings of Christmas lights. Friends and colleagues laughing at some unheard joke. An unkempt wreath full of fake holly hung on the door of the bar. Cars idled in the street with fogged windows. Women stood by the door smoking, their skirts too short for the weather.

Roy used to walk this street with his friends. They tried to sneak into the bar nearly every week. Even if they got in, the bartender wouldn't serve them. Roy and his friends had a reputation for causing trouble. Everyone in town knew them by name.

After being turned away they'd borrow a few bottles from their parents' liquor cabinets and head to the baseball field at Roosevelt Park. They'd get drunk and run the bases until they got sick all over home plate. Try to pick up girls even though they could barely string a sentence together.

They were the times you look back on and feel a sting of embarrassment. He thought he was making memories that would follow him to the grave. Lifelong friends and unforgettable nights.

Friends move away. The nights blend with all the rest. The good old days are gone before you realize you're living them.

Kids still gathered at the field from time to time. The bottles were switched out for dirty needles, and games of ball turned into street brawls and weekends in a jail cell. Different times.

Across the street the light continued its pattern.

ON. OFF. ON. OFF.

Roy tried to focus on something. Anything, except the light. He was hypnotized. Paralyzed.

ON. OFF. ON. OFF.

Blood pulsed in his temples. Pain followed the same pattern.

ON. OFF. ON. OFF.

He squeezed his eyes shut but he still saw it.

ON. OFF. ON. OFF.

He needed something to numb his headache. Take his mind off things. Linda. Georgia. His father. Omar. Margaret. Her baby. The town that was falling apart around him. It could all be out of his mind. Just for a few hours. Just for tonight, he would have some peace.

How much would one night of bliss cost him? Six months? Six years? How far down the rabbit hole would he fall before he got himself back again. He was barely back now. How much more was he willing to lose? What else was there to lose?

"Mind if I join you?"

The voice snapped him back to reality. "Hi, Hannah. Of course. Have a seat."

"How are you? How's everything going?" asked Hannah.

"I'm alright. Jane checked the hospital. Margaret checked in last Wednesday. Pelvic exam confirmed a miscarriage. She was there for three days before she self-discharged. That was Saturday around eleven. Looks like Leroy was telling the truth."

"I wasn't asking about the case."

"I know."

Silence clung to the air. Frozen in place by the cold that pressed in around them.

"Did you ever hear about that guy down in Benson County? The one who found the penguin?" asked Hannah.

Roy looked up from the concrete, confused by the question. "I don't know. I don't think so."

"Well, there was a guy, older guy. Lived off the old two-eighty-one down by Round Lake. Lonely kind of guy. No one really knew him. He's sitting on the porch in the backyard, just looking out over the trees, and he sees this penguin just walk into his yard."

"A penguin?" asked Roy. "You sure about that?"

"Yes, I'm sure. Let me tell the story. So, the guy takes the penguin and brings it inside. Calls up the sheriff says, 'Sheriff, I just found this penguin walking around my yard.' Sheriff says, 'That must be the penguin that escaped from the zoo. You need to take him to the zoo.' A couple days later the sheriff comes around to check on the situation. Sees the guy on the back porch, and he's sitting there with the penguin."

Roy gave Jane a look that went far past skepticism. "Who did you hear this from?"

"Doesn't matter who I heard it from. You gonna let me finish the story or not?"

"You're right. I'm sorry."

"So, as I was saying. The sheriff comes and sees the guy with the penguin. He says, 'I told you to take that penguin to the zoo.' And the guy says, 'I did. He loved it. This week were going to the movies."

"Wow," laughed Roy. "That joke is, truly terrible."

"Oh, shut up. You know you loved it."

A shared smile faded into a quiet Roy had grown accustomed to.

"The gun wasn't even loaded." Roy's voice choked him. "The kid- Omar. Surgery didn't go well. He's in a coma, doctors aren't sure if he'll make it. His gun wasn't even loaded. Did you know that? I shot a kid, and his gun wasn't loaded."

"It's not your fault. He attacked you. You had no way of knowing."

Roy pressed his palms hard against his forehead in frustration. "I know. The doctor said he was so high he probably had no idea what was going on. It's just- I keep hearing it in my head. The gunshot. The ringing in my ears. The way he was breathing in the ambulance. It's been one thing after another. He was just a kid. Just a stupid kid. He made some mistakes but- He had his whole life ahead of him. So many more years to keep making mistakes and he threw it away."

She placed her hand on his knee. Gentle. Like a mother would. "You still seeing that doctor in Grand Forks?"

"Sometimes." Roy looked across the street. Snow started to fall. Small delicate flakes illuminated by the streetlights. "Not really," he admitted. "She says it helps to talk about things. Just seems strange, burdening someone else with your problems. Giving up your life story to a stranger. Just because she has doctor in front of her name doesn't mean she cares about what I have to say."

He had a hundred things to say, each one harder than the last. The words sat on the tip of his tongue but when he went to speak, they caught in his throat. Strangled him.

Pain blinked in his head.

ON. OFF. ON. OFF.

Roy focused on Hannah instead of the pain. On her presence. Her smell: Antiseptic and strawberry shampoo. Her long black hair flowed down her back. Her leg brushed lightly against his, as his foot tapped a chaotic rhythm on the sidewalk.

"How's your dad?" asked Hannah.

"Good. He's good. He-" Roy's throat burned from the effort of not crying. "His memory's getting worse. He forgets. Not everything. He remembers Linda's gone, and mom, but- Georgia- He forgets she's not around anymore. Asks me to bring her over. Asks about her poetry. About school. Sometimes- all the time. I envy him for it. Not a moment passes I don't think about her. What I could've done differently."

Roy understood why Georgia left. He would have done the same in her situation. He just wished more than anything he knew where she was. If she was happy and safe.

Roy wiped away the beginnings of a tear, staring at the cold black asphalt. "The night she left was the same night we got the call about what happened in Edmonton. I was supposed to be home, but work got in the way."

"Edmonton was tough. Couldn't have been an easy decision."

In truth he decision was practically made for him. Spend the night having fun with his daughter or walk into the mouth of hell. Something inside him- some broken fucked-up part- chose hell.

Everyone knew about Edmonton in some way. Most people knew a couple pieces. Small details snowballed into some grandiose story of love and betrayal. The truth was simpler, and far more horrific. Unless you saw it with your own eyes, you couldn't imagine. The violence. The blood. The smell of death that clung to you long after you left the scene.

"No," said Roy. "It was an easy decision. At least it should have been. But I chose work. I let her down. The same way I let her mother down. Now I'm letting Margaret down too. It's my job, not just as the Sheriff but as a father, to keep these girls safe, and no matter how hard I try I can't seem to do it."

A slow burning ignited in Roy's chest. A rolling numbness spread to the tips of his fingers.

"I'm sorry," said Roy. "We can talk about something else. How about Christmas? You got plans? Gonna see your sister?"

"I don't think so," said Hannah. "She moved to Bismarck last summer, her girlfriend wanted to be closer to her family. She invited me but- I don't know- seems strange. Spending Christmas with a happy family. Why break tradition?"

They shared a morbid laugh.

"Anyway, I gotta head home." Hannah stood and put her hand on Roy's shoulder. "It may not be my business, but I think you should try and see that doctor. And if you can't bring yourself to- I know we're not as close as we used to be, but I'm always here if you need to talk."

Hannah turned and started the walk to her car.

"Hannah?" said Roy.

She turned back to look at him, amber eyes glowing against the dark.

Roy thought of his last Christmas. The day he spent alone instead of with the people who cared about him. The fight with Georgia, the words he would regret for the rest of his life.

Why don't you just leave if you hate me so much?

"Why don't you stop by on Tuesday?" said Roy. "My dad would love to see you again and- I mean if you want to. No one should be alone on Christmas."

Her smile was warm enough to melt away the cold. "I'll think about it. Goodnight, Roy."

Roy listened to her footsteps fade into the chill of the night. His breath turned to mist and floated up towards the stars. Across the street the crowds dispersed, and the cars pulled away. The streetlights went out, followed by the sign. His temples still pulsed, but not with the throbbing pressure they had before.

Tiny White Wings

On Christmas day when I was seventeen my father and I got into the worst fight we ever had.

We promised Grandpa we'd come and spend the day with him. He needed it. We all needed it. I should have remembered a promise didn't mean anything when my dad made it.

For some reason every time he made a promise, or gave his word, I clung to it. Hoped somehow, he would keep it. Every promise was a new chance for him to prove he was working towards fixing things. I should have known better.

He came downstairs that morning in a uniform that smelled like the dumpster behind a liquor store. I found him in the kitchen, acting like he wasn't having beer for breakfast.

"What are you doing?" I asked.

He didn't even respond. He just looked at me with slack jawed contempt; through me, like I wasn't worth seeing.

"Why do you have your uniform on?" I asked. "We're supposed to be at Grandpa's by eleven."

"I can't go to Grandpa's. It's the middle of the week. I have to go to work."

"It's Sunday. And it's Christmas. Or did you forget?"

"I didn't forget. I need to go." He lied so easily. He didn't even have the decency to look sorry about it.

"Go where," I said. "The station or the bar?"

"Watch your mouth. I'm your father. Show a little respect."

"Respect?" I almost laughed as I said it. "You want respect? Try saying you'll do something and then actually do it. Try spending at least half as much time with your family as you do at the bottom of a bottle."

He made his excuses. I tried to remind him of the promise he made, he said he wished he could go -which was a lie- but he needed to go to work for a little while. I knew what work meant. Time away from me; away from the constant reminder of what he lost. What *we* lost.

Our tempers got the better of us. We both said things we'd come to regret.

Why don't you just leave if you hate me so much?
I wish it was you instead of mom.

I locked myself in my room and screamed into my mattress. I turned on the shower full blast and sat on the floor so he couldn't hear me cry. I didn't want him to think I was weak or that anything he said could affect me.

On the wall, hidden among the building steam of the shower, was a moth with paper white wings. He heard the fight. Bore witness to the family falling apart at the seams.

The moth watched over me with miniature black eyes. It wasn't there to judge or degrade. It didn't prescribe us medicines we couldn't pronounce, didn't use fancy words to explain why we felt the way we did. It only observed. Uncaring and uncurious. A God with tiny white wings; watching over his experiment.

I grabbed a marker from my desk drawer and found a blank stretch of paint on my bedroom wall. I started to write. I *needed* to write. If I could get the words out of my brain, they couldn't hurt me anymore. Whisper in my ears at night and keep me awake.

Your father hates you. No one loves you. No one ever will.

I scribbled down whatever came to my head. A frantic eruption of letters and words.

I am an experiment,
A bug under the lens waiting to be burned.
A cold unfeeling mass strapped to the table under blinding light.
A rodent in a maze performing elegant tricks for scraps of molded cheese.
I am no one. Nothing. Useless and unwanted.
One day I'll be free.
Then maybe someone will miss me.

When I look back on it now, I feel ashamed. I didn't mean the things I said, but I wanted him to hurt; feel the same pain I did. The pain of knowing the person who's meant to love you the most can't stand to look at you.

I tried to change after that. Make amends. I wouldn't sit by and be a part of God's little experiment. I wanted to fight. Work towards mending the void between us.

But healing only works if both parties are interested.

Homecoming

The temperature plummeted overnight, turning rain into heavy, wet snow. Jane turned off the highway. A long, winding road led down to the shore, flanked by huge swathes of untouched snow. She rounded the bend, saw her destination. Rows of blue and yellow trailers bit through the snow like crooked teeth. The faded peeling pastels surreal against the serene blanket of unceasing white.

She drove to the end of the road and parked by the lake. She walked down to the water across snow-covered sand. The shoreline gave way to a blanket of pale blue ice. Clouds of snow danced over the surface carried by the biting wind. The mist over the ice was thick. Thirty feet out, there was nothing but a hazy grey wall of empty space. She put up her hood against the cold and stared out into the swirling tempest.

She thought of Margaret. How scared she must have been. Did she know she was about to die before it happened? Did she know no one would come forward to claim her body? Did she know in those final moments she was completely alone in a world that didn't seem to care about her?

Jane knew the feeling. Loneliness. Emptiness. Having no one in the world to care if you lived or died. For so long she feared being alone. Now, she found comfort in it- sometimes. Other times, the noise in her head got so loud she had to scream into her pillow to drown it out. Muffled voices from her past. TV static between her ears.

She watched the dance of the storm, an ever-shifting white void. An impulse blossomed in the back of her mind. Intrusive. Instinctual. What was it like inside that emptiness? How did it feel to be alone? Trapped in the cold dark, waiting for the end to come? A lump caught in Jane's throat as she gave into the impulse, stepped out onto the ice.

Every step echoed beneath the surface. A high-pitched, alien groan, an eldritch monster trying to break free from its prison. The sound was strangely soothing. It brought back memories of ice fishing with her father in early spring. Memories she locked away. The thought of her father, even in a happy memory, too painful to bear.

She closed her eyes and listened. The wind sweeping the trees, the strange metallic groan below the ice. The sharp cold gnawed at her cheeks and the tip of her nose. Snowflakes stung the hot flush of her skin.

She was there again. On the ice with her father. Pulling the sled over the lake. Setting up their bright red tent and starting a fire in the middle of the ice. Drilling down until the water gushed out over their boots. Her father taught her how to set the lines and reel the fish in, so they didn't get away. They never kept the fish; they caught them then set them free.

She always wondered what the fish thought of the experience. Swimming along, going about your business when you're snagged by a hook and hoisted towards the sky. How traumatic must it have been for the fish? Did the other fish believe them when they told the story?

Her father always told her about the biggest fish he ever caught, four feet from tip to tail- although it got bigger and bigger every time, he told the story. Out on the lake pulling the fish from the frozen water was the last time she remembered seeing her father smile.

She opened her eyes and looked at the clouds. The storm stared back with pale grey eyes. The lake waited below, patient and calm, for the storm to pass and the sun to shine.

Somewhere behind her in the labyrinth of rusted cars and mobile homes, was her mother's house. A place she hadn't stepped foot in for eleven years. Today- for some reason- she was going back. Back to the mother who hated her for being alive when her husband wasn't. Back to the angry, silent stares from the hallway as she lay in her bed at night, too scared of her own mother to sleep. The feeling in the pit of her stomach that made her not want to wake in the morning.

If she closed her eyes forever, would she see her father again? Would he be back to his old smiling self? The person he was before they shipped him off to have his soul destroyed. Before the bad spirits swam through his thoughts, convinced him there was no other way out.

An old swing set lurked in the storm, rusted, and bent. A metal grimace that sneered behind the curtain of snow. The house was smaller than Jane remembered, separated from its neighbors by a waist-high chain link fence. The gate cried in protest as she pushed it open. The five steps to the front door seemed like a marathon.

Her knock was answered immediately. Her mother must have been waiting at the door for her to arrive. To Jane's shock, her mother reached in for a hug. Jane returned it halfheartedly. Her mother smelled like hand soap and lemon cleaner. An artificial chemical stench clung to the back of Jane's throat.

"Merry Christmas," said her mother.

Jane pulled away and looked around. The kitchen was cramped but tidy. The sink emptied of dishes and the counters clear of clutter and dust.

"I wasn't sure you'd come," said her mother.

"Neither was I."

"Well, come on now have a seat." Her mother gave a weary smile and pulled out a chair. They sat together at the table, while her mother unleashed a tirade of questions. *How have you been? How's work? Are you seeing anybody?"* Her mother tried to ignore the tension. Ignore the years that had passed, and the reasons Jane had for leaving.

She ignored the masquerade of babble. Her eyes darted around the room. Not much had changed. The walls were painted the same off-white. Blue and white patterned linoleum lined the floor, peeling up at the corners. A water stain the shape of Florida clung to the ceiling over the sink.

Her gaze rested on a picture hung over the TV in the living room. A picture of her father. The knot in her stomach tightened. Fire burned behind her eyes. "Mom? Why did you ask me to come?"

The question seemed to stall her mother. She looked abashed as if to say *'Well you're my daughter. It's Christmas. Why wouldn't you visit?'*

Her mother's smile dropped, replaced by a glossy-eyed, thin-lipped frown. "I saw the story in the paper. The girl in Clareborne. The one under the tree."

Jane's father watched her over her mother's shoulder. Cold, haunted eyes. Eyes that had seen the evil of the world. The same eyes as her.

"I think about that little girl every night," said her mother. "About her parents. How hard it must have been for them. When their daughter left home, did they know they were never gonna see her again? I just thought, what if I never see Jane again? What if I never get to tell her how sorry I am?"

"Is that what this is?" Jane shifted uncomfortably in her seat. "You saying you're sorry? You finally decided to care about me. Is that it?"

"That's not fair."

"Not fair? Since when has this been about what's fair? You were too busy hating me-"

"I never hated you. It was never about you."

"You made that very clear."

"I lost my husband." Hurt burned behind her mother's eyes. "And I lost my father." Jane's demeanor broke. There were too many unsaid things for a calm reunion. Jane's eyes flooded with hot, stinging tears. "I was a little girl. A little girl who needed you. Needed somebody to tell her she was loved and cared about. That her daddy-" The words caught in Jane's throat. "That what happened to her dad wasn't her fault."

"Jane. I'm sorry."

"Sorry isn't good enough. It's been eleven years, Mom. Eleven years without a word and you call me- beg me to come and visit so- what? You can clear your conscience?"

"Please-"

"No. You don't get to beg me. After Dad died, you didn't once try to comfort me. Didn't ask what it was like to find him like that. Didn't ask me about the nightmares. About how I tried to shake him awake. How I prayed he was only sleeping. How I wished every day I could die so I could be with him again."

"You survived, Jane. Not many people can say that after what you went through. After what I put you through. But you did. That kind of trauma. That kind of *abuse.*" Her mother treated the word like poison, like she was sickened just by letting it slither passed her lips. "Those things can make you sick. They turn people into drug addicts and maniacs. But not you. You made it out and despite everything somehow managed to be a good person."

"You don't know anything about me."

"I do. I know how you feel. I know the pain tears you apart every day. And as much as you hate me, it is nothing compared to how much I hate myself. I never called you, never bothered you, because I knew you didn't want to hear from me. I knew you could never forgive me because I haven't forgiven myself. I never deserved your forgiveness."

"You're right." Jane's eyes burned as she looked at her mother. "You don't."

Jane put up her hood and walked back out into the storm. Her mother didn't chase her, but she heard her sobs over the howl of the wind.

<u>Christmas</u>

The streets sang with life. Families on their way to breakfast. Kids headed home to visit their parents. A smile crawled across every face. A Santa with a red bucket clanged his bells on the side of the street asking for donations.

Hannah idled below the red light. She watched as children pranced through the snow, trying to catch flakes on their tongues. Their parents walked behind them, scarves flowing out beneath hooded faces. Gloved hands holding steaming carboard coffee cups.

Happy families enjoying a much-needed day of rest.

Happy. The concept was foreign to her, especially when the word *family* was in the mix. She wasn't unhappy but she wasn't happy either. She existed somewhere in the middle. A limbo of contentedness.

When she thought of family, she didn't picture Sundays around the dinner table, or building snowmen with her father. She pictured screaming matches at three in the morning. Broken dinner plates and bruised ribs. Hiding her little sister under the bed so she didn't have to go through the same things Hannah did.

Her father had a temper. Describing it is a temper almost seemed funny to Hannah, but that's the word everyone used to justify his actions.

"He just has a temper is all."

"He's a good man, he just has a bit of a temper."

The correct word for her father was somewhere between animal and monster. Feral and inhuman.

Her mother was a good woman, the most decent person Hannah had ever known. Sometimes she truly believed her mother didn't know what her husband was doing in her daughters' bedroom at night.

Her mother drank just enough that you could smell it on her breath when she hugged you goodnight. Just enough that she could force her way through the day without breaking down.

It was a miracle her and her sister turned out okay. As okay as someone who went through what they did could turn out.

Hannah decided a long time ago she wouldn't let her parents' abuse control her. She wouldn't be defined by what that son of a bitch did. Or by her mother letting it happen. Victimhood was a label she would never wear.

Hannah used to spend Christmas wandering around town, looking for anything to do that didn't involve being home. Now she longed for home. Not her home, just *a* home. Somewhere people gave a shit where she was or how she was doing.

***

Roy arrived at his father's house early. No need to wait around in his apartment alone with his thoughts. The driveway was lined with blinking rainbow lights. Baby Jesus laid on the front lawn in his basinet, surrounded by misshapen plastic figures that stared down at him, observing his every move.

His father opened the door before Roy had a chance to knock. "Roy! Merry Christmas, so glad you made it."

"Merry Christmas, Dad."

"Well, come in, come in, Get yourself out of the cold."

Roy was greeted by a rush of warm air as he stepped into the kitchen. The smell of pine and sugar cookies filled the house. Frank Sinatra sang Silent Night from an old record player in the corner of the living room.

"Will your *friend* still be joining us tonight?" He could hear his father's smirk in his voice.

"She might be. Not sure."

His father scanned him from head to toe, a disapproving look in his eyes. "Is that what your wearing?"

Roy looked at himself. A light purple button-down shirt untucked and wriggling with dense wrinkles. He smoothed down the shirt with his hands. "It doesn't matter what I wear dad. I told you, it's not like that."

His father threw up his palms in defense. "Alright, alright. Just thought I'd mention it before you embarrassed yourself."

Roy walked back downstairs fifteen minutes later sporting a red dress shirt from his father's closet. He examined the pictures on the walls as he went. Black and white portraits of his grandparents in antique round frames. His father and mother on their wedding day. Him as a child, smiling wide despite two missing teeth.

He reached the dining room and was stopped in his tracks. The photo clung to the wall over the dining room table. Georgia.

His father came up from behind and put his hand on Roy's shoulder. "Just beautiful, isn't she? Spitting image of her mother, don't you think?"

Roy's hand started to shake as he looked at the picture. Georgia wore a green dress that brought out the color of her eyes. Long golden hair flowed to her waist. A golden circle on a thin chain dangled in the hollow of her throat, her mother's ring. He recognized the outfit. She wore it on her last Christmas before she went away. The Christmas he chose to spend drinking by himself in his office.

Georgia smiled in the photo. Her mother's smile. A glowing beacon of love and joy that masked unfathomable hurt. Bile burned on the back of his tongue. He swallowed hard.

"She sure is," sighed Roy.

"You remember the Christmas we went ice skating?" asked his father.

"Of course, I remember."

They woke before sunrise. Roy, Linda, his father, and a couple other parents from town. They drove down to the lake and shoveled the snow off the surface to make room for all the kids in Clareborne to come skate. The digging took a few hours. Him and Linda slogged back home and fell into bed. It couldn't have been more than ten minutes before Georgia barged through the bedroom door to wake them up for present time.

After she opened her presents, they bundled her up and drove her down to the lake, where she opened her final present, a new pair of ice skates, hot pink and lime green – Her favorite combination. Other parents brought their kids down for the surprise. Word spread and soon the whole town was on the ice. They skated and danced around the makeshift rink until the sun started to set. They practically had to drag Georgia off the ice to get her home.

That night they put on their pajamas and drank hot chocolate on the couch. They watched a Christmas movie marathon on TV until Georgia couldn't keep her eyes open anymore.

Roy carried her down the hall and tucked her into bed. He watched the softness of her breathing and wondered what he did to deserve something so perfect. He couldn't remember a time in his life when he was happier.

Eight months later, Linda was gone. Then he was gone. Lost somewhere inside himself, too broken to even try and crawl out of the dark. Fast forward through the blur of years that followed, and Georgia was gone too.

It was 9:57 at night on October 23rd- Georgia's birthday- when he found out Georgia had left. He didn't know where she went or how long she would be away. Deep down he knew he'd probably never see her again. The person he loved more than anything else in the world was gone, and he was the reason.

It was 3:04 a.m. on October 24th when Roy had his last drink.

A knock on the front door brought him back to reality. "I'll get it."

Roy walked to the door to find Hannah; her face distorted behind snow covered glass. He opened the door, surprised to see her. "Merry Christmas, Hannah. I wasn't sure you'd make it."

"Well, I figured it beat eating this whole pie by myself." Hannah held up a golden-brown pie with deep red filling. "Cherry still your favorite?"

"Absolutely." Roy took the pie and brought it into the kitchen. Hannah followed close behind.

"How's everything going?" asked Hannah. "You look good. Very festive."

Roy looked down at the vibrant red of his shirt, a warm flush crept up his neck. "Alright, I suppose. Still no leads on Margaret-"

"Listen Sheriff," teased Hannah. "I didn't come all the way to this side of town to talk about work on Christmas. So, I'll make you a deal. You don't bring up the case, and I won't ask your dad to show me your baby pictures." Hannah held her hand towards Roy.

Roy took it and shook to solidify the agreement. "Deal."

"How long has it been?" Roy's father walked into the room smiling from ear to ear. He walked up to Hannah and opened his arms for a hug.

"Too long," said Hannah.

Henry turned to Roy and clapped his hands together. "Alright. Dinners all set, just waiting on one more. Will my lovely granddaughter be joining us tonight?"

Roy's heart sank into his stomach. "Maybe a little later, Dad. She said we should start without her."

"I see," said Henry. "Too busy with that boyfriend of hers?"

"Boyfriend?" asked Roy.

"Well, I assume. Can't expect a girl like that to be single forever, can you? Beautiful, funny, charming. She was bound to get scooped up. Kids' get older, Roy. It's hard but it's true."

Roy and Hannah ended the night on the couch stuffing themselves with warm cherry pie. He hadn't thought about the case in hours. Unfortunately, the case wasn't the only thing giving him sleepless nights.

"I can't believe I didn't know Georgia had a boyfriend."

"I'm not surprised," said Hannah. "Teenage girls don't tell their fathers anything."

"She used to. We'd talk every night when I got home. She'd tell me all about her day and she'd ask what I did at work. 'My adventures' she called them. I never even realized we stopped doing it. I guess it just kind of- faded out."

"Your dad said it best. 'Kids' get older.' We're proof of that."

The conversation was brought to a halt when the doorbell rang. Roy stood to see who it was. Maybe things hadn't worked out with Jane and her mother. When Roy looked through the window to see who it was, Jane wasn't there. Nobody was.

Roy pulled the door open and stepped outside. He looked up and down the street, but no one was around. The only sign anyone had been at the door was a present, sat on the top step of the porch wrapped in sparkling green paper.

Roy brought the package inside and set it down on the couch.

"Who's that from?" asked Hannah.

"I don't know. There's no name."

Roy sat down and placed the gift on his lap before opening it. He carefully peeled the tape and unwrapped the paper to reveal a small, rectangular box.

He lifted the lid from the box. Hannah let out a sharp, stunned breath.

A pair of faded blue, size nine woman's sneakers.

Liminal Space

The station exuded an alien sense of stillness.

Jane had worked the night shift before, but this one was different. She couldn't put her finger on it, but something seemed off.

The emptiness in the station was wrong. Like a high school during summer break or an abandoned amusement park. Life was supposed to happen here. People moving from room to room. The chaotic noise of a dozen overlapped conversations.

Instead, there was nothing. A lifeless expanse of cold, beige tile. A between space people aren't meant to see.

Wind whistled over the roof. Rain tapped the windows a thousand times a second. The streetlights outside were blurred by the storm.

Jane spent most of her time the last few weeks manning the tipline. They hoped someone would come forward with information on Margaret. Someone had to know something. So far, no luck.

She heard all sorts of stories from all sorts of people. One woman swore up and down the county had been stealing her horses when she slept. Another claimed her paperboy killed her cat back in '94.

On Monday, a call came in from Park River. The caller was positive his brother in law matched the description of the man seen with Margaret. Jane informed him they hadn't released any descriptions. The caller insisted she should investigate him anyway because he was, *"a real asshole."*

Her last call was from a woman in Darby. Her husband drowned in Sixmile Bay. He got caught in a storm while fishing. Jane asked how long ago it happened.

The woman said it would be five years on Friday. She needed someone to talk to.

Jane was happy to oblige. It was nice to talk to someone who didn't think their next-door neighbor was a murderer. She was surprised how many people did.

Jane's head was clouded by a perpetual droning. Low-level static clung to the back of her eyes. Her tongue tasted bitter, like gas station coffee and out of date chocolate. Dread lurked in the pit of her stomach.

Jane's mother always claimed she could sense things. She burned cedar and sweetgrass to scare away evil. Whenever something bad happened she would say it was caused by bad spirits that put things out of balance.

She had thought about her mother every second since their encounter the day before. About the woman she used to be before Jane's father died. She got lost after that. Trapped in a bottle of little red pills. An addiction prescribed by her doctor.

Her mother didn't need antidepressants. She wasn't depressed, she was angry. Instead of making her mother happy, the pills made her stop sleeping. They made her mean. She didn't hit or yell. She hurt with words. With the blame she cast. The accusations meant to maim and humiliate.

She didn't know which version of her mother she met on Christmas. The caring woman who raised her and deserved her forgiveness, or the spiteful stranger who loathed her for existing. It seemed to be the former, but people wear convincing masks when they seek absolution.

Her stomach churned. Something deeper slithered in her gut. Past the childhood trauma and repressed memories. A hot ball of lead burned through her insides trying to escape. She tried to ignore the feeling, but it wouldn't leave. An unshakable knowing something terrible was going to happen. The bad spirits were inside her, crawling under her skin. Maybe her mother wasn't so crazy after all.

A metallic ring echoed down the empty halls as another call came along the tipline. Her heart pulsed in her throat as she answered the phone.

"Ramsey County Sheriff's Department," said Jane.

"I'm looking for Sheriff Roy Hill." The voice on the other end of the line was soft, almost childlike in its inflection.

"The Sheriff's busy at the moment but if you have information, I can pass it along to him."

"I'd prefer to talk to him myself. I don't want anything to be misunderstood."

"He's not at the station right now, but as I said, I can pass a message along."

The man let out a wounded breath. His silence was palpable. Jane's stomach tightened. The static in her head fuzzed her vision. The bitterness in her mouth overwhelmed. She wished she could scrub her tongue with steel wool.

She sensed something in the man's voice. Sadness. A pain she could feel when he spoke.

"I didn't mean for it to happen," said the man.

"You didn't mean for what to happen?"

"I didn't want to do it. She just couldn't understand. She couldn't even look at me."

"Sir, what did you do?" Jane already knew the answer. She knew before she picked up the phone.

"I want the Sheriff to know he could have stopped it. I'm sorry. I didn't want to kill her."

The word wrenched Jane's stomach.

Kill.

"Sir? Did you kill Margaret?"

"I didn't want her to die. She'd still be alive if it wasn't for him."

The line clicked as the man hung up. The lead in Jane's belly burned hotter than ever, ate a hole through her stomach and sunk into her bowels. The moment she dreaded arrived. The bad spirits had come home to roost.

PART II

We seek the wind,
Not to fly towards new heights
Or soar among the clouds,
But to let us breathe
When we feel our chest grow heavy.

We seek the earth,
Not to tread upon unfound wonders
Or venture into unknown lands,
But to have a place to lie
When our burdens press on our shoulders.

We seek the fire,
Not to warm our hands
or light our path in the night,
But to burn away the past
When we can no longer stand the memories.

We seek the water,
Not to nourish our thirst
Or clean away our transgressions,
But to live for eternity
In the tranquil world etched on its surface

The Night Of

Then

Roy stood in the kitchen. Muddy water pooled at his feet as he dripped onto the green and white checkered tile. The storm battered the windows with a jumbled tempo. 3:04a.m. glowed on the microwave in hazy green block numbers.

He hadn't realized it then, but the house felt wrong that night. The carpet was too dry beneath his feet. A sour taste filled his mouth. The storm pounded on the roof, drowning every other sound.

In the hallway, light crept beneath the bathroom door onto the carpet.

"Linda?" Roy knocked on the bathroom door. Thunder echoed over the lake. "You in there?"

"Why are you home so late?" Linda's voice was faint, muffled by the scream of the storm.

"New case came in today. I was finishing up some paperwork. Is everything alright?"

"Yeah. I'll be out in a minute."

"Alright. I'll be in bed if you need me."

He hadn't made it three steps before Linda spoke again. "Honey?"

"Yeah?"

"I love you... So much."

"I love you too. You sure you're alright?"

"Yeah. I'm just not feeling well. You go to bed. I'll be out soon."

"Alright. Goodnight, honey."

"Goodnight."

Roy continued down the hallway. His feet were sore, and his eyes stung. He couldn't keep burning the midnight oil like this. He wasn't young anymore. He had pains in his joints and soreness where he never did before. This rain didn't help any. He finally understood what his father meant when he said the rain hurt his knees. Something about the storm made his legs throb.

Another light peeked past the door at the end of the hall. Everyone seemed to be having a sleepless night. The first of many this house would see.

He went to his daughter's door and opened it.

Georgia sat on her bed on the far side of the room. Her Little Mermaid blanket wrapped around her like a shroud. She sat in silence in the dull light of her bedside lamp. She looked at him when he entered the room, as if expecting him. "Hi, Daddy."

"Hey, Peanut. Shouldn't you be asleep?"

"I couldn't."

Roy walked across the room and sat beside her on the bed. "I'm sorry, sweetheart. Is it the storm?" He wrapped his arm around her shoulders to comfort her. She shook her head. Her eyes wandered to the darkness of the hallway.

"What is it?"

Georgia looked down at her hands. She twiddled with her fingers. Anything to pass the time so she didn't need to answer him.

"Georgia, look at me." He put his hand gently beneath her chin and turned her head until she looked him in the eye. "You can tell me what's wrong. No matter what it is. Okay?"

"It's Mommy," whispered Georgia, as if telling a secret she promised she would keep.

"What about Mommy?"

"I don't know. She seems- different."

"What do you mean different?"

"She doesn't act like Mommy anymore. It scares me. Is she okay?"

Roy didn't answer. Not right away. He wanted to tell her, "*Of course Mommy's fine. Everything's gonna be alright.*" Let her live in her fairy tale with princesses, knights, and fire breathing dragons. Let her be the little girl she was. The words caught in his throat. "Well. You know how we talked about your mommy being sick?"

Georgia nodded.

"That means sometimes Mommy might act a little different than we're used to. But that doesn't mean you should be scared. No matter what, she's still your Mommy and she'll always love you. It's just that- sometimes- she might need a little help. But that's why you and me are here. To help mommy when she needs it. Okay?"

"Okay."

"Alright. Now try to get some sleep." Roy tucked her in and gave her a kiss on the forehead. "Goodnight, Peanut. I love you."

"I love you too, Daddy."

When Roy got to the bedroom, Linda still wasn't there.

The shower was running when he went back to the bathroom to check on her. Light still loomed under the door. He knocked. "Linda?"

He knocked again, louder. "Linda? You alright?"

She didn't answer. Rain pounded on the roof. Thunder clapped in the sky. Wind howled through the trees and shook the windows, but she stayed silent.

"Linda, you in there?

He tried the knob, but the door was locked. "Linda, please answer me."

He pressed his shoulder to the door. It wouldn't budge. "Linda? Sweetie? Open the door please."

He twisted the knob and threw himself at the door.

SLAM. SLAM.

"Linda?"

SLAM. SLAM.

"Honey, open the door."

SLAM. SLAM. CRASH.

The door split under the force of his shoulder. His eyes darted around the bathroom. He expected the worst, but found nothing. A shower running behind a locked door. An empty room.

He hurried into the hall and towards the kitchen. The driveway door was open. The screen hung on one hinge. The wind battered the door against the side of the house as rain soaked the floor. He ran into the storm, looked in every direction at once. He rounded the fence into the backyard. His breathing stopped. The world went blurry.

He didn't remember a lot of things about that night. His therapist told him he was repressing it. He wasn't sure how something he thought about every waking moment was repressed. He still remembered details, but other parts slipped from his mind. His brain took the memories and blurred them.

He remembered coming home. Remembered the feeling that pressed down on the house. Heaviness in the air. Smothering weight. He remembered his talk with Georgia. He didn't remember slamming against the bathroom door so hard he fractured his shoulder. He remembered trying with everything to get to his wife. Hoping when he got to the other side, she would be okay.

He didn't remember how he searched every corner of the house. He remembered the crippling sense of worry that squeezed his gut. How he scrambled from room to room praying his feeling was wrong.

He didn't remember going outside and seeing his wife face down in the water. He remembered the woman he loved. The mother of his daughter. Cold and pale. The way her body moved on the surface of the lake. Unbreathing. Lifeless. Not his wife of twenty years but some piece of wreckage washed up by the tide. It wasn't Linda. It couldn't be. If it was, his life would be over.

He didn't remember running to her. Fighting against the storm to reach her. He remembered the temperature of her skin as he clamored to find a pulse. The crack of ribs as he pounded on her chest.

He didn't remember screaming so loud he woke the entire street. He didn't remember Georgia running outside into the rain. He remembered the look in his daughter's eye when she saw her mother. His head pounded so hard he didn't hear his daughter when she cried. When she asked him if her mommy was okay.

He didn't remember calling 911, but he sat waist deep in the mud when the ambulance came. He held her even as they tried to take her away. He sat in the rain paralyzed, knowing his world had ended.

The Girl with the Golden Hair

Then

Tommy sat at the counter next to the register. He'd sat there every morning since he'd seen her. He ordered breakfast when he could afford it. If he couldn't, he ordered a drink and sat until he was asked to give up the seat to another customer. Today was his sixth day in a row coming to the Red Top. He hoped if he came every day, he would see her again.

The girl with the blonde hair.

He hadn't stopped thinking about her since he saw her. He couldn't explain it. He'd never been drawn to someone like this before. Normally, he hated people, whether he knew them or not. He hated everyone. But when he saw her, something overwhelmed him. Pulled at him. An invisible string tied them together. Pulled them towards each other. A feeling they were meant to meet. If they didn't something terrible would happen.

Their meeting had to be fated. How else could it be explained? He was eating at a diner he'd never been to before and she happened to walk through the door while he was there. He couldn't have been there for more than an hour. If he hadn't seen her, he never would have come back to this town. But he had seen her, and he was determined to see her again.

He remembered a sermon the pastor gave in church. Back when he went to church. When his father forced him to go. Now, his father spent his Sundays kneeling over the toilet, instead of in the pews.

The pastor said, *"There is no wisdom, no insight, no plan, that can succeed against the Lord."* God does not sit idle while we go about our lives. He guides us. Leads us on the path we are meant to go on.

Maybe, God led Tommy here. Maybe, God made Tommy's father drink. Beat him so bad he had no choice but to run. Maybe, God wanted him to run here. To a diner in Clareborne, North Dakota. Maybe, He wanted him here so he could meet her.

Tommy was at the counter for almost four hours with no sign of the girl. It was almost three o'clock now. He'd have to head home soon. He collected his things to leave. He would try again tomorrow.

He stood to leave when the bell rang above the front door. He turned to check, not expecting to see her.

His heart stopped.

There she was.

She walked up to the register. She faced away from him, swaying back and forth, looking out the windows as she waited for the waitress.

The feeling came over him again. That pull. A tug on the string that connected them.

"Hello," said Tommy.

She turned towards him to see if the greeting was directed at her. That's when he realized. Her hair wasn't blonde. It was golden. Her eyes weren't green. They were emeralds flecked with starlight. She wasn't a girl. She was an angel.

"Hello," repeated Tommy.

She smiled at him. "Hello."

"Sorry to bother," said Tommy. "I feel like I've met you before."

"Maybe. You from around here?"

"Sort of. I live just south of here. Across the lake."

"Where you from?"

"Nowhere you would have heard of."

"I know what you mean," she said. "Small towns are like that. I'm Georgia, by the way."

"Tommy," he said.

The waitress walked up to the register and handed Georgia her bag. She paid for her order and said thank you to the waitress.

"Well, I got to get going. It was nice to meet you, Tommy. Maybe I'll see you around."

"I hope so."

She smiled before turning and walking out the door.

<u>Omen's</u>

Now

Jane drove east down Highway 2.

A storm loomed on the horizon. A wall of clouds bruised the sky. The cars heater gave an electric hum as it wheezed out a breath of lukewarm air.

She spun the radio to zero after the approaching storm turned the signal to mumbled static.

The lake was far behind her now. The glass stillness of the water replaced by an ever-swaying sea of grass.

She distracted herself by trying to remember every license plate she passed on the way. So far, there had been three. Two semis: Montana plate G3W-098 and Iowa plate ACY644 (one hauled lumber and the other a tractor), and a red pick-up caked in dry mud. North Dakota plate 66253.

She imagined a story for each vehicle. Where they came from. Where they were headed. Whether or not the driver had a family or lived on the road. Anything to distract her from what she was headed towards.

Omar Mitchell died three days after Christmas. He was twenty-seven years old. Only a year older than Jane was. Did he know a year ago his time was almost up? That in just over three-hundred days, he would reach his last? Of course he didn't know. Only God knew. And God was damn good at keeping secrets.

Jane found herself with the job of informing Omar's mother of his passing. She had never done this before. Told someone their child was gone. She didn't want to do it now, but when the Sheriff asked for volunteers, it felt like the right thing to do.

The Sheriff wanted to tell Mrs. Mitchell himself. The way he saw it, Omar's death was all on him. To the sheriff, this entire case was somehow his fault. He was a man that carried the weight of the world on his shoulders, unaware some things were out of his control. For some things we were only observers.

Jane was having enough trouble figuring out what she would say to break the news. She couldn't imagine the kind of strength it would have taken for the Sheriff to do it himself. All that guilt, crashing down on him like waves on a stormy shore.

They ended up locating Omar's mother and Margaret's father on the same day. In the Sheriff's eyes, finding out what happened to Margaret took precedence.

In one way the Sheriff was spared, but maybe talking to Omar's mother would have helped lift some weight of his chest. He would never find out if that was the case.

Jane headed east to tell Omar's mother, while the Sheriff headed west to tell Margaret's father.

Omar's mother lived fifteen miles outside Lakota in a small town called Dorland. At one time, the town was thriving. A school, a hotel, a mechanic, stores, bars, churches. Now there wasn't even a sign on the highway to mark it.

Jane pulled off the highway onto a wide dirt road. Dorland's main street was littered with potholes.

The houses were abandoned and unattended. Collapsed roofs and exposed, mishappen frames.

Most of the families left after the fire. They bought farms and moved out into the country or went to the city to find work. There couldn't be more than a dozen people who still called Dorland home.

Jane drove past the burned-out ruin of the elementary school. Rusted bikes sat out front still chained to the rack, frames bent and tires far past rotted. The flag still swayed at half-mast. Tattered and faded by the weather.

Mrs. Mitchell lived on the north edge of town. Her small, one-story home had gone untouched by the fire. Jane pulled up in front and shut off her engine. She unbuckled, smoothed out her clothes, took a deep breath, and stepped out of the car.

On her way to the front door, she rehearsed what she would say. "*Mrs. Mitchell, your son- Mrs. Mitchell, I regret to inform you- Mrs. Mitchell, I'm sorry to have to tell you this but-*" She reached the house before working out how to break the news.

She knocked. Footsteps creaked across the floor towards the door. Each step pressed a new weight onto Jane's chest. She couldn't imagine what Mrs. Mitchell's reaction would be. Couldn't fathom the pain she was about to put this woman through.

The front door groaned as it swung open. "Mrs. Mitchell, I'm sorry to have to tell you this but-"

"Omar's dead," finished Mrs. Mitchell.

Mrs. Mitchell did not respond to the news the way Jane expected. She didn't cry, didn't accuse Jane of lying. She didn't scream at her for playing some sick joke, fall to her knees and sob, pleading with God to bring her son back. She wasn't asking if her son was gone. She knew.

Jane's breath caught in her throat. Nausea took hold of her. "Yes, ma'am. I'm very sorry."

"Not your fault darling. I've known this day was coming for a long time now. Come in, please. Get out of the cold."

Jane followed Mrs. Mitchell into the house. The scent of potpourri attempted to mask the stench of cigarette smoke. The house was well kept. Everything tidy and in its place. Not what she would expect to find in a town like this.

"I knew it would only be a matter of time before God took another one of my babies," said Mrs. Mitchell. "My daughter, Abigail. She passed. Almost a year ago now."

"Mrs. Mitchell, I'm so sorry."

"Please, dear. Call me Lou. Would you like some coffee?"

"No, thank you."

"Nonsense, I've already got a pot on. Why don't I get you some."

Mrs. Mitchell walked into the kitchen.

Mugs clinked in the kitchen as they were placed on the counter. Greying white sheets covered the furniture in the living room. The couch and the love seat were undisturbed. Waiting for company that never arrived. The only place that showed signs of life was a recliner in front of the TV. An ashtray on the coffee table held a still burning cigarette. A statue of the Virgin Mary sat atop the mantle. Chips in the paint showed the hard white plaster beneath. A rosary hung around her neck. A noose of Hail Mary's. The walls of the living room were covered in photos. A baby wrapped in a soft pink blanket. A little girl with pigtails. A teenager with long, golden hair. A memorial card tucked into the frame of a family photo. Abigail's life told in snapshots.

She walked up to the photo of a young Abigail. She looked familiar. Had Jane seen her before? Her eyes lingered on the family photo. When she looked at the picture on the memorial card, she knew where she had seen her before.

Margaret. She looks like Margaret.

Did she? The two girls certainly resembled each other. Long hair and fair skin. There were differences: Abigail's hair was darker than Margaret's, A dark honey color in place of Margaret's pale blond. The eyes were different too. While Margaret's eyes were faded green, Abigail's were a deep cerulean blue.

Maybe there was no resemblance at all. Maybe Jane just thought that because she couldn't get Margaret out of her head. The marks on her face where the blood pooled beneath her skin. Her eyes. The thousand-yard stare. The same stare her father wore when he came home from the army.

Goosebumps rippled down Jane's arm.

"Coffee's ready," called Lou from the other room.

Jane took one last look at the photo. She shook herself back to reality and swallowed hard before joining Lou in the kitchen.

Lou grabbed the coffee pot and filled two yellowed ceramic mugs. "Milk? Sugar?"

"No, thank you."

Lou pulled out a chair and sat down across from Jane. She lit a fresh cigarette and took a long drag.

Jane sipped the coffee. The acid burned her stomach, but she needed a way to fill the silence. She wanted to say something comforting, but nothing came to her. What could she say? *I'm sorry both your kids are dead. I hope me coming to tell you made it a little easier.*

"How did he go?" asked Lou. "Was it the drugs?"

Jane's mouth went dry. "He was shot. He passed away in the hospital." She tried to speak kindly, to soften the blow, but the words sounded harsh.

Lou nodded. A slow nod that said, *I understand.*

"When I lost Abby, that was hard." Lou's voice cracked at the mention of her daughter. "She was a good girl. Not perfect. No one is. But she was good. She cared about things. About people. Her problem was always that she trusted too easily. She trusted her father would come back some day. She trusted her brother would get sober and stop hurting us. She had a special spot in her heart for broken things. She was missing a week before they found her. I prayed. Every night. I prayed she got herself out of this place. That she was happy somewhere away from all this- shit." Lou ashed her cigarette into her mug. Her voice strained with the effort of holding back tears. "Eventually, I got the call. They asked me to come down to the station to identify her, but I knew. A mother knows." Lou sat up in her chair and wiped her eyes with the back of her hand. "They found her down at Stump Lake. They showed me the tattoo on her ankle. They wouldn't even let me see her face. Told me I didn't need to remember her that way." Lou choked on her sorrow. "As if I could remember her for anything except what she was. My little girl."

The sun sat low on the horizon when Jane finally got back to the station. The clouds cleared and the harsh wind mellowed into a cool evening breeze.

The stack of files on her passenger seat stared up at her. It took most of the day and a fair amount of arguing, but she managed to pull files from the Nelson and Benson County offices. She would have come straight back to the station, but something about Mrs. Mitchell's story stuck with her. Besides the obvious horror of a woman talking about the loss of her daughter, something about the whole thing made Jane's stomach lurch.

The bitter taste in her mouth when Lou told her the story had nothing to do with the stale coffee. She recognized that taste. The same acrid layer coated her tongue that night at the station. The night when Margaret's killer called.

Jane didn't know if she believed in a sixth sense or clairvoyance like her mother did. She was probably blowing things out of proportion, but she needed to be sure. Something in her gut told her evil lurked in the shadows. She had the distinct feeling more of her mother's bad spirits were coming down the pipeline.

Lamentations

They located Margaret's parents through her birth records. Her mother was an English teacher in Leeds, before she passed just over a year ago. Her father was a pastor at Saint Maria's, a Lutheran denomination in Anders, a small town off route 2 near Pelican Lake. Clareborne was like Manhattan in comparison.

The town consisted of a single intersection. Squat structures of dust-colored brick and desaturated wood. Houses that needed a new coat of paint a decade ago peered out behind dry brown shrubs. A handful of vintage storefronts with signs too faded to read. A town frozen in time, like the rest of the world moved on and Anders never got the memo.

Roy found the church at the end of a narrow dirt road, nestled in a grove of threadbare oak trees. A small steepled chapel, seated beside an old wooden trestle bridge curled over a dribble of muddied creek. The church was clean and manicured. An ivory tower amidst streets of mud.

Roy parked along the tree line and stepped out of his truck. The musk of damp earth filled his nose. Phantoms of mist drifted across the lake, spilling out into the fields, haunting the countryside.

He heard Margaret's father before he saw him. His voice spilled from the open window of the church, distorted by the cool breeze that blew off the lake.

Roy entered the church and slid into the back row. Fresh varnish gleamed on the pews with a mirrorlike shine. He sat in silence as the pastor finished the sermon.

"I ask all of you here today to look inside of yourselves. Into your heart, where your troubles weigh you down. Into your mind, where your worries hold you in their clutches. Where the devil and his disciples tell you it is too late for repentance. It does not do to dwell on regrets and mistakes. We are all sinners."

The pastor looked out at the congregation. The white of his choker glared from the collar of a crisp black suit. Roy rubbed his neck, a sudden tightness in his throat.

A thin silver cross hung on a delicate chain over the pastor's heart. His face was tight and angled. A chin sharp enough to cut. The pastor's eyes paused on Roy for the briefest of moments.

"We are all sinners," professed the pastor. "Yet, the Lord still loves us. He forgives us our transgressions. Our lapses in judgement. So, when you feel your troubles pressing down. When you feel yourself drowning under the weight of your worries. All I ask is that you feel those troubles and those worries. Feel them pulling you under the surface. Feel the power they hold over you. And let them go."

The collections basket made its way through the crowd. Every hand that touched it contributed. The town was starving, but still they gave up the little they had. They parted with their money in an effort to buy what the church promised them. Hope. An answer to the chaos of life. Hope that at the end of the road, after all the shit life shoveled at them was over, they would be rewarded.

Roy could have told them what they wanted to know for free. There was no answer. Sometimes, things just happen. No matter how hard you search, there's never a reason.

"There is sin in all of us," said the pastor. "But in all of us, there is also forgiveness. The Lord's forgiveness. Today, when you walk out those doors and back into the world, just remember, every trial we face is a lesson from God. A temporary obstacle, put in our way to make us stronger." The pastor placed his palms on the podium, closing his eyes and bowing his head. He let those final words linger with his audience. "Thank you everyone for coming. May God bless you all."

A jumbled discord erupted as the congregation stood from the pews and filed down the church's main thoroughfare, stopping on the way to shake the pastor's hand and thank him for a wonderful sermon.

Small groups gathered on their way out the door, stopping to chat or gossip about the current goings-on in town. Roy considered his options. Most places were the same. Every town was full of the same people that did the same things. However you thought a particular group of people would be was usually how they were. Not to say people couldn't surprise you, but it happened less often than you would think.

Roy spotted the perfect group just inside the front doors. Two older women- the younger well into her sixties. He sauntered over to the group and joined their conversation. "Hello, ladies."

The women inspected him as they looked up. "Hello, officer," said the shorter of the woman "You're a new face. What brings you here?"

"Well, I was just hoping to ask you young ladies a question."

"Such a charmer. Ask away, dear."

"I was just wondering, do either of you know why Jesus couldn't be born in North Dakota?"

The women looked at him in confused silence. Glancing around the room for a hint this was some kind of prank.

"Because they couldn't find three wise men or a virgin."

"You are so bad." The shorter woman gave Roy's chest a playful slap. "Why are you really here sweetie? I haven't seen you around before. Is someone in trouble?"

"No, nothing like that. To tell you the truth, I'm in the market for a new church. A fresh perspective. I was hoping I could get it here. How do you like the pastor?"

"Pastor Baker is wonderful," said the taller woman. "He came here about twenty years ago after Pastor Nelson passed, and he's been very inspiring to the community."

"That is great to hear. It was a very interesting sermon. Certainly, caught my attention."

"Forgiveness is important. Especially to the pastor," said the taller woman.

"Can you blame him?" asked the shorter. "After what happened with his daughter?"

"His daughter?" interjected Roy. "What happened with his daughter?"

The taller woman flashed a condemning glare at the shorter. "That's only a rumor."

"Well when you hear something enough times you tend to believe it," said the shorter woman. "Now, I don't make word of gossip, but people have been saying his daughter was sent to some kind of facility. Not sure why, but a lot of folks say she had a breakdown. Some sort of mental disorder. God has ways of testing us."

"That he does," said Roy. "If you ladies would excuse me. I'd like to have a word with the pastor."

The old women bickered as he walked down the aisle to speak with Margaret's father.

Upon seeing Roy, the pastor shook hands with the young man he was speaking with and hurried to meet with him. "Sheriff. What brings you all the way to our neck of the woods?"

"Nothing in particular. I was just hoping to get some information about the area. Nice place you got here."

"We're very proud of our church. It's getting harder and harder to find good honest people in these troubling times. But we persevere."

"Interesting sermon. That the type of thing you usually preach about? *Drowning* beneath your sins?" Roy's emphasis sparked no reaction from the pastor.

"I only speak the truth. We are all sinners. But it's important people understand they are forgiven. We blame ourselves for things out of our control. We allow them to torture us and define us. But we must let those things go and live on separately from our sorrows. Guilt can destroy a man if left unchecked. I'm sure a man like you can agree with that."

Roy rubbed his brow. "You know it's funny you mention guilt. Because, actually, there is a reason I'm here." Roy bit the inside of his cheek as he showed the pastor a forced smile. "I was hoping I could ask you a couple questions about your daughter. Margaret."

"Margaret." A pause. Almost imperceptible, but all too telling if you knew to look for it. "She get herself into trouble again?"

"Something like that."

"Well, Sheriff, whatever she's gotten herself into, I'm sure we can figure something out."

"How do you mean?" inquired Sheriff Hill.

The pastor scanned the church, eyeballing a group of stragglers gathered near the door. "Look, Sheriff, we don't have much in this town, but what we do have is our community. Our reputation. Margaret is- difficult. She seems determined to disobey and rebel. She has no regard for what consequences her actions may have on others."

"What about her? What kind of *consequences*, did her actions have on her?"

The pastor's mouth hung half open as he looked at Roy, weighing his response. "I'm not sure what's going on here but- What has Margaret done?"

"Margaret hasn't done anything. I just heard a rumor, wondered if there was any truth to it."

"A rumor? You drove all the way out here because of a rumor you heard about my daughter? Is that the sort of thing my taxes pay for?"

Roy took stock of the church. Polished hard wood floors. Vaulted ceiling carved with likenesses of apostle Paul and the Virgin Mary. He was sure Mr. Baker hadn't paid taxes in well over a decade.

"I heard Margaret had a problem," said Roy. "Had to be sent away for a bit to recover. Could you tell me anything about that?"

"Yes. She's staying at a care facility. Down in Devil's Lake. She has been for a while now."

"Why so far away? There are closer hospitals than Devil's Lake."

"It's not a hospital it's-" The pastor stopped himself. "I'm not sure how my daughter's medical needs are a police issue."

This wasn't working. The pastor wasn't the type of man to implicate himself. He would dance around the point unless Roy was direct with him.

"Pastor, did you know Margaret was pregnant?" *Was.* It slipped from Roy's lips before he could stop himself. Roy watched for a reaction. Anger. Disgust. Something. The pastor's face was stone.

"Pregnant?" The pastor lowered his voice to be sure he wasn't overheard. "No. I had no idea. Are you sure?"

"Positive. Does that upset you?"

"Upset me?" Confusion spread across the pastor's features. "No, I just- Why are you here?"

A sense of dread overcame Roy. Upon hearing the sermon and the way he spoke about his daughter, Roy was sure the pastor was hiding something. But what if he was wrong?

He should have opened by telling the pastor his daughter was dead, but he was too caught up in trying to get something out of him. He couldn't avoid the truth anymore. "Mr. Baker. Margaret's gone."

"I'm sorry. I don't understand. How do you mean gone?"

"I mean she's passed on. She's- dead."

The pastor closed his eyes, clutched the cross hung from his neck. He raised his head towards the ceiling and mumbled a prayer Roy couldn't hear. "I don't understand. What happened?"

Roy ignored the question. "Have you been in contact with Margaret?"

"No. No, I haven't spoken to her since she left for treatment." The pastor's hands wriggled inside his pockets. "What happened to her? Was it-" The pastor looked around the church to be sure no one would hear him. "Was it the drugs?"

"Mr. Baker. I'm sorry to have to tell you this. Your daughter was murdered."

"Murdered?" His face registered shock but something in his tone felt synthetic.

"I know this is hard Mr. Baker, but I need to ask a few questions about Margaret."

The pastor sunk down into the front row of pews. The stragglers had finally found their way outside, leaving Roy and the pastor alone inside the echoing chapel.

"I need to know where Margaret was staying."

The pastor raised a shaking hand to his head. He squeezed his temples with his thumb and middle finger, covering his eyes as though a migraine had set in. "She was staying at a sober living home. She had problems with- substance abuse. We've tried to get her help in the past but nothing stuck. We were out of options. We had to send her away. You know how people talk."

Roy was disgusted by the sentiment. Sending away your daughter for your own self-interest. But who was he to judge? Hadn't he done the same thing? Unwillingly perhaps. In the end, was there really a difference?

"I'll need the address of where she was staying."

"Yes. Yes of course." The pastor unshielded his eyes and looked to Roy. "Sheriff. Do you know who did this to my little girl?"

He looked into the pastor's eyes for a long time, attempting to catch a glimpse of his soul. Something moved. Somewhere deep in the shadows of the pastors dilated pupils. He may not be the one who killed Margaret, but he was hiding something. "No. But I'll find out."

New Beginnings

New Beginnings was a sober living house ten minutes outside of Devil's Lake proper. A two-story with a wraparound patio and a second-floor balcony. A new coat of pastel yellow paint stood out against the grey pallor of the surrounding landscape. The lawn was freshly cut. The smell of rainfall heavy in the air. A statue of two clasped hands sat atop a pedestal at the center of a small round garden. The garden was being tended by two young women. They looked at the Sheriff and waved as he walked up the driveway.

He knocked on the front door and was greeted by a middle-aged woman with wireframe glasses and short cropped auburn hair.

"Good morning, officer," said the woman, seemingly confused by his presence. "Is there something I can help you with? I don't believe anyone placed a call."

"I was hoping to speak to you about a former resident."

"I'm not sure I can help. I can't give out personal information without the patient's approval."

"I understand."

The woman stood in the doorway looking up at Roy as if expecting him to leave. "Is there anything else I can help you with?"

"Would you be able tell me anything about a young woman named Margaret Baker. I was told she's been living here for some time."

"As I said, I can't give out information on patients. If there's something specific you want to know, then it's possible I can assist you, but I can't make any promises."

A group had gathered in the living room behind the woman. Men and women of varied ages pretending they weren't listening in on the conversation. "Is there any way we could speak in private?"

"I'm sorry officer, but I'm not sure we have anything to speak about."

Roy nodded. He took a step forward and leaned in towards the woman so only she could hear.

The matron's office was tidy and well-kept, as was the rest of the property. She offered him a chair. She sat at her desk across from him and squared off a stack of papers. "I'm sorry about that out there, but I need to be careful. We get police out here all the time trying to harass us. People think because we're addicts that automatically means were criminals."

"No need to apologize," said Roy.

"So, it's true then? Maggie, she's-" She couldn't bring herself to say the word.

"I'm sorry to say she is. Did you know her well?"

She let out a soft calming breath and made a cross over her heart. "Better than some. Not as well as others. She kept to herself mostly. Wasn't really the talkative type. She was a sweet girl though. Strong. She had to be to make it through what she did."

"When was the last time you saw Margaret?"

The matron leaned back in her chair. Her hand rested loosely around her throat. "About three months back. She made so much progress. Got her three month chip. She was so proud. We all were. After that she decided it was time to part ways."

"She was allowed to leave?"

"All of our patients are here voluntarily. As I said, they're not criminals."

"I just mean- her father gave the impression she wasn't on any sort of road to recovery. Seemed to think she had no interest in it."

"Well, that is just a load of horseshit. Pardon my French."

"You disagree?"

"I disagree with a lot of things Mr. Baker has to say."

"You've met him?"

"Once. When Margaret first came here. I spoke to him a few times over the phone, but eventually he stopped calling."

"What else did her father say that you disagreed with?"

The matron sat forward in her chair; her fingers laced on top of her desk. "The world pity's people like me. Like my patients. Not because they feel bad for us, but because they're disgusted by us. They push us to the side and dismiss us. We don't make it easy for people to like us. We lie, and we cheat, and we steal. We hurt people, and we *know* we're hurting people when we do it. But we can't stop ourselves. Margaret did not wake up one day and decide she wanted to be an addict. She was pushed to it. And I'm not saying she isn't responsible for her own actions. We all are. But that girl was in pain. She was running from something. She wanted more than anything to get clean, and she was working on it every day. She just needed people who would support her instead of pushing her away. She needed someone to give her a chance."

Roy sat in silence as he took in her words. The weight of them heavy on his chest. "Why did Margaret decide to leave?"

"Like I said, it was her choice. She was going strong, three months sober. I made her promise if she left, she wouldn't go back to her father. He was poison for her."

"Do you think Margaret's father might have hurt her?"

"Oh, he hurt her. You can be sure of that. But killed? I couldn't say one way or another."

"Do you know where she went, after she left? If not back home?"

"She sent me a letter after she left." The matron opened a drawer on her desk and shuffled through the contents. "Here it is." She pulled out a cream-colored envelope and handed it to Roy. Margaret's name was sprawled in the top right corner above an address.

"She mentions the family she was staying with. A young man she was seeing."

"Thank you, ma'am. You've been very helpful."

***

His name was Daniel Summers. He was seventeen years old. He lived on the north edge of town, with his parents, in a cluster of houses off State Highway 20. Two dozen homes walled in by a border of well-manicured hedges and trees.

Daniel's house was at the top of a shallow hill in the far northeast corner of the community. The driveway snaked up the slope towards a two-story colonial with beige vinyl siding and a two-car garage. The afternoon sun glared off the pale blue surface of a pond at the bottom of the hill.

Roy stood on the front porch, looking down the hill at a cluster of snow shrouded houses as he waited for someone to answer the door.

The door was answered by a man with curling black hair and a salt and pepper beard, who Roy assumed to be Daniel's father.

"Mr. Summers?" asked Roy.

"Yes." Mr. Summers leaned out the door and looked up and down the street. No doubt searching to find a reason the Sheriff was at his door. "Can I help you with something?"

"I was wondering if I could speak to Daniel. Is he home?"

Mr. Summers gave a quick glance behind him before pulling the door closer to him to block Roy's view of his home. "What do you want with Daniel? He's been here all day."

"Daniel hasn't done anything, Mr. Summers." Roy's insides tensed, unsure whether the statement was true. He hoped it was. Hoped a seventeen year old boy hadn't killed his pregnant girlfriend. Hoped he wasn't the monster they were looking for.

He hoped Daniel was innocent, but he found as he got older, fewer and fewer things surprised him. "I was hoping I could speak with him about a friend of his. Margaret Baker."

Mr. Summers clicked his tongue at the mention of her. "Margaret doesn't come around anymore. We did her the courtesy of allowing her to stay with us, against my better judgement, I might add. Then she up and disappears without so much as a thank you or goodbye. Broke Daniels heart when she left. I tried to tell him he was better off, but you know what it's like when you're that age. First heartbreaks always the hardest." Mr. Summers stared at Roy in silence for a moment. His eyes widened when he realized why the Sheriff had come knocking. The bitterness drained from his voice. "Is she alright?"

"I'm afraid not."

"Dad?" said a voice from inside the house. "Did something happen to Maggie?"

Mr. Summers turned towards the voice as he opened the door to reveal Daniel, standing behind him in the hall.

All the blood drained from Daniel's face. He looked at Roy with terror in his eyes. The Sheriff's presence was answer enough to his question. "What happened to Maggie?"

They sat around the kitchen table, Daniel across from Roy. His father sat beside him; his arm slung over his son's shoulders. Daniel's eyelids burned red as he fought off the onslaught of tears.

Roy explained what happened to Margaret. How she died and where she was found. He left out the more gruesome details. The discolored streaks on her face. The delicate placement of her hands. Her frosted flesh, frozen solid from so many hours alone in the cold.

The pregnancy had to remain a secret for now. Roy hated himself for it, but he needed to use that information carefully. Needed to see their reaction to the news. Both Daniel's and his father's.

"How did you and Margaret meet?" asked Roy.

"Leevers. I cashier there on the weekends. She would always come through my line. We got to talking. Started spending more and more time together. I can't believe she's-" Daniel choked on a sob before he could say the final word.

Roy gave him a moment to calm himself before continuing. "When was the last time you saw Margaret?"

"Three months ago. A few weeks before Christmas."

"Did she say anything about where she was going?"

"No. I woke up one morning and she was gone. No note or text or anything."

"And you've had no contact with her since?"

"No, sir."

"Had the two of you been fighting?"

"What exactly are you trying to say?" interrupted Daniel's father.

"Mr. Summers, please. I'm not accusing your son of anything. I'm just trying to fill in the blanks."

Mr. Summers eyed Roy, hatred plastered on his face. Hatred at Roy for bringing his son such devastating news. He looked at Daniel and nodded for him to continue.

"No, Sir. We hadn't been fighting."

"Was she acting strange? Doing anything out of character?"

"No, sir. She seemed normal."

Daniel hesitated for a moment as if deciding whether he should mention something. "There was something strange. A couple of nights before she left. I woke up and she wasn't there. I got up to look for her. I heard her in the kitchen. The lights were off, and she was sitting in the dark. I thought she was talking to herself, but she wasn't. She was on the phone, and she was crying. I turned on the lights and she hung up."

"Do you know who she was talking to?"

"No, sir. I asked her but she wouldn't tell me. She looked upset. Scared almost. I tried to talk to her about it, but she just kept telling me everything was fine."

"Mr. Summers," said Roy. "If you wouldn't mind, I'd like to speak with Daniel alone for a moment."

Mr. Summers stared daggers into Roy.

"Mr. Summers, I don't consider your son a suspect." He didn't. Not anymore. Criminals -especially psychopathic killers- often made good liars. They smiled when they should, cried when they needed to. Acted the part of human so well, they sometimes fooled you into thinking they were.

Daniel was in no way disingenuous. His reaction to the news seemed authentic. A heartbroken kid, devastated by the news of his girlfriend's passing.

"I just have some questions he may be more comfortable answering if his father wasn't sitting beside him," said Sheriff Hill.

Mr. Summers glanced towards his son.

Daniel nodded.

"I'll be in the living room. Just shout if you need anything." Mr. Summers shot one last piercing look at Roy and stepped out of the room.

Roy waited long enough for Mr. Summers to be out of earshot. He was probably just on the other side of the wall, listening in to make sure the big bad sheriff didn't accuse his son of anything indecent. Roy couldn't blame him. If someone had come to his door asking Georgia questions about a dead teenage girl, he'd have thrown them out onto the curb. Assuming they came at a time when he was functioning well enough to understand what was happening.

"Daniel. How long did you know Margaret?"

"Three or four months."

"And she was already living with you? Your father was okay with that?"

"It was his idea. Heard she was staying at a motel. He acts tough, but he cares about people."

"Why was she staying at a motel? Didn't she have a home? Parents she could stay with?"

"Motel was all she could afford. One of those by the night places off the highway. She couldn't go back to her dad's place. He didn't treat her very good."

"How do you mean? How did he treat her?"

"She didn't really like to talk about him. Whenever I asked, she would change the subject. I think she just wanted nothing to do with him."

Roy wrote down Daniels responses in his pad. Emphasizing Margaret's strained relationship with her father.

"Are you aware Margaret was an addict?" asked Roy.

"Yes." Daniel's response was delayed. His face wooden, as if admitting to it would get Margaret in some sort of trouble. "But she was past that. She was coming up on six months sober. She was happy. She- she *seemed* like she was happy. I got her a job at the market. We talked about getting a place after I graduated." Daniel's voice stuttered as he tried to get out the words.

Roy tried to swallow, but his throat was too dry. Now it was time for the hard part. "This may seem like a strange question but were you and Margaret- intimate."

A pink flush crept up Daniel's neck. "Does this have something to do with the case?"

"Yes. Unfortunately, it does."

"Yes, sir. We were."

Roy interlaced his fingers and placed them on the table. He stared at his knuckles as he called Daniel's father back into the room. Mr. Summers returned to the seat next to his son.

Roy looked Daniel in the eyes. He let a breath he didn't know he was holding and told Daniel about his baby.

***

Roy got permission from Daniel's father to check the phone records. If they could find out who Margaret had called. They might find the next piece of the puzzle.

He sat in his office. The sound of room tone buzzed in his ears. He continued his search while he waited for the records from the phone company.

The motel where Margaret was staying, and the supermarket she and Daniel worked at both came up dead ends. If anyone had noticed someone watching Margaret, seen or heard her having any sort of confrontation, they had forgotten or chosen to remain ignorant.

Roy read through Margaret's case file for the thousandth time. Every time he looked, he hoped to find something he'd missed, some nugget of information that would crack the case wide open. He never did. The crime scene had been barren of physical evidence. The shoes had been the same; ragged and well worn, but clean. There wasn't even anything on the shoes that could prove they belonged to Margaret. The cloth and laces had been washed. The soles scrubbed free of dirt and debris. No DNA. No Fingerprints. No nothing. A piece of material evidence, literally gift wrapped and left on his doorstep, and it got him no closer to an answer.

He thumbed through the file, knowing nothing of value would emerge. He needed to do something, feel like he was making progress on the case. Sitting around didn't do anything but allow him to be alone with his thoughts.

He tried to focus on the file, reading every word and studying every diagram. Nothing could stop his mind from wandering to Daniel. His reaction when he told him about Margaret's miscarriage. Roy saw the way the pain tore through him. The torment danced behind his eyes. Daniel didn't even have his driver's license. He wasn't old enough to drink or vote. But he already knew the pain of losing a child. A pain that cruelly and ironically would not fully set in until, somewhere down the line, when he had another child. When he watched them grow and become their own person. When he realized his child with Margaret never had that chance.

A tight knot formed in Roy's chest. A tumor of anger and anxiety. *He's going to get away with it.* The thought pressed on his temples and rang in his ears. This wasn't the first time the thought slipped into his mind.

He couldn't get away with it. He wouldn't live the rest of his life after destroying so many others. But the thought lingered, and every day that passed made it seem more like the truth. Every day they took a step and were no closer to finding the killer, that thought moved closer to becoming reality.

He didn't know how long Jane had been standing in the doorway, but when he noticed her, she looked concerned. "You alright Sheriff?"

Roy forced himself back to reality. "Fine. What is it?"

"We got the phone records. We know who Margaret talked to."

A Deceitful Tongue

Jane stared at Mr. Baker through the one-way glass that separated her from the interview room. Deep lines marred the gaunt features of his face. He looked older than he was. Frail, like a soft breeze would send him across the county in a tailspin. Like he had a dark secret inside, eating away at him with every passing moment.

He was still dressed in his preaching clothes. A pressed dark suit, all black besides the strip of white tucked beneath his collar. She pictured it closing around his throat. Tightening until it choked the life from him. Until his face turned purple, and he begged for air.

Jane's breath caught as the imagery of bulging eyes and pulsing veins formed in her mind. She forced the thought away as hot bile roiled in the back of her throat.

She turned her attention to the interrogation.

The sheriff sat across from Mr. Baker. His hands clasped together. A manilla folder on the table in front of him. "Last time we spoke, you told me you hadn't had any contact with Margaret since she left for treatment."

"That's correct."

"Okay." The Sheriff raised his shoulders, sitting up straighter. He was an imposing presence. Tall and broad, where the pastor was hunched and spindly. "Why did you tell me that?"

"I don't understand. What do you mean?"

"I mean why did you lie to me?"

The pastor's mouth opened and closed like a fish out of water, no sound escaped his lips.

"Why did you tell me you hadn't spoken to Margaret? Was it something you said to her? Something you didn't want me digging into? Something that may ruin your oh-so-shining reputation?"

The pastor stayed silent, but the guilt was painted on his face. In the beading sweat on his forehead and the subtle tremble in his lips.

She thought of Margaret. The cold grey of her skin, the emptiness in her eyes as she stared out towards eternity. Then she thought of Mrs. Mitchell and her little girl, Abigail. Cold and alone in the water for God knows how long. She might have wondered how someone could do that to their own daughter, but she knew. She understood how cruel a parent could be towards their child. The malice that could build if life hurt them in the right ways.

Her eyes burned as she stared at the pastor. He was the one to blame for this. The face of evil, responsible for all the girls who were lost and alone. The girls whose faces stared up at her as she flipped through file after file, searching for answers she may never have.

She could read the pastors sin on his face, plain as day. He might as well have stood and proclaimed his guilt for the world to hear. But it was all wrong.

The man across from the Sheriff couldn't be who they were looking for. His voice was wrong. *He* was wrong. The feel of him. The led in her belly. The sour rust in her throat when they spoke. None of it was there.

The Sheriff opened the file and slid it across the desk. He placed his finger on the page to show the pastor how they discovered his deception. "Is this your phone number, Mr. Baker?"

"Yes."

"What did the two of you discuss when you spoke? Did she tell you she was pregnant? That she wanted to keep the baby?"

The pastors only response was a continuation of his shocked silence.

"Did you push her?" asked the Sheriff. "Tell her to get rid of it? Tell her to get rid of your grandchild? Did she refuse? Did you get so mad that you did something drastic?"

"No."

"Did you find out where she was staying? Drive up there to talk some sense into her? Did things get out of hand?"

"That's not what happened. I did not hurt my daughter."

The Sheriff snorted with derision. "No?"

"No. And I don't appreciate you suggesting I did."

"I didn't suggest anything. I'm just asking questions. Questions you still haven't answered."

"And I won't answer them. Not until I see my lawyer." The pastor sat back in his seat with his arms crossed. A tight-lipped grimace slapped on his face.

"Alright," said the Sheriff. "If you don't want to answer my questions, I'll do my best to answer for you."

The Sheriff stood and placed his palms flat on the table. He loomed over the pastor, a dark specter, daring him to contradict what he was about to say. "I think your daughter called you after she found out she was pregnant. I think she told you she was clean. She was doing well, and she was in a good place to raise her child. I think you disagreed. You told her she needed to have it taken care of. Your junkie daughter having a child out of wedlock? You know how people talk. You know what that would have done to your *reputation.*"

"Stop," muttered the pastor.

"I think what you said hurt Margaret. Her father, the man who's supposed to love her more than anyone else, telling her having her baby was a mistake. She should go and have her baby killed to spare you from the embarrassment."

"Stop," begged the pastor.

The Sheriff didn't stop. He couldn't. That anger trapped inside- the anger Jane had only glimpsed those weeks ago during Leroy's interrogation- came boiling over.

"Do you know what that kind of thing can do to a young girl? The confusion it can cause? Your daughter was sober for six months before the two of you spoke. I suspect her relapse came soon after. You weren't there for her. You weren't there when she needed you, so she ran away to find peace in the only way she knew how."

"Stop."

"Mr. Baker, your alibi for the night of Margaret's death checks out. You may not have been the one who killed her. But for as long as you live, don't you ever even think about saying you didn't hurt her."

The Sheriff stood and walked from the room. The door closed behind him.

Pastor Baker began to sob.

Blame

One of the things Hannah liked about Roy was he was stubborn. He stood his ground when others walked away. Fought even if it wasn't his fight. He stood up for people who couldn't stand up for themselves. He cared about people. He'd been like that since high school.
She looked up at him from where she stood by the edge of the water. The man who she'd known for all those years was not the one who stood at the top of the embankment.

Roy hadn't been the same since the call came in. The call all but confirmed Margaret had been murdered. Hannah could see the changes in the way he carried himself. The way he seemed to drag himself through the day. Dark patches swelled beneath his eyes. A fog circled him. Blurred who he was and left him in a constant haze. He lived inside his own head, like the world around him didn't exist. She could hear the conversation that played behind his hollow eyes. The way he blamed himself.

"I didn't want her to die. She'd still be alive if it wasn't for him." That's what he had said. Whatever monster had done this.

Hannah could practically hear the words in Roy's head. Playing like a broken record. The needle etched his wrong doings on the inside of his skull. Every sin he'd ever committed bounced around behind his eyes like a rogue pinball as he tried to identify what he could have done to deserve this.

She tried to tell him it wasn't his fault. He couldn't blame himself for someone else's sick delusion. No matter what she said, it wouldn't get through.

Roy worked at the case even harder than he already had been. He spent late nights with endless cups of coffee and weary bloodshot eyes. Roy blamed himself. He'd been doing it as long as she'd known him.

Hannah had the shoes from the mysterious present sent to Fargo for testing. They came back clean. The killer knew they would. They were just another taunt. Another way to crawl beneath their skin and burrow into the bone.

The weeks passed. Late winter turned to early spring. The first signs of life blossomed into the world. The sun rose to the sounds of birdsong and the world got a tad warmer.

No clues. No leads. No nothing.

Until now.

The body was face down in the water when Hannah arrived on scene. A couple of school kids found her tangled in the weeds along the shoreline as they walked home from the bus stop.

Jane stood off by the road, far enough away so the kids wouldn't have to look at the body anymore. She asked them questions about how they came upon the body and if they had seen or heard anything.

If they'd noticed anything, they wouldn't remember, not yet anyway. Right now, Jane's questions would blow through their minds like leaves in the wind, scattered before they had a chance to rest. They would never be the same. No one was after an experience like that.

The girl had been dead for a while. Hidden somewhere beneath the ice. Waiting for some warmth to melt away her prison.

They wouldn't find any evidence. The lake would have washed it away. She thanked God the body had been face down. If those kids had seen her face they wouldn't have slept for a month. She knew she wouldn't.

She made sure to cover the body before they brought it up the slope. No one else needed to see this. Roy sure as hell didn't need to see it. She would have to tell him eventually, but right now, he wouldn't be able to handle it. He didn't need another thing to keep him up at night.

"Roy." Hannah moved up the hill towards him. He didn't look. He didn't respond at all. He didn't even move, except for his eyes. They were locked on the girl.

Hannah recognized his expression. She'd seen it before. The same expression her mother wore on the day Hannah's father died.

Vacant and lifeless.

Hannah's mother wore that look for the rest of her life. Even on the rare occasions her mother would smile or laugh, those eyes pierced through, frigid and haunted.

"Roy?" Hannah called again.

Roy's eyes stayed fixed on the water. "I was supposed to catch him."

"We don't know it's him," she lied. She knew and so did he. The sick fuck did it again and this time it was worse. So much worse.

"It was," said Roy. "I feel it. I feel- him. He's been here. I can taste it in the air. Bitter." He turned to her. "How many times has he done this already? Two? Three? Ten? How many more little girls are hidden underwater waiting for us to find them."

"You can't blame yourself, Roy."

He could. He did. She knew every part of him was convinced.

"It's my fault," he said.

"It's not. You did everything you could."

"Well, it wasn't enough, was it?" Anger burst from him. "He called the station. Called and told us he did it and we still couldn't catch him. Now, I have to go tell someone else their little girl is gone and she's never coming back. I wonder if they'll care this time. I wonder if they'll come claim her body and have a funeral or leave her to rot on a slab of metal in the morgue."

Hannah took a step back. A reaction that became ingrained in her. When a man got angry you moved away. Roy looked in her eyes. She tried to hide the fear but couldn't.

"I'm sorry." Roy's eyes darkened with shame. "It's not you, it's- I promised myself nothing like this would happen again." Roy let out his breath and turned back to the water. The body bag was being hauled up the slope on a gurney. Another nameless life zipped away in a plastic bag.

Did She Suffer?

The sun hid behind a wall of fog. The grey-white mist covered the sky and drowned the grass. Stagnant and brooding, the fog went on for miles, smudging out the horizon. Roy drove the single road that pierced through the center of the colorless void.

Roy thought of the girl. The most recent victim in some senseless, deranged game. Her name was Jennifer Hanson. She was ID'd through her dental record. Two months ago, she had celebrated her sixteenth birthday. Six weeks ago, she hadn't come home from her shift at Dollar General. Three days ago, she was found dead in Creel Bay, drowned, and beaten beyond recognition. Someone needed to go and tell her parents. Roy took the job. He needed to. Hannah volunteered to join him, and protocol dictated that Jane- being his partner- accompany him, but he insisted it was his burden to bear alone. His responsibility.

His fault.

Up ahead a bright orange water tower stood out against the dull sky. Huge arched letters spelled out the town's name. RUGBY. The high school mascot- The Rugby Panther- proudly displayed next to it for the world to see. Roy recognized the mascot from the picture in Jennifer's file. A patch on the jacket she wore over her cheerleading uniform.

He drove slow, stopped at every yellow light and stop sign. Took every turn unhurried and reluctant. His temples pulsed. Acid tickled the base of his throat.

The GPS signaled for the final turn. A robotic voice alerted him, *"Your destination is on the left in two-hundred feet."*

Two hundred feet before he broke the news. Destroyed any hope Jennifer's parents had their daughter would be home one day. Two hundred feet before he caused someone's entire world to drop out beneath their feet.

"You have arrived at your destination." said the robotic voice.

He pulled up in front of the address and turned off the engine. Two cars sat side by side in the driveway beneath a shroud of mist. A boat sat on a trailer against the side of the house. A couple of old coolers rested on top of the boat, waiting to be filled for the next family fishing trip. A small garden ran across the front of the house, populated by statues. A family of plastic baby deer peered out of the fog. Empty pots lined the garden. Spring flowers replaced by tangled dry vines.

Roy swallowed the lump in his throat and knocked on the door.

Jennifer's father answered. Upon seeing a police officer on his doorstep, he assumed the worst.

When Roy told him about his daughter, Mr. Hanson fell to his knees, his sobs more animal than human.

Mr. and Mrs. Hanson sat together on the couch. Mrs. Hanson placed her hand on her husband's leg. He pulled away from her despite their need to comfort each other. They might get through this and stay married, but the odds were against them.

"Did she suffer?" Mr. Hanson's voice was thick with grief.

Roy thought of Jennifer. The bruises on her chest. The way she fought for air over and over as water filled her lungs. How she used every ounce of energy she had to get one more breath. He thought of her face. Blackened flesh, torn and ragged. Shards of bone that pierced the bloody sludge inside of her cracked skull.

He wanted to puke.

To cry.

To scream.

To apologize for letting their little girl suffer.

"No," said Roy. "It happened quick. She didn't feel a thing. No different than falling asleep." *Except she'll never wake up*, thought

Roy. Never run into your room in the morning excited to start the day. Never call you at work to say she missed you. Never run to you after a long day and hug you like her life depended on it. You'll never hug her back, knowing your life did depend on it. Never start to take those moments for granted.

"Part of me hoped she ran away," said Mrs. Hanson. "She always wanted to go to California. See the sunset over the ocean."

Roy thought of Georgia. He was always thinking of Georgia. He told himself she was better off away from him. Away from this town. The town that took her mother and her childhood. The town where her father left her to fend for herself. Georgia always wanted adventure. Ever since she was a little girl, pretending an old barn was an unbreachable castle.

Roy wanted adventure once. That's why he joined the force. He got it- for a while. Soon, adventure became time away from his family. Fights with his wife for never being home on time. An excuse to get away from that house. The unendurable silence that lurked in the halls.

"Mr. and Mrs. Hanson," said Roy. "If you're ready, I need to ask you a few questions about Jennifer."

Mr. Hanson burst into a new round of tears, but he nodded and agreed to answer the questions.

"The last time you saw Jennifer she was headed to work, correct?"

"No," said Mrs. Hanson. "The last time was that morning. She didn't have work until later. She walked there when she got out of school."

"And how far is the walk from school to her work?"

"Not even ten minutes. Less than half a mile. She walked it almost every day. She had been for the last few months."

"I was never comfortable with it," said Mr. Hanson. "She was still so young."

"She was sixteen," said Mrs. Hanson. "She wanted some independence. It wasn't even half a mile."

Mrs. Hanson looked at her husband. She begged him with her eyes. Begged him to understand it wasn't her fault their daughter was dead. Begged him to forgive her.

"That morning?" asked Roy. "Did Jennifer mention she was doing anything after work? Going out with some friends? A boyfriend, maybe?

"No," said Mr. Hanson. "She wasn't dating."

Mrs. Hanson wrung her hands in her lap, unsure for a moment if she wanted to speak. "She was seeing someone. I'm sorry, John."

"I thought we decided she was too young."

"No, you decided that."

"Why didn't you tell me?"

"I knew you'd react this way. You've always been so protective of her."

"Maybe if you were more protective, my little girl would still be alive."

Mrs. Hanson recoiled as if slapped. As if she knew her husband blamed her but couldn't bear to hear him say it out loud.

"Mr. Hanson," said Roy. "I understand you're angry and confused. But this isn't helpful. Why don't you take a break. I think it'd be better if I spoke to the two of you separately."

Mr. Hanson stalked from the room. He looked back at his wife with scornful eyes. A door slammed as he disappeared into the garage.

"Mrs. Hanson," said Roy.

"Call me Mary, please."

"Mary. What can you tell me about Jennifer's boyfriend?"

"She was seeing him for a few weeks. Never brought him around here if she could help it. Didn't want her father to know about him. She asked me to keep it a secret. She didn't really have friends. I thought it'd be good for her."

"Wasn't she a cheerleader."

"Yes." Mrs. Hanson's hands wriggled on her lap. "But the other girls weren't very- welcoming."

"How do you mean?"

"She was bullied. They would call her names and make fun of her. That sort of thing happens in high school, I understand. She said it didn't bother her, but I could tell it did. I'm amazed she even stayed on the team. I think she did it for her dad, he always wanted a boy. An Allstate football star. I think she felt like cheerleading was the closest she could do for him."

"The bullying? Did it ever escalate to violence."

"Dear God no. They were just kids. I'm sure they were all sweet girls, but you know what high schools like. All sorts of pressure to be someone you're not. Jenny only ever wanted to be who she was. I went down to the school and told the faculty about what was happening. They said that's just the way it is with high school girls. Said hazing was just a part of growing up."

Roy nodded as he scrawled notes in a tattered memo pad. "What else do you know about Jennifer's boyfriend?"

"Not much. I told her I wouldn't tell her father, under the condition I got to meet him. John was really against her dating and- well, he has a temper, she thought if he found out he might try to hurt him."

"Your husband's temper. Has it ever caused him to hurt people before?" Roy didn't say he meant her and Jennifer, but Mrs. Hanson understood the implication.

"No. John wouldn't hurt Jenny. Never in a million years. He can get loud, but he's really a sweet man."

"What was he like? The boyfriend?"

"He seemed nice enough. Friendly. Respectable."

"And what did he look like?"

"Normal."

"Normal? How do you mean?"

"Well, he was tall. About your height. He had black hair. Thin little thing. Some sort of rash on the back of his right hand. Could have been a burn maybe. I'm not sure. I only met him the one time."

"Would you be willing to sit with a sketch artist?"

"Yes, of course."

"Is there anything else you remember about him?" Roy could tell by Mrs. Hanson's voice she wanted to say more. She knew something. Something she didn't want to say.

"Mary, I want more than anything to find out who did this to your little girl," said Roy. "To do that, I need you to be honest with me. Tell me everything. No matter how small the details may seem."

"He was a little strange, is all," said Mrs. Hanson.

"Strange in what way?"

"I don't know really. Something about him seemed- forced. The way he talked and answered my questions. Like everything he said was calculated to try and win me over. Scripted. Like he planned every answer beforehand. I figured he was a highschooler trying to impress his girlfriend's mother. I know what boys are like at that age. I figured it wouldn't last very long anyway. You know what relationships are like in high school."

Roy thought of his father's barn. The way he would sneak Hannah in at night, so she didn't have to sleep at home. The musty smell of hay and the sweet scent of her hair. He would hold her to keep her warm. Let her know she didn't have to worry as long as they were together. He planned to marry Hannah back then. Spend the rest of his life keeping her safe. He never knew why they grew apart. Things like that happen when you're young. He should have known it wouldn't last, but he was still naive then. The world hadn't taught him the harsh truth. He couldn't keep anyone safe.

"Was there anything else he did that seemed strange to you?" asked Roy.

"Yes. There was something else. I thought I was paranoid at the time. Looking for things about him I didn't like. He was Jenny's first boyfriend, and I wanted to make sure she would be safe but- The way he stood. Between me and Jenny. The way he held onto her arm. It left a bad taste in my mouth. Like he was protecting her from me. My ex-husband used to do the same. He couldn't stand it when I would talk to other men. He was the jealous type. He would-" Mary touched her cheek bone, as if reminded of the bruise from all those years ago. The humiliation and the shame. "But Jenny's boyfriend couldn't have been like that right? He was just a kid. She really seemed to like him. Told me about him all the time. Do you think- oh my God." A sob wrenched Mrs. Hanson's throat. The anguish she had held back for the past months released. "Do you think he hurt Jenny? Did he hurt my little girl?"

Roy was sure this wasn't the first time she thought it. But he knew that if she admitted to herself that Jenny's boyfriend did this, if she thought she noticed something strange about him and didn't make a move to protect her daughter, she would never forgive herself.

The mind was curious in that way, jumping through hoops and taking odd turns. Working as hard as possible to blame itself for things it had no control over.

Roy sat back in his truck. He rubbed his eyes with cold red hands. He told Mrs. Hanson it was very unlikely Jenny's boyfriend was the one who hurt her. A lie. He said most people were killed by people they didn't know. Another lie. Most people knew the person who killed them, especially when it came to girls around Jenny's age.

A flush crawled up Roy's face. His throat burned. His saliva took on a sour taste. He opened the door of the truck and threw up on the street out front of the Hanson's house.

Hard Truths

Jane and Roy traversed a long echoing corridor washed in sickly green light. The hallway was infused with a chaotic mixture of smells: gym clothes, cologne, cleaning supplies, and God knows what else.

Jane hadn't been inside a school in almost a decade. She never made a habit of reminiscing about school life, but the symphony of smells and the empty sound of resonant footfalls brought everything rushing back.

Her high school career was lackluster to put it mildly. Her life experiences up to that point hadn't painted her as a *'cool girl'*. Native, crazy mom, dead dad. A trifecta of traits that shallow high school kids could use as ammo (and use it they did).

Things in school weren't so bad. If she ignored the bullying and the constant nagging from her brain that the world would be better if she didn't exist.

She'd always done her best to fly under the radar. Remain unseen. For a lot of people her insistence on not bothering others was an open invitation to torment her even more. High school is fun like that. Hundreds of kids trying to discover who they are and deciding the best they can be is an asshole.

She found herself stopping in the main foyer as she came across the trophy case. Shining gold and silver gleamed under a strip of too bright fluorescent bulb. Pictures of star athletes were scattered throughout. Group photos of all the teams deemed worthy of being displayed.

On the bottom shelf all the way to the right, a framed picture of the cheerleading squad leaned against the back wall. Twelve girls lined up in two neat rows of six. Several of them were holding ribbons and plaques to show the team's accolades.

She recognized Jennifer in the bottom row. Second in on the left-hand side. Her hands were crossed on her lap. She smiled, but her eyes told a different story. She was surrounded by people. People who were supposed to be her teammates, her friends, and she was so alone.

"Did you know sociopathy can't be diagnosed in people under eighteen?" said Jane.

Roy stopped mid step. His echoing footfalls faded as he looked back at Jane in confusion. "I'm sorry?"

"They don't diagnose kids as sociopaths. They can't. Kids naturally display similar traits to people with antisocial personality disorders. They act impulsively and have trouble planning ahead. They show a lack of remorse and disregard for social norms. They have trouble respecting and understanding the feelings of other people. Schools are basically just a gathering place for little sociopaths."

"That actually explains a lot," said Roy.

"I'm nothing if not insightful."

Footsteps sounded from down the hall. Jane and Roy turned towards the noise. A middle-aged woman wearing loose black sweatpants and a worn spandex running jacket approached them. A greying ponytail sprouted from her head beneath a Rugby Panthers baseball cap.

"You must be Sheriff Hill." The woman reached out for a handshake.

"I am," said the Sheriff, accepting the offer. "This is my partner, Officer Barlowe."

"Nice to meet you both. My name is Beth Dawson. Around here they call me Coach Beth. I'm the P.E. teacher. I also coach the cheerleading team and the girls' basketball team. I heard you had some questions for me."

"We do," said Roy. "We also have some questions for the girls on the cheerleading team. It's my understanding they have practice today."

"They do. Can I ask what this is about?"

Jane reached into her bag and pulled out a photo of Jennifer Hanson her mother had provided for them. "One of the girls on the team, Jennifer Hanson."

"I know what Jenny looks like." Coach Beth ignored the photo. "I heard what happened to her. I just can't believe someone would do that to a child." She put her hands on her hips. Her head hung in a slow disbelieving shake. "What do you want to know?"

"We were just hoping to get a little more insight into what she was like," said Jane. "Who she spent time with. Places she liked to go. Anything that might help."

"She was a sweet girl. Shy. Kept to herself. I tried getting her to open up, but she never really took to it." Coach Beth let out a deep sigh. "I suppose it's the other girls you want to talk to. They'd know better than me who Jenny spent her time with. I'll take you to the gym. The girls are in there now."

They followed Coach Beth through a labyrinth of identical hallways. The walls and floors the same dreary off-white, below row upon row of migraine inducing fluorescent tube lights. The only way to distinguish these halls from those of a prison were the burnt orange lockers that seemed to span every available inch of wall.

The girls were gathered in the gym. Huddled in a group on the bleachers laughing amongst themselves. They looked up as Coach Beth entered. There expressions shifted when they saw two police officers enter behind her.

Coach Beth addressed the group. "Girls, this is Sheriff Hill and Officer Barlowe. They came all the way here from Devil's Lake to ask you a few questions. I have a meeting with Mr. Fuller in a few minutes. While I'm gone, I expect you on your best behavior. Am I understood?"

"Yes coach," answered the girls.

The girls watched Coach Beth as she walked across the gym and made her exit, her sneakers squeaking on the freshly polished floor with every step. Their eyes followed her with the same slow crawl, as though each of them was psychically linked.

Sheriff Hill stepped forward to face the pack.

Jane joined him as eleven sets of eyes focused on her. The way the girls moved in perfect unison- backs straight, shoulders back, slight turn of the neck- reminded Jane of something from a horror movie.

"We're here to ask you a few questions about a friend of yours," said Sheriff Hill, "Jennifer Hanson."

"She wasn't our friend." The response came from a girl who sat in the center of the group, ringed by her teammates.

"And what's your name?"

"Ashley."

Ashley was tall and blonde. High sharp cheekbones. Bright blue eyes accented with winged eyeliner. The other girls looked upon her with admiration. A queen surrounded by her court.

Jane almost laughed at the scene. The stereotypical head cheerleader from every high school movie ever made.

"Well, maybe she wasn't your friend, Ashley," said Sheriff Hill. "But I don't think you speak for the rest of your teammates. Were any of you friends with Jennifer?"

He was wrong about Ashley not speaking for the rest of them. Jane could tell by the way their eyes lingered on Ashley, like pleasing her was their means for survival.

"None of us were friends with her," said Ashley. "We didn't even want her on the team. But Coach insisted."

"Why didn't you want her on the team?" asked Sheriff Hill.

"Because she was a freak."

"A freak? In what way?"

Jane didn't know how the Sheriff was staying so calm. Anger welled inside her chest, growing with every cruel dismissive retort that dripped from Ashley's mouth.

"Like she was a loser," answered Ashley. "Always sitting alone, mumbling to herself and shit. Like being friends with her would be social suicide."

Jane eyed the group with disgust as the girls laughed. All except one. She sat in the back, a few rows above Ashley. Nervous eyes hid behind a curtain of copper hair. She wore a disappointed frown she wouldn't dare put on if she was in sight of Ashley.

Jane nudged the Sheriff, asked for silent permission to take over the questioning.

She pulled a picture from her file. A copy of the sketch created based on Mr. Hanson's description. A depiction of a thin faced young man. Average looking. A long triangular face with a pointed chin, thin lips and a mop of tussled black hair.

She held the sketch up to the girls. "Do any of you recognize this person? We have reason to believe he was Jennifer's boyfriend."

"I doubt it," said Ashley.

"Why's that?"

"Because there's no way anyone would want to touch her," Ashley laughed.

The other girls followed suit. Some genuine. Some halfhearted.

The only one who didn't laugh at all was the girl in the back. She looked uncomfortable. She rang her hands in her lap. Her eyes flicked between the sketch of the man and the top of her feet.

Jane jotted something down in her notepad and showed it to Sheriff Hill.

She knows something.

With her eyes, Jane gestured to the girl in the back row.

Sheriff Hill glanced towards the group and nodded in understanding.

"Do any of you know what happened to Jennifer?" jane looked Ashley in the eyes, the anger in her gut rinsed her face with . "Jennifer's body was found in a lake less than an hour from here."

The statement caused visible discomfort among the girls, even Ashley, who shifted in her seat, looked to the floor to avoid Jane's burning gaze.

"She was drowned. Several times. Someone beat her until her skull caved in."

Sheriff Hill placed a hand on her shoulder so she would back down.

Jane brushed it away, stepped forward. Her gaze bore into Ashley's soul. She was determined to make the girl realize the people she bullied and harassed were not her punching bag. They were not expendable bodies she could use to climb some bullshit social ladder. They were people. Human beings with feelings and families just like her.

"We had to identify Jennifer through dental records because there wasn't enough left of her face. Her parents had to have a closed casket at her funeral. They couldn't even look at her when they said goodbye. So, maybe you didn't like Jennifer. Maybe she wasn't your friend. But she didn't deserve that. So, next time you decide you should torment someone because they don't fit in with you and your delusions of grandeur, I want you to think about Jennifer. How she fought to stay alive. Over and over again, for hours. And then you'll ask yourself if you've ever actually done anything to make you deserve the praise you're so desperate for. And if you think about it enough, who knows, maybe you'll develop some qualities that people might mistake for decency."

Jane turned and walked from the gymnasium, staying calm until the doors closed behind her.

The moment she was out of sight she collapsed against the wall and took a deep choaking breath, trying not to sob. She put her back against the wall and sank to the floor, head on her knees as she did her best to calm herself.

By the time Sheriff Hill joined her, she'd gotten her breathing under control. He found her pacing part way down the corridor that led back to the main foyer.

Sheriff Hill was accompanied by the girl Jane suspected of knowing something.

The girl stood with her head down, arms hung at her sides as she clenched and unclenched her fists.

"Officer Barlowe this is Sarah. She has a few things she'd like to tell us."

"Hi Sarah," said Jane. "I'm sorry about-"

"Jenny was my friend," said Sarah. "All that stuff you said. Was that true?"

Jane tried to swallow past the choking lump lodged in her throat. Unable to get out any words, she nodded.

She watched in real time as the air went out of Sarah. Her shoulders slumped; soft sobs pulsed in her ribs as her eyes filled with tears.

Sheriff Hill crouched down in front of Sarah and placed a hand on her shoulder. "I know what it's like losing someone you care about. I'm very sorry you had to hear all that."

Shame welled in Jane's ribcage. She shouldn't have said those things. How could she let a child get to her so easily? She was so caught up in her anger. So caught up in the fact that no one seemed to care. About Margaret. About Jennifer. About all the lost girls in the files she obsessed over in some misconstrued hope she would happen upon a case-breaking miracle.

"I'm sorry," croaked Jane. "I shouldn't have said those things."

"Yes, you should have, they needed to hear it. Jennifer was sweet and kind and beautiful. She was the best person I've ever met." A new round of sobs racked Sarah. "But Ashley told us we weren't allowed to be friends with her. And for some reason I listened. I should have been nicer to her. I should have told her- I should have let her know she was important to me."

Sheriff Hill stood and led Sarah to a stone bench against the wall of the foyer. He didn't speak to her or ask her questions. He only sat beside her and gave her time to collect herself.

"I saw her with a guy once."

"Do you know who he was?" asked Jane.

"No. I'd never seen him before. She'd mentioned a guy a few times but never told me his name. All she ever said was *'my boyfriend.'*"

"And you saw him? The guy she was talking about."

Sarah nodded. "I was waiting for my mom to pick me up after practice. The rest of the team had already gone home, so it was just me and Jenny. Some guy pulled up in a big truck. She got in and they drove away."

"And you're sure it wasn't Jenny's father who picked her up?" asked Sheriff Hill.

"No sir. I know Mr. Hanson. I used to go over Jenny's back in middle school when my mom had to work late."

Jane's breath caught in her chest as she sat down beside Sarah. "What did he look like? The guy who picked up Jenny?"

"He was tall, and real skinny. He had black hair, longish, kind of messy. He was only there for like a minute."

"And you're sure you didn't recognize him?" asked Jane. "Jennifer's mother said he was a student here."

"He doesn't go here. He was like, old."

"What do you mean?" asked Sheriff Hill. "Like an old man? Like your grandparents? That kind of old?"

"No- I mean- I don't think so, but I was across the parking lot. It's just that Jenny was always talking about how the guy she was seeing was older and how he was so much more mature than guys in high school. And she was always saying how she loved him and they were gonna move away together and get married. I knew it wasn't right. I should have told someone after I saw him, but everyone was already so mean to her, and she seemed so happy when she talked about him. And now-" Sarah's voice cracked as fresh tears flooded her eyes. "He killed her. Didn't he?"

Jane took the girl's hand in hers, disgusted she'd caused a little girl so much pain. "No sweetie, he didn't hurt her. But we think he knows who did. We're just trying to find him so we can ask him some questions."

Sheriff Hill pulled a card from one of his pockets. "You've been very helpful Sarah. If you remember anything else or if you just need to talk, this is my number. You can call any time okay."

Sarah took the card and nodded.

"Alright. You can head back now."

***

Fog covered everything. Long curled fingers sunk their claws into the earth. Wrapped themselves around the trees and the houses. Holding everything in place. Making sure no one and nothing would ever go anywhere. This place was stagnant. Unmoving. Nothing would change. Nothing would get better.

Jane found herself in a familiar position. Staring out Sheriff Hill's passenger window at windblown fields, ramshackle towns swallowed by the sweeping landscape. She was lost in her head. Angry. Paralyzed by her own voice screaming inside her ears. Telling her she wasn't doing enough. Reminding her she'd never done enough.

Her mind wandered back to the cheerleaders. The girls who could have been Jennifer's friends. They could have been kind and welcoming but chose instead to be cruel.

How could they talk about Jennifer like that? Knowing she was gone. That she was lost somewhere, and no one knew where to find her. They didn't even care. Didn't lose any sleep. Meanwhile, she couldn't get them out of her head. Not just Jennifer, but Margaret, and all the other girls in the endless stack of files she rifled through.

She couldn't sleep. Couldn't be awake. Couldn't fucking think without seeing them. And when she did see they always just looked at her. Stared like she was supposed to be helping them, and they knew she was nowhere close to finding out who did this to them.

She turned from the window, observed Sheriff Hills face. A blank, impassive stare, eyes watching the road as he drove mindlessly down the monotonous stretch of highway.

She was suddenly hyper-aware of the silence. The way it hung in the air between them, manifested as a weight on her chest, shortness of breath. If she didn't fill this silence, didn't make the hundred thousand thoughts rampaging through her brain known she would implode. Consume herself until nothing was left of her but anxiety and dread.

"Doesn't it make you mad?" She only meant to ask the question in her head, think it so hard she could send the words, unspoken, right into the Sheriff's mind.

She continued to watch him. The only indication he'd heard her was a slow blink that seemed to bring him back from whatever thought he'd been lost in.

"Something on your mind?" Sheriff Hill continued to watch the road. "I hear it can help to talk about it."

"And do you believe that?"

"It's what they tell me. I've never been too good at it myself."

"Me   neither."

"Well to answer your question. Yes. It makes me mad. Though I suppose that depends on what you mean by '*it*.'"

"All of it. The case. The people around here. The way none of them seem to care about what's going on." A wave of nausea overtook her, boiled from the pit of her stomach to the base of her throat. She took long slow breaths through her nose as she did everything in her power not to be sick in the Sheriff's truck. "And then today with those girls. Those fucking girls."

"I know what you mean," said Sheriff Hill, "I mean that girl Ashley. She was like something out of an eighties high school movie."

"I know right. It's like she based her personality off *Bring it On*."

They shared a laugh that somehow managed to lift some of the weight off Jane.

"We'll find him," said the Sheriff.

"How do you know?"

"Because I know you, and I know me. And I know we won't stop until we do. And after today we have our biggest breakthrough yet."

"What would that be?"

"We're looking for a white guy that drives a truck. How hard could they be to find in the middle of North Dakota."

Jane was so caught off guard by the comment she snorted with laughter. "Thank you, Sheriff. For listening."

"Anytime."

The truck settled back into a familiar silence. The steady sound of the engine, tires rolling down the empty strip of highway.

The Box

Roy's truck idled in the driveway. The bar was a five-minute drive. He needed something to take the edge off. A release from the pressure that pushed at the back of his eyes. What did he stand to lose? Everything he cared about got swallowed up by the lake.

His migraine had somehow managed to get worse. He couldn't focus through the ringing in his ears, the way his temples throbbed. His eyes stung from the struggle of holding them open.

Rain dinged off the hood of his truck. He tried to focus on the sound of passing cars. He could count on one hand how many hours he'd slept in the last week.

He couldn't get it out of his head. The way she bobbed up and down in the calmness of the tide. Face down, staring into murky darkness. An image straight from his darkest nightmares.

He was haunted by the way Jennifer's father broke down in front of him, by the look of revolt in her mother's eyes when Roy came to the door. He witnessed Jennifer's parents learn their little girl was never coming home.

The after image of their pain was seared into his retinas. The scene played on a loop every time he closed his eyes.

He shuttered when he thought of Jennifer. The way they pulled her from the lake. Cold and pale. Even paler than Margaret had been. She was all alone, hands and feet purple from the cold. Waterlogged skin barely clung to her frame. Reeds and twigs knotted her hair. A horrid crown.

The lake grabbed her and sucked away everything it could before it coughed her back up for the world to see. Another little girl taken away on his watch.

He could feel her skin beneath his fingertips. Clammy and cold, pocked with gooseflesh. The warmth of life gone from her body.

His hands trembled as he squeezed the steering wheel. His knuckles burned white as he imagined himself finding the man who did this. Wrapping his hands around his neck. Making him fight for air with everything he had. Bringing him to the brink of death, giving him one last taste of air before he felt the coward's bones snap.

He released his grip, pressed his fingers into his eyes to relieve some of the pressure building inside his skull.

He convinced himself to go inside. He was too angry. Too emotional. He could have gone to his apartment, but he knew if he drove off, home wouldn't be where he ended up.

His father was asleep when he went to check on him. His frail body absorbed by a bed far too large for only one person.

Roy peeled off his uniform and sat in front of the TV. Images and color from the television flashed across his eyes without leaving a trace behind in his mind. His head overflowed. He was sure it would burst from the pressure that thudded beneath his skull.

His mind drifted to the closet in the corner. To what was hidden there. His shameful secret stowed away. Safe from judgmental eyes. He stared at the TV screen, trying to focus on the meaningless pictures and jumbled noise, but he couldn't.

He stood and went to the closet. The smell of dust and stale air filled his nose. He reached up to the top shelf and searched along the back wall until his fingertips brushed a small wooden box. He slid the box from the shelf and sat back down in front of the TV.

He ran his hands reluctantly over the rough grain and breathed the earthy scent of old wood. The latch popped and the lid squeaked open. He reached inside.

The bottle was heavier than he remembered but the weight was comfortable in his hands. The world went quiet. He stared into the deep amber liquid. He could taste it. Feel the burn in his throat. Hear the thoughts being snuffed out with every sip. A couple of swigs and everything could be better.

He placed the bottle on the side table and looked back into the box's depths. A smiling family stared back from a faded polaroid.

Georgia was young. Only seven or eight. Roy had his hands on her shoulders as he laughed. Georgia swam in a red jacket much too large for her. Her wet hair plastered to her forehead. She held a small brown frog in her outstretched hands. She smiled from ear to ear, blissfully unaware what life would throw at her over the next few years.

Linda smiled as well. A beautiful, radiant smile that lit every room she entered.

He looked at that smile and saw the deep sadness beneath it. Or did he only see that now because he knew what would happen to her? Did she already know her fate? Did she know how she would leave them?

He placed the picture next to the bottle and went back to searching. He sifted through birthday and Father's Day cards until he reached what he was looking for. A small, brown envelope. The corners bent and worn with time. No stamp and no address.

He blew out a sharp puff of air from breathless lungs. His chest tightened like someone had reached into him and squeezed his heart with all their strength.

Roy lifted the flap of the envelope and pulled out three sheets of paper. He flipped the pages between his fingers several times before unfolding them. Every page had a section missing. A chunk in the bottom left corner where the pages were ripped from Georgia's poetry book. He ran his fingers over the torn edges. The missing piece was identical on every page.

The pages were a letter. Three pages. Six hundred fifteen words. One thousand eight hundred thirty three letters.

Those words were the only thing he had left of Georgia. The only explanation for why she left. Roy didn't need an explanation. He knew the reason. He *was* the reason. His drinking and his lies. His absence when his daughter needed him. Every promise he broke. Every time he swore he wouldn't break another.

He never told anyone about the letter. No one else had read or heard a word of what Georgia had to say to him. Those words were for him.

Someone shuffled in the hallway. Roy's heart leapt into his throat. He threw the contents of the box back inside and slid it beneath his seat as his father entered the room.

"Roy. What are you doing here so late?" asked his father.

"Sorry, Dad. Must have fallen asleep. I'll get out of here." Roy stood to leave.

His father put a hand on his shoulder to stop him. "Wait. Wait for a second, not so fast. Sit down. Tell me what's bothering you."

"Nothing's bothering me, Dad. I'm just tired."

"Oh, just tired." His father took his hand off Roy's shoulder and gave a sarcastic shrug. "He's just tired is all."

His father looked at him, stared through the facade in the way only a parent can. Past all the bullshit and fake smiles. Past the constant insistence everything was magnificent, and life was beautiful. He didn't see some broken man. A useless, washed-up excuse for a human being. He saw his son.

"I'm your father, Roy. I know what tired looks like, this ain't that. Is it about Georgia?"

Roy's stomach lodged in his throat. His eyes seared when his father said her name. "No. No, it's just the case. They found another little girl. She was only sixteen. She was- in the water. She got trapped under the ice."

The silence thickened the already humid air.

 His father sat on the couch and gave a measured nod. "Did I ever tell you about Elizabeth Cane?"

"No, not that I remember."

"It was back in '66 during the Blizzard. You were only 6 months old. You wouldn't even remember. Thirty inches in three days, worst I've ever seen. A young woman named Elizabeth Cane. A friend of your mother's from work. First night of the storm, she didn't show up for her shift. Your mother called me. Told me she was worried. We started looking and she wasn't at home, wasn't answering her phone. We figured she'd show up, but we looked for her anyway. Then she didn't show up. We searched for days, through the storm, and the cold and- through everything. We didn't find the car until a week later when the snow started to melt. She slid off the road and hit a tree. The snow kept coming and the plows came by and- that was that. We started digging and we got her out and- she was unconscious, in a coma, but she survived in the end. Thank God."

"Well, that's good," said Roy. "She's lucky you were there."

"I thought so too but-" The words caught in his father's throat. He looked at the floor and swallowed back tears. "Elizabeth had a son. Five years old. He was in the back seat when the accident happened. He- he didn't make it. He, ah- suffocated. Elizabeth woke up a few days later. I thought I should be the one to tell her but- she already knew."

"I'm sorry, Dad. That must have been hard."

"Hard? No. I thought my life was hard back then. Long hours, crying baby. I had the easiest life in the world. What did I have to be troubled by? Happily married, good job, a new son at home happy and healthy. But whenever I looked at you, I thought about Elizabeth. About her little boy, and what they went through. What she felt every day knowing no matter how hard she tried, she couldn't save the person who meant more to her than anyone else in the world, and knowing the crushing weight it must have put on her. Like she was drowning and no matter how many people tried to help her, they couldn't pull her out. I remember I used to ask myself, how did she survive after something like that? It's been more than forty years and I think I finally know the answer. Her child was gone, and he was never coming back, but her memories of him kept her alive. Memories, whether good or bad, are the most important thing we have. When life deals us something so devastating, something we don't know how to pull ourselves out of, we get stuck. Being a parent is the hardest job in the world, but it's the best one there ever was, and before I'm gone, I may not even remember who I am anymore. But even after they put me in the ground, I will remember the most important thing in my life, and so will you. No matter how painful that memory is." His father's voice cracked. Tears welled at the corners of his eyes.

Roy pretended not to notice. His gaze lingered on the television. The unfocused disarray of colored lights interwoven with static. For so long, he resented his father. Loathed the fact he didn't need to suffer the pain of losing Georgia. Now he would give anything to make his father forget again, to spare him the pain of knowing Georgia was gone.

Regret

I walked to the Red Top every day for a chance to see Tommy. We met around the corner from the diner, in a small patch of trees in the back of the parking lot where we couldn't be seen from the road.

We walked through the woods and around the lake, away from prying eyes. We talked about everything. Every day we learned a little more about each other. After a couple months he knew me better than anyone else ever had. Knew me not just by what I like or disliked, did or didn't do. He knew me in the way you know a person when you're not afraid to share how you feel.

We were open with each other. When we were together, we could talk about everything. No holding back. We called it 'trading trauma'.

I told him about my mother dying, and the problems my dad was having.

He told me about his father. How he would get angry and hit him. He quoted the bible as he beat him. Told Tommy he was a sinner who needed to repent.

Some of the stories Tommy told me were terrifying. I didn't like hearing them, but I listened, the same way he listened to me.

For the first time in a long time, I wasn't alone. I could open myself to someone. Let the truth spill out of me. When I talked to Tommy, I felt the same way I did when I wrote my poems. Honest and real, a pressure lifted from my shoulders.

We both dreamed of a better place. Somewhere fresh and new outside the pull of our normal lives. We lived in a stationary orbit, never straying too far from the center, never venturing far enough to make the path we were on memorable.

Most people around here wanted to find a way out. A way to break free from monotony. The constant cycle of waking up, hating yourself, and going back to sleep. Even in wanting to be free from the grasp of that town we were unoriginal.

We talked about leaving. We'd jump in Tommy's car and disappear. Follow the road until we reached the ocean. Climb the mountains until we touched the clouds. Sail across the sea of endless fields and see what waited for us on the other side. Travel to all the places the birds sang about. Free from the claustrophobic weight of an ever-shrinking town. Run and never look back.

I didn't think it would ever really happen, but it was a nice dream.

For our first date, Tommy took me on a picnic. He called and said, "Come to the lake."

He told me he had a surprise for me. I didn't know it was a date when I went. I wouldn't have gone if I had. I liked Tommy, but not in that way.

He set up a blanket on the shore. One of the red and white checkered ones you see in all the movies with happy families in the park.

He gave me flowers he picked himself- pink prairie roses.

We ate fruit and chocolate and shared a bottle of cheap champagne.

Everything about it seemed awkward- in a sweet kind of way- like he read about first dates in a magazine and followed the instructions to the letter.

When the sun set, he rowed me out onto the lake on an old rickety boat someone abandoned years ago. He rowed us all the way out to the sunken house. My castle on the lake. I was scared he'd ask me to go inside. Until then, the house only existed in my imagination. I didn't want to see what it was really like.

He never asked to go inside. We watched the sun set and the stars come out. They reflected in the water like a hundred thousand fireflies. We drifted through space. Quiet and alone in the vast nothingness.

He kissed me then. Maybe it was the champagne, or because nobody ever did anything that nice for me, or maybe just because I knew he wanted me to, I kissed him back. His lips tasted sour, like the lemon candies they sold at the gas station. I expected my first kiss to be magical. A beautiful moment I'd remember for the rest of my life. It didn't feel beautiful or magical. It felt strange, awkward and fumbling, our lips never quite connected in the right way.

I never told my dad about Tommy. Not that he would've cared. If it wasn't work or a bottle, he didn't take much interest. I didn't tell my grandpa either.

I wasn't ashamed of Tommy. I just delighted in having a secret. Something for myself. Something I had the entire town didn't know about.

Grandpa did find out eventually.

Tommy and I were at the lake one day when he showed up. I was worried he would be mad. Upset I took someone else to our special place. He wasn't. He sat down with us, and we talked for hours.

Grandpa never asked if Tommy and I were seeing each other. To be honest, I didn't know if we were.

What me and Tommy had didn't feel like love. At least not to me. Love was supposed to be something out of a fairy tale. Like Westley and Buttercup from the Princess Bride. A force so powerful nothing could stop it.

I knew I liked Tommy, but the idea of falling for someone. Loving someone. Giving them your heart. Trusting them with your secrets-

The idea of knowing someone that intimately set my teeth on edge.

I told Tommy everything. I trusted him with the deepest parts of myself. What we had was beautiful. A genuine connection. I should have loved him. But I didn't.

The only other person who knew about me and Tommy-whatever we were- was Abby. Tommy knew her brother Omar and he thought me and her would get along. We did. I liked having another girl to talk to. I didn't realize how much I missed it. Besides Grandpa, she was the best friend I ever had. We started hanging out all the time. She even started going to my school after the one in her town burned down. Most days we didn't go. We'd drive around in her car listening to old folk music. John Denver and Bob Dylan. It reminded me of when my mother would play records on rainy days when she didn't feel like leaving the house. Me and mom would take our shoes off and dance barefoot on the carpet. We sang at the top of our lungs and laughed until we couldn't breathe.

Abby's mother used to tell her a bedtime story about a town lost beneath the waves. Down under the water where the sun danced in beautiful patterns across the rooftops. Where no one could see you cry. No one could scream or fight. Nothing but peace and silence. I always wanted to go to that place. An oasis beneath the surface. A calm down below. Away from all the noise.

Abby and I used to see each other almost every day.

On the west side of town there was an old water tower. At one time the tower was blue, light blue, like the sky on a spring morning. *Clareborne* was painted across the side in bold black letters. Over the years the rain and the wind did their damage. Stole away the blue and changed it to rust, faded the name until it disappeared altogether.

High schoolers used to drive out to the tower with cases of beer. They'd get drunk and climb to the top. There were more than a few injuries. Some were from falling, but most were from fighting. Drinking and fighting were pretty much the only two activities Clareborne had to offer. Everyone seemed to be an expert at one or the other.

I'd been to the tower a few times with Abby, but it wasn't for me. I wasn't much of a partier. I drank, like every high schooler. I just didn't see the point of getting black out drunk and making a fool of myself in front of every kid in town. The risk always seemed to outweigh the reward.

The last time me and Abby went up to the tower, we lost interest pretty much right away. Neither of us wanted to go home, which was the default feeling for both of us most nights. I'd borrowed my dad's truck for the night. He wasn't in any condition to notice it was gone. Me and Abby drove down the road with the windows down. Abby was halfway through a bottle of whiskey she stole from her mom's liquor cabinet.

I turned off the headlights and drove us out into the fields. We laid in the bed of the truck for hours, staring at the night sky, listening to the shouts from the tower as the varsity football team lit off fireworks from the top.

"Georgia?" Abby's voice was just above a whisper.

I rolled on my side to look at her. She'd finished off the whiskey. Her lipstick left a violent pink ring around the mouth of the bottle. How long had she been crying?

"Abby? Are you okay?"

Abby shook her head, tears streamed down her cheeks. "Do you ever get scared?"

"What's wrong? Did something happen?"

Abby stayed quiet (which was against her nature). She stared up at the stars. She clutched the bottle against her heart.

"You know you can talk to me, right?" I asked.

Abby leaned her head against my shoulder. Tears streamed down her flushed cheeks. "I just- I've been having these dreams. I'm running down the street. I run and I run, and I try to reach the end of the road, but I never get there. I don't know what I'm running from. I never stop to look back, but I know there's something behind me and if I don't run fast enough it'll catch me." Abby wiped away her tears with the heel of her palm. Eye liner and mascara streaked across her face. "Then I wake up. And I'm so terrified, and when I look out into the hallway, I swear I can see him staring at me."

"Who?"

Abby sat up straight. She dabbed at her eyes with the hem of her shirt. "Omar."

"Omar? Your brother? Did he do something to you?"

"No." She shook her head. "But sometimes he scares me. He's just- he's not himself anymore. He hasn't been himself in a long time, but lately it's been- different."

"Different how?"

"I don't know. Every time he's around, he's so angry. He's always asking my mom for money. She's not stupid, she knows what it's for. But when she won't give it to him-" Abby turned and looked at me for the first time. "I'm afraid he's gonna do something bad."

I didn't do a great job comforting Abby at the time. I told her everything was going to be alright. That I was always there for her if she needed me, and I wouldn't let anything happen to her. Those things were true, but they weren't what she needed to hear. She needed me to tell her I understood. Tell her she wasn't alone, and she wasn't the only one feeling the way she was feeling.

She wasn't.

I knew all too well what it was like. Living with an addict. Seeing the way they changed when they got there fix- when they didn't. Telling yourself the person you've known your whole life is somewhere beneath but never knowing if you'll see them again. Being afraid of someone who's supposed to love you. I knew those feelings. I understood.

I dream about Abby sometimes. Her smile and carefree attitude. The soft rasp of her voice when she sang. She floats along in the lake singing *Shelter from the Storm*. Her dark golden hair floats around her head like a crown.

Sometimes, her face looks strange. The details faded, like a stone smoothed by a river. Sometimes it doesn't look like her at all. Somethings off about her. Her hair's the wrong color and her smile is gone. The hopeful glimmer in her eyes replaced with darkness. Fear of what she's seen. It's hard to believe it's Abby, but I know it is- the way you do in a dream.

I never told Abby I understood about Omar. I knew what it was like being afraid like that. There were so many things I never got to tell Abby. I left so unexpectedly I didn't even get a chance to say goodbye. Maybe someday I'll see her again. We'll cross paths somewhere on our journeys from here to there, and I can tell her all the things I wanted to, back when we were still living our old lives.

I've tried not to have regrets in life, but that's not realistic. We all have regrets. Moments we look back on and wish we could change. I would change my whole life if I could. I would have said how I felt. Spoken my mind when someone asked me a question. Told people I loved them more. Most of all, I would have said goodbye.

I've missed so many goodbyes in my life. Grandpa, Dad, Abby. My mother was the first. I remember being afraid the night she died. I don't know why, but something in her eyes terrified me. I was looking at my mother, but someone else looked back. I didn't realize what she was going through. If I was old enough to understand, I would have held her hand. Told her I loved her and everything was going to be okay. Instead, I went to bed without saying goodnight and never saw her again.

For a long time, I was mad at my mother for what she did. For leaving me. Every time I thought about her, I would get so angry. That rage lurked under the surface for years, waiting to burst through.

I blamed my mother for everything that went wrong in my life. Dad drinking and never being home, not having any friends, always thinking something was wrong with me. The voice in my head that told me I would never amount to anything. I was unlovable. No matter how hard I tried, I would never be good enough. I would be stuck in this town forever, waiting to turn to dust.

Maybe it was just easier to blame her than to blame myself.

<u>Home</u>

Nothing about the house had changed. The elm tree still sat on the front lawn. The first traces of flowers budded on its branches. A tire swing hung from its thickest limb on frayed rope. The same fence still ran along the driveway. The last five pickets newer than the others from when Georgia crashed into it after she got her permit. The same front door. Bright yellow. The door Linda picked out.

Honey, I know I said get whichever you liked but why so- yellow?
That's the one that spoke to me. Makes me feel warm on my rainy days. A reminder the sun will always shine again.

The sun hid behind an overcast sky. The little bit of light that managed to pass through desaturated the world. Dimmed every color, leaving everything muddy and grey. Not the door, though. The door smiled at the street, bright as ever. Yellow. The color of sunshine. A color this town never got to see anymore.

Roy hadn't been to the house in over a year. Not since Georgia left.

He stayed after Linda died. He could have moved. Left everything behind and started over somewhere else. Maybe he should have. He wanted Georgia to stay at her school and be with her friends. Live like a normal kid (as if she could after what happened to her mother). So, they stayed, and he drank enough to forget what happened in that house.

After Georgia left, nothing could keep him there anymore.

He tried, at first. Tried to sit around and pretend Georgia had gone off to college or gotten her first apartment. Only a phone call or a short drive away. Pretending didn't help. Pretending Georgia was around reminded him she wasn't. He couldn't see her or talk to her, and he may never get to again. That's what he was reminded of every time he walked into that house. When he saw the cold expanse of tile in the kitchen.

The empty rooms screamed at him with unfathomable silence. The walls started to press in around him. The ceiling came down to crush him. Every picture, every sound, every board, every nail, every inch of scratchy carpet a reminder of what he lost. He couldn't stand another second of time inside those walls.

He ran.

Ran away from his problems like he always did. Better to forget. Better to close the pain away and keep it locked up forever.

He moved into a one-bedroom apartment on the outskirts of Devil's Lake. Halfway between the station and his father's. His father needed someone to take care of him, and Roy didn't want to spend another second in that house.

He thought about selling it a few times. He even had a few offers, but he could never pull the trigger. What if Georgia came back? What if she knocked on the door one day, expecting to see her father, and ended up face to face with a stranger? Maybe the two were one and the same.

Roy stood in the street and looked at the house. He stared down the monster that tormented his every thought. He wouldn't run anymore. Whatever happened in that house. Whatever he did or didn't do. Whatever led to the nothingness. He needed to face it, even if it only made him blame himself more.

He breathed deep and walked up the driveway. The same driveway where he taught Georgia how to ride a bike. She smiled ear to ear the first time she made it all the way to the street without training wheels.

Daddy, Daddy, I did it. I did it all by myself.
Yeah, you did Peanut. And guess what we're gonna do to celebrate?

He reached the door at the end of the driveway. The yellow door that screamed into the street. He walked up to the door and unlocked it. For some reason he was surprised the key still worked. The house didn't feel like it belonged to him. It belonged to his family. To the memories of them. To the life and love they brought to the world. If they weren't here with him then it was no longer a home. It was nothing. Four empty walls where tragedy made its nest.

The front door opened into the living room. He ran his hand across the back of the green velvet couch. His fingers came back thick with dust. He stood in the middle of the living room and took it all in. The TV where they would watch movies on Saturdays as a family. Georgia loved *The Princess Bride* and asked to watch it every time it was her turn to pick. She would stand in front of the TV acting out every part and saying every line.

'My name is Inigo Montoya. You killed my father. Prepare to die.'

She picked up the remote and pretended it was a rapier as she bound around the room to fight Count Rugen.

Roy smiled despite the burning in his stomach. The acid on the back of his teeth.

He walked into the dining room. He ran his hand over the small wooden table. The table just big enough for the three of them. Roy was sitting at that table when Linda gave him the news that would change his life forever.

Honey, I was feeling a little off. I thought I knew what it was, but I went to the doctor to be sure.

What's wrong? Is everything alright?

Roy, I'm pregnant. You're going to be a father.

Eight months later Georgia was born. Red-faced and screaming. Roy had never been happier than when he looked into his little girl's eyes for the first time. So pure. How could he make something so beautiful? He had never been perfect. He'd never even come close. But she was perfect.

He made a promise to himself. He would protect her. Keep her safe even if it meant giving his own life. He was never good at keeping promises. Even the ones he made to himself.

Roy walked down the hallway. He passed the bathroom with the missing door. Scraps of wood hanging from bent hinges. The door he never replaced.

He continued down the hallway until he reached the room he needed to see. He turned the knob and pushed the door across the carpet. Dust clung to every surface. He brushed off the light switch and flipped it on. He braced himself and stepped over the threshold.

He was greeted by a familiar silence. A silence that bore itself into his ears and kept him awake at night.

The room was exactly how Georgia left it. Roy hadn't touched anything. He hadn't even been inside the room since Georgia left.

The bed was still unmade from when Georgia woke up, excited to celebrate her birthday. Georgia never made her bed, no matter how much her mother nagged her.

A library worth of books filled the room, stacked on the nightstand and lining the shelves. The books he used to read to her.

Alright, Peanut. Time for bed.
One more chapter Daddy, please.

There were no more bedtime stories after Linda died. There wasn't much of anything after that. No warmth. No time spent making his daughter laugh or letting her know she was loved.

A lot of his time was spent in a haze. Too drunk to remember he had a daughter who needed him. Too stupid to realize it wasn't about him. It was about her. Georgia. A confused little girl who lost her mother. Whose father shut down and became a different person. Not the loving father she had known her entire life, but a hate-filled shell of a man that screamed at her instead of encouraging her.

She did.

She turned eighteen and disappeared. No calls, no visits, no nothing. Nothing but a letter letting him know why she was leaving.

The walls of Georgia's room were burnt orange. The color of fallen leaves. Roy had driven her to the hardware store to pick out the paint. They looked at hundreds of swatches before she decided on one.

In the empty spaces, where some might have hung posters or pictures, the walls were covered in words. Scribbled on at all angles with thin black marker.

Poems.

Her poems.

She stopped showing him her poetry years ago.

He moved his hands across the writing. Georgia's writing. Neat, thin, and slanted. He moved across the walls reading his daughter's words. Every letter a piece of her left behind. Every line a look into her soul.

Warm wind dances through the grass,
Whispering secrets to the sky.
The water watches,
Mirroring every move.
A silent copy of reality,
Distorted by the rippling surface.

The words of the poem gathered inside of Roy. They collided with each other and formed into a tiny ball. A black hole in his chest. The ball pulled on him, getting tighter and tighter until he couldn't breathe. He forced out his breath in a shaking sob. His legs buckled, and he stumbled. He caught himself on the bedframe. Roy looked down at the mound of blankets pushed up against the wall.

He grabbed a new set of sheets from the linen closet, stripped the old set and threw it out into the hall. He unfolded the new sheets and made the bed. He tucked them in and smoothed out the wrinkles. When he was done, he collapsed onto the mattress.

He looked up and saw a picture. The only picture in the entire room, stuck to the ceiling above. A picture of them: Roy, Linda, and Georgia. They looked down at Roy through smudged glass. The three of them sat on a bench outside of the Red Top. Chocolate ice cream dribbled down Georgia's chin. Linda scrubbed her clean with a damp napkin. Dottie had taken the picture. They went for ice cream to celebrate Georgia's report card. Straight A's. The last picture they took together as a family. Three weeks later, Linda was gone.

Beneath the photo, Georgia had written two lines.

I do not cry for those who move on.
I cry for those left behind to miss them.

Roy laid in his daughter's bed staring at the ceiling. The taste of dust clung to his throat. He read the two lines over and over as the silence gathered around him.

A soft rain began to fall. Soon the rain would be a storm. Roy closed his eyes and drifted off, thoughts of his family smiling in his head.

<u>Repentance</u>

Then

The storm crashed through the clouds. Thunder cracked the sky, bathing the landscape in harsh white light. A camera flash covered the whole world. Tommy's windshield wipers slapped back and forth, fighting against the pounding rain.

He should have stayed at a motel or slept in the car, but he had made his decision. Tommy had spent the entire day with Georgia. He met her grandfather too. He ran into them when he was out for a walk.

He seemed surprised when he saw Tommy, but he didn't say anything. He just said hello and introduced himself. They all sat together and talked about life. Her grandpa told them stories about growing up. About how he met Georgia's grandma. He said he knew the first time he saw her she was the one. He could feel some invisible force pulling them together, and Tommy knew he wouldn't spend another day without seeing Georgia.

Tommy's car flew down the road. Long fingers of mist trailed behind him in violent swirls. His mother always told him storms were a sign of God's anger. Despite the ground shaking storm, God's anger would be nothing compared to his father's.

After tonight, his father wouldn't matter. This was the last time Tommy would have to face him. He would walk into his father's house one more time. He would grab his things: some clothes and the money he kept hidden in an old alarm clock. If his father tried to stop him, he'd tell him to mind his own business. He wasn't going to put up with his bullshit anymore.

Tommy pulled up to the house with the headlights off. He prayed his father wouldn't hear him over the storm. He stepped down onto the flooded sidewalk. Water rushed down the street, sweeping away anything in its path. Storm drains roared as they sucked down the onslaught of rain. Maybe God was mad enough tonight to wash this whole town off the map; send his father down to hell in a torrent of water and debris.

Tommy slogged through the backyard. Mud sucked at his boots, trying its hardest to pull him down into the earth. He stood by the back door and waited.

Through the window, the television flickered with ambient light. His father should have passed out by now, but Tommy wasn't taking any chances.

Lightning flashed. The world glowed. He opened the door as the thunder cracked to mask the squeal of the hinges. He closed the door softly behind himself and stood in the kitchen soaked to the bone. Rain and mud pooled at his feet, reaching out across the stained tile.

The clock over the kitchen table showed 12:17. On the TV, a late-night host joked with his guest. The audience went wild with canned laughter. Tommy crept towards his room. He reached for the doorknob.

"Thomas?"

Shit.

The audience's laughter died as the TV powered down. Any remnants of joy left in the house snuffed out.

"Where were you, boy?" said his father from the living room.

"Nowhere," said Tommy. "I went for a drive."

Beer cans clinked to the floor as his father stood from his chair. His bare feet slapped on the tile as he rounded the corner. The lights flipped on.

"Don't lie to me. Where were you? You had your mother worried sick." He imagined his mother. Tucked away in her corner of the living room. Arms around herself as she stared at the screen. Her eyes glazed over. Too numb to be worried about anything.

"I wasn't anywhere. I was just out for a drive. Getting some air."

Tommy couldn't tell his father anything to stop what was about to happen, but he damn sure wasn't going to tell him about Georgia.

"I said don't lie to me boy. You better have a damn good reason for coming home so late. I warned you about waking me."

"I hoped you'd be so drunk you'd never wake up," Tommy said it before he could stop himself.

Stupid.

The outburst would cost him.

A smile crossed his father's lips. A thin, menacing smile no God-fearing man should ever wear.

"You're under my roof. You know what the book says." His father took a heavy leather-bound bible from the table. "'Honor your father, that your days may be long in the land that the Lord your God is giving you.' If you keep lying and disrespecting me in my house. Your days on this earth won't be very long." His father held out the bible, using it to gesture at the kitchen table.

"Sit."

"I'm sorry. I didn't mean to wake you. I just needed a few things. I'll leave. You'll never have to see me again."

"You're not going anywhere. Now **sit.**"

Tommy walked over to the table and sat down. A shiver ran up his spine that had nothing to do with his soaked clothes. He looked into the living room. His mother was asleep in the corner. A fresh bruise graced her left eye.

"You must think I'm stupid, boy. Is that it? You think I'm stupid? You don't think I know what you're up to on those little drives of yours? What's her name? The little whore whose been inviting sin into my house?"

Tommy lowered his head to his lap as the blood drained from his face. He balled his hands into fists, clenching until his knuckles turned white to stop his fingers from twitching.

He was bluffing. He had to be. He couldn't know about Georgia.

"So, it's true." His father stared into his soul. A smug smirk plastered his face. "What's the whore's name?"

Tommy gave him nothing. Georgia was his. His father's punishment he could handle, but telling him about Georgia, hearing her name from his grinning lips. The thought churned his stomach. His father didn't deserve to hear her name. Didn't deserve the satisfaction of Tommy's obedience.

"You don't want to tell me? That's okay. Maybe, I already know her name."

Tommy's heart stopped. A dull squeeze spread from his chest to his throat.

His father moved closer. Leaning in until Tommy could see the cigarette stains on his teeth. "Maybe, I'll drive around town. Find all those little harlots you've been spending time with. Pay them a visit and make sure they never tempt my family with sin again."

Hot bile filled Tommy's stomach. Churning magma threatened to erupt onto the kitchen floor. He gathered the courage to look his father in the eye.

He knew it was a mistake the moment he did it, because what he saw there filled him with fear. An unmatched terror. Not for himself, he could handle himself. Something in his father's eyes spoke of a promise. His words were not an idle threat. Not the words of a broken man to long at the bottom of the bottle.

Tommy looked into his father's eyes and knew he meant every word.

"On the table, boy." His fathers breathe stunk of beer and stale cigarettes.

Tommy didn't move. He sat paralyzed. Yellow newspapers and old cigarette butts littered the kitchen table.

"On the table. Don't make me say it again."

Tommy did as he was told. He pulled his hands from his pockets and placed them palm side down on the table.

"You seem to be too stupid to understand me when I speak. But maybe this will help you understand."

His father lifted the bible over his head and brought it down like an axe. The spine slammed into Tommy's knuckles. Tommy winced in pain but he refused to scream.

His mother wasn't asleep anymore. She sat in her chair in the corner cradling herself. A child, woken from a bad dream, only to discover real life was worse than any nightmare. She looked at Tommy like he was a ghost. Through him, like he wasn't worth seeing.

She sat in her corner, too broken to stand or speak. Too afraid to protect herself. To afraid to do anything. She watched with vacant eyes as the man she married used the word of God to beat her only son.

The Visitor

Now

Hannah ran the shower hot enough to burn away the memories of the last few days. She would have scrubbed her eyes out if it meant she wouldn't have to see that girl anymore.

She was used to bodies; she had seen them all day every day for the last twenty years. This time it was different. Most of the bodies she worked on were of the elderly. People who lived their lives and went out when their clock ran out of time. The occasional accident and the more occasional overdose. Somehow, she managed to separate those. Compartmentalize. File them away somewhere she didn't need to see it. Accidents happened. Nothing would stop that.

This time she couldn't file it away. The girl's face followed her everywhere she went. Haunted her. Soft flesh sloughed from fractured bones. Skin so bruised it looked burned. Beaten until fragments of skull lodged into her brain. She had never seen the likes of it before. The anger. Pure rage taken out on an innocent girl.

She scoured her skin so hard she started to bleed. She watched the patterns the blood made as it hit the water. She stayed in the shower until the water turned to ice, transfixed by the whirlpool of red ribbon that spun down the drain.

The storm howled. The primal yelp of a community in pain. Every crack of thunder another blow to the town's gut. How much could a place take before it waved the white flag and faded away.

Her nerves were shot to hell. She lit a candle and put on an Elvis record. She laid down on the couch and closed her eyes. She tried to focus on the music but all she could see was the girl. The face would haunt her for the rest of her life.

This wasn't the first monster she'd dealt with. She'd been dealing with them her entire life. She used to fear the dark. The monsters lurking under the bed or in the closet, waiting for your foot to slip out from under the blankets so they could grab you and pull you away.

When she was a little older, she was taught about a different kind of monster. The ones who waited in dark alleys for unsuspecting girls that were trying to make their way home before dinner time.

Monsters were always portrayed as strangers, faceless beasts looming in the dark. Preying on the innocent like wolves drawn to blood.

Reality was different, simpler, but infinitely more complicated. Monsters don't always hide in the dark or prowl through parking lots at night. Sometimes they tuck you into bed at night. Hold your hand while they walk you to school. Tell you they love you and they'll never hurt you.

The King warbled *Kentucky Rain* through the old speakers when someone knocked on the front door. Her heart leapt out of her chest. Who was knocking at this time of night? In the middle of a thunderstorm?

She grabbed her shotgun from the cabinet above the dining room closet. She flicked on the porch light before opening the door to a torrent of rain.

A man stood on her porch soaked to the bone. Despite the rain she could tell he'd been crying.

"Roy?" she asked in disbelief. "Is everything okay?"

He seemed surprised to see her, like he was expecting someone else to answer the door.

"Yeah, everything's okay. I- I'm sorry to stop by so late. I uh- I know I haven't been all that- present, recently but- I uh- I tried calling that doctor again, the one down in Grand Forks. I couldn't make myself go but- she said- she said sometimes it can help to talk about things and I- I thought-"

"Roy," said Hannah.

He stopped talking and looked at her like a lost puppy.

"Let me get my umbrella."

<u>Empty Walls</u>

A cool wind blew through the crack in Jane's office window. The corner of her files flapped in the breeze as she read through her growing collection of case files.

Missing girls.

Dead girls.

More than she could comprehend. Each file a new face. Each page a new tragedy. She wanted to stop. Shove the files back in the boxes and burn them. Destroy all traces of them so no one else had to see. So no one else could be burdened by what happened to these girls.

What would people do if they knew what waited for them in the dark? Could they still live their lives if they knew what people were capable of? Would they lay awake at night with those images burned into their eyes. The faces of those girls. Scared and alone. Their cries unheard. The people who hurt them walking free.

Jane put down the file and leaned back in her chair. She pressed her knuckles into her eyes, tried to douse the burn. She didn't want to look anymore, but she had to. The answers were here. Hidden somewhere inside the endless pages, the stack of boxes in the corner of her office. She knew it was there, some detail, some tiny shred of evidence that would put her on the path to catching this monster.

Jane looked out the window. The world outside was quiet. Streetlights shined on empty roads. Insects buzzed and chirped somewhere out in the dark. Branches swayed in pale silver moonlight, waving goodbye to the town they were so desperate to be gone from.

The cold emptiness reminded her of home. Blank white walls. They should have been covered in her mother's art, filled with her father's laughter. A mother and father who loved her. A home that was happy until the world decided to take that away.

She often thought of her father. What life would be like if he was still here. What her relationship with her mother would be like if he was with them.

The picture of him on her mother's wall was the clearest she'd see her father in years. She was young when he died. Over time his face faded from her memory. Bit by bit and then all together. Seeing his picture shocked her. She was surprised how different he was from what she remembered. The slight curve of his smile. The way he put his hand on his chest when he laughed. The color of his eyes: Dark brown, almost black. The same eyes as her.

Her father had been gone for so long, but some days she felt him next to her. She saw him in the way the wind blew the leaves. Heard him whisper when the rain danced on the rooftops. A soft presence, watching her move through life.

She wished she could talk to him. Even if it was only one more time. Ask him why he went away. Why the world was so cruel.

Her father knew what people could do to each other. He saw it when he was in the army. Bodies piled in mass graves. Teenagers turned to soldiers. Guns in their hands, riddled with bullet holes in the middle of the street. Children shredded by bombs. Girls taken from their homes at night. Sold to the highest bidder. Forced to do things no child should even have to think of.

Jane was only six when her father left. He got on a plane and flew to the other side of the world.

He never came home. Someone did. He looked like her father, sounded like him, but he was someone else. Her real father got lost somewhere in the jungle eight thousand miles away.

It started with little things. Always looking over his shoulder. Getting overwhelmed when there were too many people around. The nightmares were the worst. When his screams woke the whole house. The way he cried when he thought no one could see him.

One day it all became too much.

Jane found him in the garage with an extension cord around his neck. His eyes bulged so far she was amazed they didn't pop out of his head.

Her father stared at her with those dark, bloodshot eyes. The same eyes as her.

She turned back to her desk and pulled the next file from the top of the stack. She would find out who did this. Find the answers so no one else needed to go home every day to those cold, empty walls.

A Dream Beneath the Waves

Then

The fire towered over Tommy's head, casting strange patterns across the grass. An ever-changing dance of light and shadow. Here and then gone. Each moment unique, something never seen before, never to be seen again.

A cyclone of sparks spiraled upwards around a column of white smoke. The sparks drifted towards the clouds. Higher and higher, until they blinked out against the star-strewn cobalt sky.

Pick-ups and rusted out station wagons made a ring around a massive bonfire in the middle of nowhere. Groups of teenagers stood in circles sipping beer, casting overlong shadows across the unending field.

Parties didn't suit him. People he didn't know in a place he was unfamiliar with. Kids getting so drunk they lost track of themselves. Made bad decisions as though it was something to be proud of.

He floated near Georgia, hands in his pockets, pretending to be one with the shadows. He wasn't one for small talk. He wasn't one for talk at all.

Abby stood at Georgia's side, their fingers interwoven, head perched on Georgia's shoulder. Her other hand held a red plastic cup. The smell of its contents reminded him of home.

Two men stood across from the girls. Omar and Leroy. Omar was Abby's brother, tussled brown hair that looked like he'd just woken from a coma. Nothing shone within his deep-set eyes.

Leroy was his best friend and "business partner." He stood a head above everyone else at the party. Rail thin. He swayed in place as if the wind was trying to grab hold and pull him away.

Tommy didn't particularly like either of them, but they could get him pills. Something to take the edge off. He didn't see a need to get along with his dealer, but he was kind enough to them when they were around, for Abby's sake.

"So, are you two like dykes or something?" asked Leroy.

"What do you mean?" asked Abby.

"I mean do you like- go down on each other and stuff."

Omar put a solid backhand into Leroy's stomach. "Come on, dude. That's my sister."

"It's fine Omar, we don't mind." She looked into Georgia's eyes, biting her lower lip in mock flirtation.

"Why?" asked Georgia. "Do you like to think about us doing it?"

"No. it's nothing like that I just-"

"Then what is it?" asked Abby. "Is it because we spend so much time together? You and Omar live together. Are you two gay?"

"What? No. I mean it's just like you guys are always holding hands and hugging and stuff."

"Oh, you mean like this?" Abby downed the rest of her drink and planted a long kiss on Georgia.

Leroy and Omar looked on in disbelief, but Tommy knew it was just part of Abby's game, always doing her best to be the center of attention. She loved the shock value, and Georgia was always right along for the ride.

Abby pulled away and wiped her lips with the back of her hand. Her and Georgia started howling with laughter until they fell backwards into the grass, kicking their feet in the air.

The smile that accompanied Georgia's laugh reached from ear to ear. Tommy had never seen something so beautiful, but that didn't stop the ache in his stomach, the tightness in his chest and throat.

Georgia loved Abby, not in a romantic way, but in a way Tommy new he could never experience. Two friends who knew each other on a level that reached down to the very fiber of who they were. He thought he had that with Georgia. A true connection. No secrets. No lies. Two souls laid bare for the other to know. But as he looked at Georgia and Abby laughing in the grass, something deep inside him pained to be closer to her.

***

The fire had dwindled down. The chatter faded into hushed conversation. Tommy sat in the grass, the moon illuminating the field, the trees that loomed on its edges. Moonlight glowed against the gold of Georgia's hair, firelight flickered in her eyes.

Abby was a few too many drinks in. The way she usually was. Trying to chase away a monster who would forever lurk in the shadows. Her high from earlier in the night crashed into a substantial low. She laid on the grass with her head in Georgia's lap, doing a bad job at trying not to cry. "I just don't understand why the world hates me so much."

"The world doesn't hate you." Georgia ran her hands through Abby's hair to comfort her. Curling her honey-blond locks around long slim fingers. "It just doesn't understand people like us."

"I just wish I could get out of here. Find a place where no one knows me. Somewhere to start over. Somewhere there isn't so much- nothing."

"I understand," whispered Georgia.

She did.

If anyone could understand what Abby was going through it was him and Georgia. For some reason the world kept dealing them shittier and shittier hands. His father would have said, *Every trouble we face is a test from God.* But why would God want to put people- good people like Georgia and Abby, like his mother- through so much hardship? What was the purpose of it? What lesson did He need so bad for them to learn?

"My mother used to tell me a story," sniffled Abby. "To help me get to sleep. We'd sit on the back porch and look out over the water. She told me there was a city. Down beneath the waves where light danced on the rooftops and all your problems floated away. A reflection. Our world. But better. Where everyone cared for each other. Where people couldn't see you cry or tell you you weren't good enough. Where fathers didn't leave, and brothers didn't break their promises."

Abby wiped away her tears. Her eyes burned with longing as she admired the fire. "You know when my school burned down, I was glad. I remember seeing the smoke outside my bedroom window. I thought it was a dream. I'd wished for it to happen so many times that it couldn't have been real. But it was, and for a second, I thought I was the one who started the fire. I wished for it so bad. Prayed for it. And I remember thinking all my problems were gone. Burned up. Blown away on the wind with the smoke. Sent off to some other town where they would become someone else's problems. I remember thinking, if burning that school down was the only thing God ever did for me, then that would be alright."

Abby rolled onto her back, her head on Georgia's thigh as she looked into her eyes. "I thought we would move away. Drive until this place was nothing but a distant memory. But we didn't. And now I'm stuck here and I'm pretty sure I'll never get out."

Something shifted behind Georgia's eyes. She looked afraid, as though she heard her worst fears put into words.

Tommy looked around the party at a jumble of faces he didn't recognize. Shadows danced across them, hollowing their features, turning their eyes to empty pits. The fear he sensed from Georgia was all around him, written on the face of every stranger. Everyone was the same. One flock. Afraid of being trapped in their pen for the rest of their lives. Existing but never really living. Until they ended up like everyone else. Broken and alone.

Tommy knew that feeling. He wasn't going to let it happen to Georgia. No matter what it took.

"If only the world worked like that," said Georgia. "I would have sent my problems away a long time ago."

A Decent Man

Now

Roy and Hannah walked to Roosevelt Park. The rain had stopped. They sat on the bleachers that overlooked the baseball field, too soaked through to bother wiping away the puddles that formed in the dented metal, the dull yellow glow of the streetlights too dim to make out the details of each other's faces.

They sat in silence. Not an awkward silence that screamed of past wrongs and overdue apologies. A gentle silence that didn't beg for someone to break it. He knew, if he spoke, Hannah would listen.

That's why he didn't. He wanted to, but he couldn't.

They sat like that for a long time. Maybe minutes. Maybe hours.

Roy mulled everything over in his head. Everything his father said. Everything he wanted to say to Hannah. Every thought of failure and inadequacy that plagued him night and day.

Every attempt to speak filled his mouth with sand. Numbed his throat. The idea of speech made his tongue forget how to form even the simplest of syllables.

If he spoke, he wouldn't stop. The torrent inside of him would burst through the floodgate. An endless barrage of unsaid words and pent-up emotion. Hard truths and bitter resentments.

A thousand thoughts ran through his head but whenever he went to speak, one stopped him. A single thought screamed over the tumult of all the rest. The voice in his head told him to keep his fucking mouth shut. Keep it to yourself before she figures it out. You're too far gone to bother with. Too broken to care about.

Roy was terrified of telling Hannah the truth. Once she saw the real him, she would leave. Everyone did. He forced them to. Everything he did or didn't do pushed away everyone in his life.

"We were supposed to be together." Roy spoke before his brain had a chance to stop itself. "The day Georgia left. We were supposed to be together. It was her eighteenth birthday. I promised I'd be there. We were going to go to the movies. I told her to take her friends. She didn't want to hang around with her old man on her birthday." Roy sighed. A deep, pained sigh, overflowing with regret and loathing. "But she insisted. And I did want to go. I did. I really did but- I was on my way home when the call came in. Husband and wife down in Edmonton. Must've been the worst thing I've ever seen. I'd seen bodies, but this- Local cops couldn't even walk into the house. She put two shells in his chest. She was on the back porch with a bottle of whiskey and a stomach full of pills. She was just looking out at the sunset like nothing happened. I called Georgia on the way up to tell her I wasn't going to make it. She told me it was alright. She understood, but- I knew she wanted me there, and I knew- I knew how much I was about to hurt her. Wasn't the first time, not by a long shot. I should have been there for her."

"You can't put it all on yourself, Roy. People make their own choices."

"I know what everyone says about me, Hannah. I hear them whispering behind my back. That I was too caught up in work to take care for my sick wife. Too caught up in myself to notice my daughter leaving. I'm not the person you think I am."

He knew the things they didn't say as well. The words they only thought, because speaking them out loud wouldn't be decent. *You're the reason they're gone. You're the reason they left.*

They did leave. In different ways, but they left all the same. Everyone did eventually. His mother left. Cancer took her before his eighteenth birthday. Then Linda left. Then Georgia. His father was leaving too. A little more every day.

A lump lodged in Roy's throat. Tears burned his eyes. He was glad it was too dark for Hannah to see. "I just- between her mother and the drinking- I lost myself. I kept making promises I couldn't keep. I told myself at the time I was grieving. I lost my wife. But Georgia lost her mother- and her father. I should've been there for her. I should have been there for Linda, and I *chose* not to be." Roy waited among the stillness. Waited for Hannah to do- something. To call him a terrible father. Stand and walk off into the night so she didn't need to see him anymore.

"You know I haven't been here since high school," said Hannah. "Me and my sister would steal my mom's chardonnay and get drunk after the games ended. My father would be so mad when we came home. Stinking like booze and swearing we hadn't done anything. He'd chase us around screaming at the top of his lungs, *'Get over here girls. I'm not fuckin' around.'* He said that every single time." Hannah laughed at the memory. "My father was a mean son of a bitch. I always wondered what made him so angry at the world. Sometimes I think he was just lonely. Trapped in a marriage with a woman he loathed, raising two kids he never wanted."

Hannah wiped a tear from her eye with the back of her hand. "I was sitting right up there when Sheriff Blake came and slapped the cuffs on you." Hannah turned and pointed to the far top corner of the bleachers. "You were down by second base smoking like a chimney in your leather jacket. Hair slicked back like a regular Danny Zuko. I'm amazed your hair didn't catch fire." Hannah slid down the bench, moving closer to Roy. "What did Blake say he was bringing you in for when he came to get you?"

"He didn't say anything. Just told me to get in the car and keep my mouth shut."

"Yeah, sounds about right. Truth is, everyone in town knew what you did to my father. 'The Great Jimmy Harris put to the ground by that punk Roy Hill.' Everyone in town talked about it for weeks and when they asked you why you did it, do you remember what you said?"

"He said he didn't like my hair."

"Yes." Hannah clapped her hands together and laughed. "You were ballsy, I'll give you that." Hannah's smile faded. Her eyes shifted to the stars overhead. Her voice became solemn. "I appreciated you lying about why. I still do. The thought of everyone knowing the real reason you did it terrified me. Everyone knowing made me feel weak and dirty. Of course, everyone already knew why you actually did it. Everyone knew for a long time what went on in that house. The drinking and the yelling. Two little girls at school with new bruises every week. My mom in the grocery store barely able to walk. Everyone knew. Everyone saw. But you were the only one who did anything. Not because you wanted something. You had nothing to gain. You did it because you cared. That's what you do, Roy. You care. Sometimes you care so much you want to tear the world down to make things right. Unfortunately, we're past the time where you can break my father's jaw to solve a problem, but that doesn't mean we can't do the right thing. You're a good person, Roy. An actual, decent man. Maybe the first one I ever met. Not caring is not the answer. You're not capable of not caring."

The tears came then, stinging his eyes. They streamed down his face and disappeared into his beard.

I do not cry for those who move on.
I cry for those left behind to miss them.

Maybe his father was right. Maybe Georgia was right. Maybe the people left behind were the ones who had to suffer. Linda was at peace and Georgia was out living her life. He didn't need to worry about them anymore.

Roy's phone buzzed in his pocket. He wiped away his tears and answered. "Hello."

"Is this Sheriff Roy Hill?" asked the caller.

"Yes. Whose calling?"

"How do you live with yourself?"

"Excuse me?" Roy cleared his throat.

"How do you live knowing you've destroyed so many lives?"

"Who is this? How did you get this number?"

"How can you just sit there. Do you want to ruin her life too? Don't you think Hannah deserves better than you? How long until she ends up like the rest?"

Roy looked at Hannah. Who was calling and how did he know who Roy was with? "Who is this?" Based on the sour taste in his mouth he already knew the answer. He scanned the fence around the baseball diamond, searching for any sign of movement.

"You're a disgrace," said the caller. "Even your own daughter couldn't stand to be around you."

"Who are you, you sick son of a bitch?"

"You know who I am. Or at least you would if you took the time to care about anyone other than yourself."

The line went dead. Across the baseball field an engine roared to life. High beams ignited. Roy and Hannah were flooded with blinding light. Tires spun in the mud and a truck took off across the parking lot. Roy was on his feet. He was past second base before his body realized he moved. The streetlight lit up the truck. Red with North Dakota plates. He was too far away to make out what they said. He reached the fence at a full sprint and vaulted over. He ran across the lot. Mud sucked at his boots. He reached the sidewalk as the truck's taillights disappeared around the corner.

<u>Go With Me</u>

Then

The morning breeze off the lake brought a harsh chill. Tommy gathered a pile of twigs and branches and lit a fire in a rusted old barrel he pulled from the water. He sat on the rocks with Georgia beneath the setting sun, warmed by the fire. Georgia used a rag to clean the blood from Tommy's knuckles. "I can't believe he did this to you. It's not right."

"I've had worse." A smile touched Tommy's lips. "You know this isn't even the thing I remember about that night."

"What do you mean?"

"Well, this happened the same night I met your grandfather. When we were all talking, he was telling us stories about him and your grandma."

Tommy stood and held out a hand for Georgia to join him. "He told us about how they used to walk along the shore. They'd find a place with a beautiful view and dance in the moonlight."

He took Georgia's hands in his and they began to sway back and forth. They moved to the rhythm of gentle waves and the melody of singing insects.

He placed his hand on her back, pulled her close. Her head rested against his chest, breath warm against his skin.

"Why do you keep going back there? You know he's gonna keep hurting you."

Tommy didn't answer. He didn't know what to say. There was a part of him, a tiny piece somewhere inside, that hoped his father would change. He could somehow break free from whatever demon had him in his grip and go back to being who he used to be. Not for Tommy's sake, but for the sake of his mother.

"He wasn't always like this, you know. He used to be decent. That's what my mother says at least. He was an electrician. He worked on the wires. Those big, tall towers that run across the valley. When I was little, I thought they kept going on and on forever. I used to ask my mother where they went. She said they went everywhere. For thousands of miles all over the country. That blew my mind back then. I couldn't imagine something so-huge. All I knew was a dirt road in a town with a couple dozen houses. But seeing those towers made me want to find out what was at the end of them. Across the fields. Over the grass where things actually happen."

"I know the feeling." Georgia looked up at him with shining eyes, out of place in such a dull town.

"Well, it's not too late," said Tommy. "We could go together. Take off and leave this behind us."

"I've thought about it. You know that. But we can't just go. What about my dad? My grandpa? What about your mother? You said you wanted to get her out of there. Get her away from him."

Tommy thought of his mother. Her blank eyes. The way she looked through him.

"My mother," said Tommy. "You know, she was my best friend growing up. We used to go grab old bread from the dumpster behind the bakery. We'd pull it into little pieces and feed it to the ducks at the park. We'd make up stories about them. Give them names. She'd take me for ice cream after. We'd spend the day laughing and talking. She would read to me every night. Robin Hood, Treasure Island, The Swiss Family Robinson."

For a moment, Tommy caught himself smiling. The memory of his mother's smile warmed something within him.

"What went so wrong?"

"My dad lost his job. There was an accident at work. A bucket truck malfunctioned while he was working on one of the towers. The company sent him home for a few weeks to recover. Weeks turned into months. The doctor wouldn't give him more pain meds, so he picked up a different bottle. I was eight the first time I saw him hit my mother. He'd done it before but- that was the first time I saw it happen. I woke up in the middle of the night. I could hear them arguing. I walked down the hall to check on things. He was yelling so loud, and I just wanted to make sure my mom was okay. I walked into the kitchen. The floor was soaked, glass everywhere. The whole house reeked of booze. I made it to the living room where they were arguing and that's when it happened. He punched her. Right across her face. She had a bruise for weeks. She was so upset."

Tommy swallowed hard. The scent of alcohol stung his nose. "The worst part was, she wasn't even upset with him. She was upset with herself for letting me see it. Something in her broke that night, like any chance I had to escape died when I found out what my father really was. I can see it when she looks at me. Like she doesn't know who I am. Her eyes are empty. Soulless. To tell you the truth, I don't think there's anything left of my mother in there." Tommy wiped a tear from his eye. "I'm sorry. You don't need to hear all that."

"No, I'm sorry," said Georgia. "I'm just not really sure what to say."

"Say you'll go with me."

Georgia pulled away. Nervousness in her smile.

"Not right now," said Tommy. "But one day. When you're ready. When the time is right. Will you go with me? Leave this place behind and find out what's out there?"

Georgia smiled at Tommy. A sad smile, but a smile all the same. "That's the problem. What if the time is never right?"

Punishment

Now

Roy sat in the briefing room in a hard plastic chair. The kind you would sit at in the cafeteria in elementary school with tennis balls stuck on the legs. Jane stood by the case board at the front of the room. One by one she taped up the pictures. Five faces looked out over the room with accusing glares. Ten eyes pierced through Roy. *"You did this,"* they said. *"You did this to us. You should have stopped him. How could you let this happen?"*

The air in the room tasted like rust. Acid burned in Roy's throat.

"Abigail Mitchell. Sixteen years old." Jane pointed at the first picture in the lineup. "Omar's sister. As far as I can tell, she's where all this starts. Her body was found last February. She'd been missing for six days when a group of high schoolers found her drifting along the shore during a party at Stump Lake. The coroner's report says she was in the water between forty-eight and sixty hours. Cause of death was determined to be accidental drowning."

"So, she was already missing for four days before she died?" asked Sheriff Hill.

"Correct," said Jane. "And the local police spent none of that time looking for her."

"How soon after she went missing was it reported?"

"Less than six hours. Abby had gone for a drive with a few friends. When it started to get dark, and Abby hadn't called, Mrs. Mitchell got worried. She took a cab to Lakota to report it in person. She explained everything. The police took Mrs. Mitchell's statement and told her not to worry. She should go home and sit by the phone because Abigail would call soon to check in. Mrs. Mitchell didn't know at the time, but when they told her, 'Don't worry,' it meant they weren't going to either."

"They didn't look for her at all?"

"No," said Jane. "It was the view of the Nelson County Sheriff's Office that the Mitchell family had a history of *'unsavory behavior'* and at the time they had *'no reason to suspect she was anything but a runaway.'"*

Jane moved down the line of victims. She pointed to the second picture. A young woman with shoulder-length, dirty blonde hair. Freckles ran from cheek to cheek across the bridge of her nose. "Jackie Hope, seventeen. Body found last April in Sweetwater Lake outside of Fort Totten. Tribal Police suspected foul play. They called in the FBI, but the M.E. listed the cause of death as accidental drowning. The Feds walked. Tribal Police tried to investigate further but didn't have the resources."

Jane continued down the line putting a name, place, and date to each of the girls.

Bethany Burke. Minnewaukan. July. Accidental drowning.

Margaret May Baker. Crary. November. Homicide.

Jennifer Hanson. Devil's Lake. March. Homicide.

"How does this happen?" asked Sheriff Hill. "Five girls drowned in the last year within a fifty-mile radius, and no one noticed a pattern."

"No one was looking," said Jane. "Abby was found in Nelson County. Bethany in Benson County. Jackie's body was on reservation land. There were no two bodies found in the same jurisdiction until Margaret and Jennifer. Nobody saw a connection because nobody had anything to connect."

"And you're sure these are all the same guy?"

"As sure as I can be," said Jane. "When he called. When I heard his voice, I knew. Before he even told me what he did to Margaret, I knew. I could feel it. I could-"

"Taste it," finished Roy.

"Yes," said Jane. "And I got the same feeling when I talked to Abby's mother. The same taste when I read those girls files. I didn't know for sure until I saw all their pictures."

The girls stared down at Roy. They were not spitting images off one another.

Margaret had green eyes, sharp features. Her hair long and pale.

Jennifer eyes were green as well but with hits of blue. Dark golden hair fell above her shoulders, framing the soft features of her face.

Five girls. Each one different in small ways. Variations in the shade of their hair and the angle of their features.

The real similarity was the eyes. Not the shade or the size, but the look. Something within that couldn't be described with words.

He'd seen the look before on Linda, other times on his daughter. Profound sadness, masked by a radiant smile. He looked into those eyes and his stomach imploded.

"He called again," said Roy. "Last night."

"Here?" asked Jane. "At the station?"

"No. He called me directly. Somehow, he got my cell number."

"What did he say?"

Heat rose in Roy's ears. A cold sweat trickled down his neck. "Just more taunts. He said I would know who he was. That if I cared about anyone other than myself, I would know who he was."

Roy tasted it again. A pinprick on the tip of his tongue. Ash. Metal. Blood. Sour candy and burnt coffee.

The taste slithered to the back of his throat. A sickening bitterness clung to his teeth, burned up through his nose. The taste of a killer.

<u>Dinner</u>

Hannah drove through town beneath an overcast sky. Another night of rain. What else was new? She drove slowly, letting the breeze roll over her face.

She watched the people walk down the street, studied their faces, tried to read their emotions. Were they scared? Worried? Nervous?

Everyone knew about the girls. About Margaret. The way she sat beneath the tree. Peaceful and still. The bruises on her chest. The never-ending stare. They knew about Jennifer's face. The brutal, gut-wrenching marks that forced her parents to have a closed casket at her funeral. Soon, they might find other bodies. She gagged at the thought of another little girl on her table, pale and cold.

Did one of these people know something?

Did one of them do this to her?

Were they doing it again? Now? While everyone searched for them?

She continued to study the faces as she passed by. She tried to gain some semblance of what was going on in her town. All the faces looked the same. Weary. Worn down. Tired of the monotony of their day to day.

Hannah was tired too.

Tired of waking up to bad news. Tired of wondering when someone would find another girl's body. Tired of watching the man she cared about fall deeper and deeper into despair. Tired of watching her town drown in front of her eyes.

The lake had been rising almost half her life, but she never really saw it that way. The water was getting higher, but it wasn't because the lake was rising. It's because the town was sinking.

She scanned the faces on the street. She did a double take when she saw the old man. He had a ring of snow-white hair. He stumbled through the McDonalds parking lot in shorts and a tank top. His hands shook as he mumbled to himself. She pulled into the parking lot and got out of her car. She approached slowly.

"Henry?" The man looked at Hannah, confused. "Henry, is that you?"

"I saw her," said Henry. "I saw them together."

"Who'd you see, Henry?" She walked him over to a bench and asked him if he wanted to sit down. She spoke calmly, trying to figure out what was going on. "Henry? Do you know where you are?"

Henry looked around. Confusion plain on his face. "Looks like Fourth Street. Near the movie theater."

"That's right," said Hannah. "Do you know how you got here?"

"I walked. I think," said Henry. "I'm- I'm not sure. I remembered something. I think it was important. Something I had to tell Roy."

"I'm sure it'll come back to you. Why don't I take you home? I can call Roy, let him know you have something to tell him."

Henry looked at Hannah for the first time since she pulled up. A smile spread across his face. "Hannah? How are you sweetheart?"

"I'm good. Could I give you a ride home?"

"Works for me. I got to get the barn stripped down so Roy can help me repaint it. Been bugging him about it for months now. Say, maybe you could ask him. He always listens to you."

"I'll do that. Why don't I call him on the way?"

Hannah helped Henry into the car and pulled out onto the street. She picked up her phone and called Roy. He answered after the first ring.

"Hannah? Everything alright?"

"Hey Roy. You'll never guess who I ran into."

"What? Who?"

"You're dad. I ran into him on the way home from the station."

"Near the station. Why? Is he alright?"

"Of course. I'm driving him home right now."

"I'm sorry, Hannah."

"No worries. I'll have him back in no time. Will I see you there?"

"Yeah- of course. I'll be there as soon as I can."

"Alright. Bye Roy."

She hung up and smiled at Henry to assure him everything was okay.

"He doin' alright?" asked Henry. "I don't mean to bother him if he's busy."

She hesitated. Only for a moment. Roy was far from alright. He hadn't been '*alright*' for years now.

"He's good," said Hannah.

"Good. I know he's been nervous lately."

"How do you mean?"

"Well, you know with prom coming up. Young men act tough, but they're just as nervous as the girls. Hell, I'd say they're even more nervous. You should have seen the state of him before he asked you. Pacing back and forth. Practicing his lines in the mirror. You looking forward to it?"

Prom? She hadn't thought about that night in a long time. How long had it been? *Twenty years?*

God, had it really been that long?

She remembered her dress. All lace and sequins. Roy, handsome in his tuxedo. Pink undershirt and slicked back hair like John Travolta.

"I am," said Hannah. "I'm really excited."

"That's good." said Henry "He is too. He'd kill me for telling you this but, I can tell how much he cares about you. He talks about you all the time. You're very special to him."

"He's special to me too."

"Well, that's good. I'm glad to hear it. You know Roy's been troubled lately. Only natural with his mother being sick and all. He's worried we're gonna lose her, but I have faith. She'll pull through. She's one tough woman. A lot tougher than I am. Hell, all those machines and pills. I don't think I could stay positive like she has."

Tears welled in Hannah's eyes at the thought of Mrs. Hill. The days spent in her hospital room with Roy. The endless beeping of machines. Mrs. Hill still smiled every day. Always cracking jokes and making everyone feel better. Even when the chemo took the last of her hair. *"I've always wanted to try shaved,"* she said. *"Very punk rock."*

Mrs. Hill passed a week after Roy and Hannah graduated high school. A part of Roy died along with his mother. The way it does when someone close to you leaves. Something irreplaceable you know you'll never get back.

Roy and Hannah would go into his father's barn at night. They used to spend all their nights there. The smell of hay and dirt. Roy's arms wrapped around her. The night after his mother died Roy cried on Hannah's shoulder, the first time she saw a man cry. That night she told herself she would marry him.

Things didn't work out.

Roy joined the force right out of high school. Hannah moved to Fargo for college. They grew distant. It happens as people get older.

Hannah and Henry sat at the small round table in Henry's kitchen. Hannah untied the knot in the takeout bag. The salty sweet smell of Chinese food filled the room. Hannah reached into the bag, containers still damp from the steam.

"Steak and peppers for you, Henry?" She laid the container in front of him.

"That's the one. This place is the best. You're gonna love it."

A truck screeched to a halt outside the house. A few seconds later Roy came through the door, breathing heavy like he'd run all the way home.

"Hey Roy," said Hannah. "We got Mandarin Palace." She pulled two more take-out boxes out of the bag. "Orange chicken and fried dumplings. That still your order?"

"It is," said Roy.

"Sit down then. Food's still hot."

Roy pulled out a chair and joined them for dinner. He gave Hannah a worried look. "So, how's everything going." Roy nodded towards his father.

"We're having a great time," said Hannah. "Me and your dad were just talking about prom. He tells me you practiced in front of your mirror before asking me."

"You told her that, Dad?"

"It slipped out," said Henry.

"Well," said Hannah. "Is it true, Roy?"

Roy's cheeks flushed like they were back in high school.

"I might have gone over it a few times."

Henry pushed his chair back and stood from the table. "Well, kids this has been fun. Hannah, thank you so much for the ride and the meal. I'm stuffed. Think I'll go to bed early tonight."

Henry placed his hand on Roy's shoulder and leaned down to talk to his son. "Hold onto that one. She's a keeper."

Henry walked from the kitchen and disappeared into the hallway.

"A smile looks good on you, Sheriff," said Hannah.

"I'm sorry about him," said Roy.

"Don't be silly. He was a perfect gentleman."

Roy shifted in his seat. "Hey, Hannah?"

"Yes?"

"I just wanted to say I appreciate what you said the other night."

"I didn't say anything that wasn't true."

"I guess it's hard for me to see myself as a decent person."

"That's hard for a lot of people."

"Yeah." Roy opened his box of dumplings and took a bite. "Wow. These are just as good as I remember."

"I know, right." Hannah picked up a fortune cookie from the pile in the middle of the table. "You remember senior year when we stole that box of fortune cookies from behind the counter?"

"Oh, I remember. Mr. Kim ran out after us screaming *'Damn kids. I fucking kill you. I fucking kill you.'*"

"That's right, he did say that." Hannah laughed. "I must have had thirty of these things that night. I still get sick when I smell them." Hannah took the cookie in her hand and crushed it into powder."

"How about that time we were night fishing down under the causeway," said Roy. "When Greg and Charlie thought it's be a good idea to play drunk chicken?"

"Oh yeah. And Sheriff Blake almost turned Charlie into roadkill." Hannah crushed another cookie beneath her fist. "Look at us now. A couple of narcs. I think my eighteen-year-old self would try to kill me."

"Try? I don't think you'd stand a chance against her."

"How dare you." Hannah punched Roy's shoulder playfully. "You're probably right though. I was mighty feisty back then."

Hannah and Roy laughed together. They lost track of time as they reminisced about the past.

Roy rubbed his eyes. He hadn't realized how tired he was. He looked at his watch. 11:44.

"Is that the time already?"

Hannah looked at the clock above the stove. "I guess it is late. I should get going."

"Before you do," said Roy. "I have something I need to give you." Roy stood from his seat. "I'll be right back."

Roy walked out of the kitchen into the darkness of the house. He returned a few minutes later holding a wooden box with a small metal latch. Roy slipped an envelope into his pocket as he walked into the kitchen.

"I need you to take this," said Roy. "Throw it away. Burn it. I don't care."

"What's inside?"

"Something I don't need anymore. You can look if you want, just- don't look until you leave."

Hannah looked into Roy's eyes. Emerald with flecks of gold. The eyes she fell in love with as a teenager. Back then they were warm and inviting. The years had stolen their glow, tarnished the emeralds, dimmed the golds luster.

"I won't look." Hannah took the box from Roy and placed it on the table. She stepped closer to him and took his hands in hers. "We can't let the past control our future." She pushed up onto her tip toes and kissed him.

<u>Faces in a Crowd</u>

The kiss took Roy by surprise. He didn't get much sleep after. He offered Hannah his room. Told her he'd sleep on the couch. He didn't want her driving home tired.

She insisted she had to leave, but she would see him soon. She took the box and drove away. She wasn't in a hurry. She wasn't rushing out the door ashamed of what she'd done. Hannah was never ashamed. She did what she wanted. She was bold and outgoing. She always had been. She kissed him because she wanted to. That much he was sure of. What he wasn't sure of was how he felt about it.

He wanted to kiss her. It crossed his mind that night at the baseball field. The thought was brief. A sudden moment of temptation. Fleeting. He hid the urge away, deep down, somewhere behind the self-loathing and unexplainable need to push away anyone who cared for him.

Now that it happened, he found he was ashamed. Like kissing Hannah was a betrayal. To Linda. To Georgia. He knew it wasn't. They would want him to be happy. Right?

They would want this to work out for him. Let him have something to care about.

He wanted to, but he knew himself. The guilt of moving on would eat at him every day. Take over his life until he pushed Hannah away like he did everyone else.

Roy laid in his bed until the early morning, overthinking like a teenager after a first date. His eyelids were heavy. He stared at the ceiling, half dreaming half awake, until he gave up on a good night's sleep.

The sun was still down when Roy got to the station. The brief was scheduled for eight o'clock. If he wasn't going to sleep, he figured he could make himself useful. Set up chairs, make coffee, anything to busy his mind.

Jane's car was in the lot when Roy pulled up. She'd probably slept at the station again. He'd have to talk to her about that, but today wasn't the day. The smell of coffee greeted him as he entered the briefing room. A dozen chairs were arranged in a semi-circle in front of the case board. The board was covered in maps and files only Jane would be able to make any sense of. At the top of the board, the girls watched over the room, waiting for their retribution.

The room was quiet. The electric hum of the heater was the only sound. The girls' eyes followed him as he moved through the room, like the statues of Jesus he used to see at church. Watching over him. Judging him.

Jane was in his office when Roy entered. She sat on the couch with the stupor of someone who had been woken from a deep sleep. Her eyes searched the room before settling on him.

"Morning Sheriff," said Jane.

"Morning Jane." Roy jabbed a thumb at the set-up in the briefing room. "Where'd you find the time to get all that done?"

"Couldn't sleep. Figured I'd make myself useful. What time is it?"

"Just before six. Still a couple hours until the briefing. You can sleep here if you want. No one will bother you."

"No. That's alright. Thank you but, I'm actually here to ask you about something."

"Alright." Roy maneuvered past the labyrinth of file boxes and sat at his desk. "What's on your mind?"

"Well, I was thinking about the case. About the girls that- you know. I read through the files over and over and something just didn't make sense to me."

"What's that?"

"The phone call. The one you got the other night when you saw his truck. He couldn't control himself. Maybe his emotions got the better of him, or maybe he was so caught up in taunting you he made a mistake. But it wasn't the first one he made."

"What was his other mistake?"

"Margaret," said Jane. "She's the only one that doesn't fit. Abby, Jackie, Beth, Jenny, all of them were found in the water. It was only by chance any of them were found. But Margaret wasn't in the water. She was out in that field, right off the side of the road."

"Do you think someone else killed Margaret?"

"No. It was the same person, but something changed when he killed Margaret. Why? Why leave her in the field? It's like he wanted her to be found. He said on the phone call you could have stopped it. I thought he was just taunting you because you were the Sheriff, but what if that's not it? I talked to Hannah. She said Jennifer's body was frozen solid in that ice. She could have been killed before we found Margaret."

"So, he killed Margaret because he was upset we didn't find Jennifer?"

"Jennifer was the only other girl found in Ramsey County. All the others were in places he must have known we wouldn't have heard about." Jane paced back and forth in the cramped office. She picked at her fingernails unconsciously. "That field. The one we found Margaret in. It's less than a quarter mile outside of Clareborne on the way to the station. I think- I think he wanted *you* to find her."

"He mentioned my daughter."

Even your own daughter couldn't stand to be around you.

"And he knew Hannah's name."

How long until she ends up like the rest.

"I'm sorry, sir," said Jane. "But why would someone do this? Why would they want you specifically to look for them? What is it he thinks you did?"

Let my wife die, thought Roy. Abandoned my daughter when she needed me the most. Drank away the days with no regard for anyone around me.

He was right. Georgia hated him- rightfully so. Her letter said otherwise, but he knew deep down how badly he hurt her. Maybe he deserved to be punished. Maybe he drank himself to death years ago and this was his own personal hell.

Roy looked at the picture on his desk. The picture he took from Georgia's room. The picture of a happy family enjoying ice cream, unaware they were about to fall apart.

Georgia looked so much like Linda. She had her hair, her smile, her sense of humor. She was like a miniature version of her mother. Except for the eyes. Georgia had his eyes. He was grateful he could pass on one good thing to his daughter.

"I see their faces everywhere," said Roy. "People on the street. Pictures in the newspaper. I see them when I look at those girls." Roy looked out across the hallway. The five faces leered at him through a crack in the blinds. Five Georgia's. Five Linda's. Wondering why he let them down.

"I see my father." Jane's voice was soft, as though if she talked too loud, she would lose the courage to speak. "I saw him when I looked at Margaret under the tree. Her blank, unseeing stare. Whenever I look at those pictures, I see him looking back at me. Sometimes when I look down the street, I see him standing in the middle of a crowd. Standing real still, while everyone moves around him. I know he's gone but part of me thinks it might be him. It might be a miracle and somehow, he found his way back to me."

"He's with you Jane. He'll always be with you. The people we love never leave. Not really."

***

Roy made sure no one knew about what they were doing before the meeting happened. Someone in the station had been letting information slip. That was the only way details about Margaret and Jennifer could have gotten out.

Whoever was behind the leak, Roy didn't think they had malicious intent. They could have mentioned something to their wife or husband in passing.

How was work, sweetie?
It was a hard one today. They found another girl. Her head was all smashed in. I've never seen something so evil.

However the information got out, Roy couldn't risk it happening again. If word got out about what they had planned, everyone in the county would know by lunch-time. It would ruin everything. A knock sounded on the door to Roy's office. He glanced at the clock. 7:15. Still forty-five minutes until the briefing. "Come in."

Jane reentered his office. She was tense, her face drained of blood as she attempted to hold back panic.

"Jane? What's wrong?"

"A call came in from Rugby. Missing girl. Went out for a walk night before last and never made it home." Jane held out a picture.

Roy's throat tightened. He sat paralyzed as he stared at the photo. "Change of plans. Move up the meeting. Call everyone and tell them to get down here. Send out his picture. I want every cop in the state looking for this son of a bitch."

Ten officers gathered in the briefing room waiting for Jane and Roy to tell them why they were there. They looked up at the girls on the board.

Bloated. Beaten. Humiliated.

The officers shifted uncomfortably in their chairs. They mumbled to each other, wondering what was going on.

The mumbling stopped as Roy walked into the room. Jane followed behind carrying a stack of files. She placed the stack on the desk and joined Roy at the case board.

"Good morning, officers," said Sheriff Hill.

"Morning, Sheriff," said the officers all together.

"I'm sure you're all wondering why you were asked here. I'm sure based on the pictures you've figured out why."

"But Sheriff," said Officer Henderson. A short portly man with a graying mustache. "I thought they only found two girls. There's six on the board."

"Correct. Over the last four months, we found the bodies of two girls. Using what we knew about these girls, Officer Barlowe worked tirelessly to find three more victims."

"Sheriff," said another officer. "Are you saying the same person killed all six of these girls?"

"Five." Jane pointed to the last picture in the row. "This is Sarah Morris. Reported missing yesterday morning. So far, there's been no trace of her."

"What does she have to do with these other girls?" asked Officer Henderson.

"Several weeks ago, we spoke to Sarah Morris in an effort to identify this man." Jane pointed to the picture of Jennifer's alleged boyfriend in the center of the board. "While she couldn't identify him she did confirm seeing our latest victim, Jennifer Hanson, get into his truck only a few days before she went missing."

Jane pointed to the first picture in the lineup and went down the row. "Abigail Mitchell, Jacqueline Hope, Bethany Burke, Margaret May Baker, and Jennifer Hanson. Each of these girls drowned. Each showed signs of CPR-related injuries. They were drowned and someone attempted to resuscitate them. In the case of Jennifer Hanson, she was drowned and brought back up to four times."

A wave of shocked muttering passed over the room at this piece of information.

"And you think he'll do the same thing to that girl?" asked one of the officers.

Roy looked down the line of officers and nodded. "Someone has been killing young women. Daughters. Friends. Mothers." A lump forced its way into Roy's throat. "They've been doing it in your town. The place you and your loved ones call home. They've been doing it for a while now. We don't know much about them. We know that the man in this sketch is our most promising suspect. We believe he is in his mid to late twenties but it's possible he or the person responsible is older. He may have a scar or a burn on the back of his right hand. The only thing we know for sure is they drive a red pickup, and they need to be stopped."

"I'm sorry, Sheriff, but what do you mean 'him or the person responsible'" said Officer Henderson.

"It is important to note," said Jane, "that although we believe this sketch to be of the man responsible for these killings. Do not rule out anybody based on this picture. It's possible this man is only an accomplice or that he isn't involved at all."

"So, all we really know is what he drives? No offense, but how the fuck are we gonna find him if that's the only thing we know."

Jane picked up the stack of folders. She walked down the row of officers and handed each of them a file.

"There are forty-eight red pickup trucks registered in Ramsey County. The addresses of their owners are inside your file. You and your partners will be going to eight of these addresses. You will knock on the door and ask the questions listed in your file. Stay with your partner at all times. This man is dangerous and desperate. We don't know how he'll react if we get him in a corner. If you think someone's suspicious. Go back to your car and call it in. Watch the address until backup arrives. It is of the utmost importance you get to all eight addresses by the end of the day. Once word gets out about what we're doing, our guy will ditch the truck. If he does, we're back to zero."

The officers looked at each other confused.

Roy didn't blame them. This was the longshot of longshots, but something had to be done. They couldn't afford to sit around. No telling when another body- Sarah's body- would turn up.

"Officers, I understand this is a bit unorthodox," said Roy. "I know the odds of us finding this guy like this are low. But this is what we've got. What we do today could be the difference between five bodies and six. You're dismissed."

Abby & Tommy

Then

"I can't believe she just left." Abby sat on the front lawn of her old school. Tears ran from the corner of her eyes, leaving small dark blotches on her shirt. She ran a finger over the tattoo on her ankle- a small valentine's style heart, split down the middle that peeked out above her sock.

Tommy sat beside her, looking at the school. Empty windowpanes where the glass exploded outwards from the heat. Black tongues of char bruised the faded orange bricks. The school was a shell of what it once was. The town was the same. Nothing inside and nobody left to miss it.

"She didn't want to," said Tommy. "I mean, she did want to leave, but I don't think she wanted to leave us."

"But she did." Abby rolled back onto the grass. She sprawled out her limbs like she was about to make a snow angel and watched the clouds drift across the sky.

She had. She might not even have wanted to. Not really. The truth is, Tommy would never know what it was Georgia wanted. For all the times they talked, all the hours spent spilling out the deepest parts of themselves, maybe Tommy didn't really know Georgia at all. He liked to think he did. But he also always thought him and Georgia would leave together. It hurt him more than anything he'd been wrong about that. "We'd talked about it, you know. Leaving. Getting in the car and just- going. Driving until we got to the place we wanted to be."

"Where was that?"

"Not sure. Always figured we'd know when we saw it." Tommy looked away from the school and let his eyes rest on Abby. "I asked her to leave with me. When the time was right."

Abby rolled onto her side. She rested her head on her hand, doing nothing to wipe away her tears. "What did she say?"

"She said she didn't know if the time would ever be right."

"Guess she changed her mind."

Tommy looked away from Abby, unable to meet her gaze. "I don't think she wanted to leave. Not the way she did. But we all do things we don't really want to do. Decisions in the spur of the moment we wish we could take back. Problem is, by the time we realize we messed up, it's too late."

"I don't know if I could ever really leave." Abby rolled onto her stomach. She tore up handfuls of grass and threw them into the air to be taken by the wind. "I know I talk about it. But I think that's all it really is. Talk. I guess I'm surprised Georgia left because I thought that's all it ever was. Just talk."

"People can surprise you," said Tommy. "But maybe it's for the best. Maybe now she'll be free."

"I know it's for the best. I just wished we could have gone with her. At least that's what I tell myself. If it came down to it, I don't know that I could ever leave my mom behind. I'm all she's got left."

A knife twisted in Tommy's gut. He looked back at the school. Then to the sky. He thought of Georgia. The way her voice and her presence still followed him everywhere he went. The look in her eye during their last encounter. He knew he'd never get to see her again.

He looked into Abby's eyes and his breath caught in his chest. That look. Hope, worry, fear, all rolled into one. The same look Georgia always wore. Maybe she wasn't as gone as he thought she was.

The Search

The truck was parked on the side of the house, nestled between a screened in patio and the tree line. Ribbons of dried mud covered the bumper and speckled the hood.

Roy thought of the baseball field. Tires squealing in slick mud as he chased after phantom taillights.

The door shook in its frame when Jane knocked. Roy stood behind her, his jaw taut as they waited to see who would answer the door. He would know when he saw him. Before he spoke or answered any questions, he would know.

"Hello?" The door creaked open to reveal a whisp of a woman with long silver hair. She gazed at the officers on her doorstep with silent confusion.

"Hello, ma'am," said Jane. "Sorry to bother you. We were hoping to speak with Robert Parker."

"What's this about?"

"We just have a few questions," said Roy. "Is that Robert's truck on the side of the house?"

The woman leaned out to inspect the truck as if unsure what Roy was referring to. "Yes."

"And is Robert here?"

"He's out back."

"Could we speak with him?"

A look crossed the woman's face that was difficult to read. She hesitated for a moment before inviting them both inside. They followed behind her. Roy studied the house as he walked. White linoleum stretched across the kitchen, peeling up in the corners. The counters were clean except for an assortment of pill bottles and yesterday's newspaper.

"My names Dorothy, by the way," said the woman.

"I'm officer Barlowe," said Jane. "And this is Sheriff Hill."

"What is it you want to speak to Robert about?"

They passed the basement door as they followed Dorothy. A rusted steel latch held shut by a shiny new padlock. Roy's stomach churned. "We just have a few questions about a case we're working on. We're hoping he can help us clear things up?"

"Good luck with that. He hasn't been very talkative lately."

The yard was framed through the kitchen window. The property was all but baron. An empty wooden frame housed a withering garden. A snake of garden hose slithered across the yard, caked in dry mud. An old wooden shed waited by the fence line; its roof collapsed. Just past the shed sat an old willow tree. A curtain of grey-green leaves hung from the branches like a shroud, hiding whatever rested beneath it.

"You're our first visitors for a while. No one really stops by anymore. That's what happens when you get old. People just see you as a burden. Someone to be pitied. Don't bother me none. If people want to act like I'm already dead, then so be it. Makes it much easier to get things done." Dorothy stopped by the back door and leaned her head outside. "The police are here."

"What?" shouted a voice that must have been Robert's.

"The police are here."

"I don't know any Bernice."

"No. The police." Dorothy turned back to Roy and Jane. "You see what I deal with?"

Dorothy leaned back outside and shouted as loud as her voice would allow. "The police are here. Why do you have the hearing aids if they don't work?"

"What do you want, woman?" asked Robert. "I'm watching the game."

Dorothy closed the door and walked over to Jane. "Well, he's all yours. Good luck learning anything from him. And if you need to arrest him, you'll hear no complaints from me. Maybe I can finally get some peace and quiet."

Dorothy ambled back towards the kitchen as Roy and Jane stepped out the back door. Robert sat on an old wooden chair in a screened in patio. An old tube TV showed a fuzzed image of a Timberwolves game. Above the TV hung a wooden crucifix. Below the cross on a small shelf rested three war medals beneath a thick layer of dust.

Robert grabbed the remote and muted the television. "Something I can help you folks with?" He gestured to a pair of plastic chairs in the corner. Jane followed Roy's lead as he took a seat.

"Hello Mr. Parker." Roy raised his voice so the old man could hear him. "The truck out front- "

"No need to shout, son. I got the hearing aids fixed months ago. I just like the quiet." Robert leaned back in his chair. "Sixty-five years with that one. Married when we were fifteen. Despite how it may seem, we still like each other. We have the occasional fight, but making up is still just as fun." Robert laughed to himself.

"Your wife tells us that's your truck out front," said Jane.

"Sure is. I don't drive much anymore though. My eyes aren't what they used to be."

"Does anyone drive it?" asked Roy. "I noticed the mud."

"My grandson takes it from time to time. He drops off the little ones and goes trail riding. I don't mind. Gets me time with my granddaughter. Well, great granddaughter that is. Cutest damn thing I ever seen. Troublemaker though. Had to put a new lock on the basement door so she wouldn't play on the stairs."

"When was the last time your grandson borrowed the truck?"

Robert raised his eyebrows in thought. "Hard to say. Haven't seen him in about six months. I just don't bother cleaning the damn thing."

"And your grandson. What's his name?"

"Well, I got a few of them. One who borrows the truck is Samuel. My oldest daughter's son. He headed up to Boston a few months back. Law school if you can believe it."

"You must be very proud," said Jane.

"Oh yeah. He's a smart kid. Always has been. I knew he'd make it out of here. I always told him, if you want to be something you got to leave, cause you're sure as shit not gonna do it here."

"Mr. Parker just one more question." Jane pulled a small pile of photos out of the folder and handed them to Robert. "Do you know any of these young women."

Jane handed the pictures to Robert. He shuffled through them slowly. Squinting through the thick yellowed lenses of his glasses.

Roy watched him closely for any hint of recognition. Roy thought it unlikely Robert had anything to do with those girls, but nothing was impossible.

"I do." Robert looked up, his gaze shifting between Roy and Jane. "This one here." He took the picture of Sarah Morris from the pile and showed it to them. "Seen her on the news last night, been missing, right?" Robert leaned back in his chair. "I heard she run away."

Jane stood from her seat and retrieved the pictures. "She most likely did, Mr. Parker. We're just covering all our bases."

"All them other girls? They missing too?"

Jane looked from Robert to Roy. She swallowed hard. Roy could practically hear the dryness in her throat. "Not anymore. We found the others."

Robert looked away from Jane. Somewhere off into the distance. Past the overgrown yard and the crumbling shed and the willow tree. Somewhere in the past where the horrors of his own life lived. "I used to be in the army. I fought in three countries. Germany was the worst. Everything rubble. Everything burned. We came across a woman on the side of the road. The place was torn to hell. No one should have been there, but it was her home. She was holding something in her arms, wrapped up in a blanket. A mortar shell hit her house. Landed in the living room where her daughter was playing. There was nothing left of her. Burnt pieces wrapped up in a quilt. She showed them to us. Showed us what our war did to her little girl. Then she turned around and walked into the flames. I still hear her screams when I'm sleeping. Same as when I'm awake."

Robert wiped a tear from his eye with an arthritic hand. "I'd like to say times used to be simpler. But that just ain't true." His gaze wandered back to Jane. "I hope you catch whoever it is hurt them girls."

Jane gave a gentle nod and a half-hearted smile. "Thank you for your time, Mr. Parker. Sorry to bother you."

***

The fifth address was the farthest from the station. An hour north, where the only paved road was a two-lane highway, and the landscape was pocked with so many little ponds they didn't even bother to give them names.

Sheriff's Hill's truck rolled over loose gravel and felled branches as it crept towards the address. They found the house a few miles off State Road Thirty-Two, a bend that was more trail than road.

They spotted the truck in the side yard, half hidden in a tangle of dried ivy and thorn bushes that edged the fence line. The dull arhythmic thud of half a dozen wooden wind chimes sounded from the porch as Roy approached. He knocked on the door as Jane went to investigate the truck.

Roy raised his hand to knock again when Jane called to him. "Sheriff. You're gonna want to see this."

Roy rounded the front of the truck. He was hit by the smell of rust. Potent and sour. The tailgate hung open. Thick smears of dark curdled blood stretched along the length of the truck bed. Roy pulled his gun. Jane followed suit.

They moved around to the backyard, following the marks where something had been dragged across the dirt. The tracks led across the yard to a weather worn shed in the far back corner. Pistols raised, they approached.

A radio played somewhere in the shed. A static filled broadcast leaked out into the yard. Beneath the broadcast was another noise. A wet squelching, like a blade being dragged through meat. Flies buzzed around the shed in a frenzy, diving in and out of the half-closed door searching for the source of that heavy metallic smell.

As if sensing their presence, a man walked out of the shed. He wore only a pair of jeans and an apron. Each soaked through with vibrant red. He held a long, curved knife in his right hand. Blood gleamed from the razor-sharp edge of the blade.

"What are you doing on my property?" The man looked them over. His eyes widened when he realized they were police.

"Drop the knife," yelled Roy.

The blade fell to the grass with a soft thud. "You can't just walk onto my property waving guns around. I've got rights."

"Move away from the shed."

"You can't just walk onto my land like this."

"Away from the shed. Now. Hands on the back of your head."

The man did as he was told.

"On your knees." Jane held her gun on the man. She nodded to Roy to let him know she had him under control.

Roy approached the shed, still cautious. The smell grew stronger with every step. Flies landed in his hair and on his face. He batted them away and pulled the door open.

A yellowed butcher block stood on metal legs against the wall of the barn. A magnetic strip nailed to the wall held a large assortment of knives, in every size and shape imaginable. Blood dripped from the butcher block onto the cement floor. The floor and the butcher block were both stained with blood, old and new. Whatever scene of horror Roy was expecting, he didn't find.

A dead deer rested on the butcher block. Half of its skin peeled away to reveal the deep red flesh beneath.

"I don't have a license to butcher on the property," said the man. "I'm just doing it for a friend. I didn't think it was that big of a deal."

"Stand down Jane," said Roy. "It's just a deer."

"Of course, it's a deer," said the man. "What the fuck did you think it was? On my property waving guns around. I ain't out here hunting ferrets."

***

Roy knocked on the front door at the penultimate address. He had already accepted today wasn't going to uncover any answers. They would finish here and go to the final address, hope one of the other officers had found the man they were looking for. He knew no one would. They had nothing. No evidence. No name. No motive. Nothing to lead them in the right direction.

He's going to get away with it. The sickening thought invaded his mind once more. Over the past few weeks, he had managed to push the thought away. Dampen the crushing hold it had on him. Now it was back, and it dug its talons in with no intention of letting go.

Jane stood beside him as he knocked on the door. A woman in a red knit sweater with greying black hair answered. Her face filled with the same surprise everyone else had shown when they discovered the Sheriff at their door. "Can I help you, officers?"

"Hello, ma'am," said Jane. "Are you Mrs. Larson."

"Yes."

"Do you own a red nineteen-ninety Chevy pickup."

"Yes. Why? Is everything alright?"

"Everything's fine ma'am," said Roy. "We just have a few questions. Should only take a few minutes."

"Well alright then. Would you like to come in?"

Roy and Jane followed Mrs. Larson into the living room. Mrs. Larson sat on a stool by the kitchen door and offered the couch to Roy and Jane.

"Mrs. Larson, is your husband home today?"

"Yes, he's in the garage. Should I get him?"

"No that's okay." Roy sat beside Jane on the couch as he looked around the room. A TV sat atop an entertainment stand in the far corner. An old wooden coffee table stood in front of the couch; small cork coasters painted with various birds sat on top. A white carpet stretched from wall to wall, changing to tile as it entered the kitchen. The walls were covered with small shelves which housed a variety of knick-knacks. At the bottom of the staircase against the living room wall sat a pile of luggage and travel bags.

"Planning a trip?" Roy gestured towards the bags.

"Oh no. Returning from one actually. Just got in last night."

"Where to?" asked Jane.

"Maine. Went to visit my sister."

"How long was the trip?" asked Roy.

"Just over a month. My sister's in-laws have a place out in Bar Harbor. We usually go in the summer, but we figured we'd surprise her for her birthday. Hadn't seen her in a few years."

Behind Mrs. Larson a young woman plodded down the stairs. She held the phone to her ear, a long coil of cord trailing behind her. She lowered the phone and wrapped her palm around the receiver. "Mom, can I go to Becka's tonight."

"We just got home, honey. You really want to run off so soon."

"Please, Mom. I haven't seen her in like forever."

Mrs. Larson let out a sigh of reluctance. "Okay. Get dad to drive you."

Mrs. Larson's daughter darted up the stairs in excitement.

"Sorry about that. Teenagers. She used to love going on vacation with us. She'd always get so excited when we told her to pack her bags. She'd run along the beach with her cousins, and we'd all go out for ice cream." Mrs. Larson looked at the wall. A picture of her daughter hung in a round wooden frame above the television. "I swear she was on the phone the whole trip. Like spending a little time with family would kill her, you know. But times change, I suppose. She couldn't stay a little girl forever."

"Kids get older." Roy echoed his father's words. "It's hard. But it's true."

"You can say that again." Mrs. Larson let out a breath, eyes lingering on the photo of her daughter. "Sorry. I tend to ramble. What was it you needed to ask about?"

"We had reports of a red pickup speeding through the neighborhood. People we're worried someone might get hit," said Roy.

"Oh. Around here?"

"Yes, ma'am, but not to worry. Couldn't have been you. You weren't even here." Roy stood from the couch and thanked Mrs. Larson for her time.

No need to trouble her and her family. Ask them questions about missing girls and dead bodies. It would only make them worry. Make them scared to leave the house or let their daughter out of their sight.

But maybe they should have been scared.

For a moment, Roy considered telling them. Keep your daughter home. Don't let her go anywhere. But what good would that do?

Roy thought of the girls. Abby. Jackie. Bethany. Margaret. Jennifer. Sarah. The fear they must have felt. The terror that pulsed in their veins. The horror of their final thoughts.

He thought of the voice. Coarse and mocking. That voice lived beside him. A whisper in his ear, screaming of his shortcomings. Telling him all the truths he hated about himself. His inability to help the ones he cared for.

How do you live knowing you've destroyed so many lives?

Even your own daughter couldn't stand to be around you.

He would no longer be a slave to that voice. He wouldn't let anyone else feel that fear. He was going to bring this to an end. He would find the man who did this and make him pay. Pay for all the lives he destroyed. All the girls and their families. It wouldn't change the past. Wouldn't cancel out his failures. As a husband. As a father. But maybe he would be able to rest. Lay his head down knowing there was one less monster in the world.

The Voice

The world was flat here. That's the first thing Jane noticed when she moved here. Flat. Empty grass with the occasional copse of thin bare trees.

Even the sky was flat. Cloudless grey, like a base coat of primer on a living room wall. The flat ground met the flat sky somewhere off in the distance and made a line that somehow ignored the curve of the earth.

Out here there weren't any neighbors. Nothing but you and your thoughts for miles in all directions.

Jane's parents were born on the Fort Berthold reservation. Their house was nestled along a bend in the Missouri River. Nothing but mountains and sky.

When Jane was a little girl, she'd sit on her father's lap and watch her mother set up her easel. Her mother painted the landscape in beautiful strokes of color. The deep navy of the water. The blended purple and orange of the setting sun as it dropped below the lush blue mountains, rippled across the horizon.

She'd sit with her family and watch as the river flowed away to somewhere far beyond what she could see.

"How far does the river go?" Jane asked her father. He told her it flowed for thousands of miles. From Montana all the way across the country, down south to Mississippi. To Jane that sounded like forever.

Jane and her mother moved away after Jane's father died. They hauled the boxes across North Dakota and settled in Devil's Lake, she was never sure why. Maybe because it was the exact opposite of the home they left. Rolling mountains and rushing rivers, replaced by vacant lots and placid water.

 Her mother never unpacked after they moved. Never hung her beautiful paintings. Never spoke, unless it was to blame Jane for what happened to her father.

Her mother's words still haunted her.

She told herself she didn't care what her mother thought, but the words still stung. Somewhere so deep in her heart she couldn't even reach inside to tear them out. As much as she tried to ignore the words, that was the one thing her and her mother both agreed on. They would have been better off if it was Jane who died that day.

She should've moved away. Got in the car, put the lake in the rearview and never looked back. She thought about it for a long time, but whenever she was about to leave, one thing stopped her. She had nowhere to go.

Jane watched the vast nothingness out the window as Sheriff Hill drove them to the next address on their list.

"You ever wonder why people choose to live here?" asked Jane. "In the middle of nowhere."

"They don't choose it," said Sheriff Hill. "They just live here."

"Don't you think they get tired of it? No one for miles. Just grass and silence. No one to talk to."

"Some prefer silence. You might, if you gave it a try."

"No," said Jane. "Silence isn't for me. I'll take the noise and distraction. That way there's always something to think about."

Something besides my own thoughts, thought Jane.

"I know what you mean," said Sheriff Hill after a pause.

Another town passed on the right. A handful of houses, a post office, a church. One of the many that dotted the county. Tiny, unincorporated towns, connected by infinite miles of nothing.

Jane looked at the GPS. Their destination displayed in the bottom corner: **183 45th St. NE. Stevens, ND.**

Jane flipped open her file. "Is this really the last address?"

"Yep. This makes eight." The Sheriff seemed calm, but she knew under that shell, he was just as upset as her about today's outcome.

Jane looked over the page. The list of addresses where their killer might be waiting. "Do you think anyone found our guy?"

"Honestly. I doubt it," said Sheriff Hill. "We knew this was a longshot. We're looking for one guy across an entire county. Based on the assumption he lives in the county at all. If anyone found something, they would have called it in."

"If we don't find him then Sarah-"

"Half the uniformed officers in the state are looking for Sarah. I know it's hard. I know it feels like we need to be the ones who gets him. But it doesn't always work that way."

"But what if she's-"

"She's not. They'll find her, and when they do, we'll have him."

The truck's radio chirped with static. *"Dispatch looking for Sheriff Hill, Come in Sheriff. Over."*

"Sheriff Hill, responding. Did we find something? Over."

"Negative Sheriff. We have a situation at HQ that requires your attention. Over."

"What kind of situation? Over."

"There's a man hear who claims he's your father. He's very upset about something. Dr. Harris is with him now trying to calm him down. Over."

"Shit," muttered Sheriff Hill through gritted teeth. "Affirmative. ETA twenty minutes. Over."

Sheriff Hill hit the brakes and turned the truck around. He hit the gas and raced towards the station.

***

Roy burst through the station door. Behind the small plastic window that separated her from the outside world, the receptionist jumped at the sudden disturbance.

"Where is he?" asked Roy.

"I'm sorry Sheriff," said the receptionist. "He walked in and started yelling. I couldn't tell what he wanted, and I was afraid he might get violent and-"

"Beverly." Roy cut her off. "Where is he?"

"Interview three."

"Thank you. I'm sorry about all this."

Roy moved through the hallways. Every room he passed grew silent. Word had already spread who the crazy old man in room three was. Every step echoed down the silent corridors. The girls on the case board stared him down as he passed the briefing room.

Why are you here? You're supposed to be out there. You're supposed to find the person who did this to us. Don't you care at all?

Roy pushed the voices from his head.

He passed the bullpen. The officers dropped what they were doing. They muttered amongst themselves as they peered and pointed.

Roy rounded the corner to the interview rooms and almost collided with Hannah.

"Roy. I tried to calm him down but he's a mess."

"Are you alright?"

"I'm fine. But I don't think this is just an episode. Something's really upset him."

"What's he saying?"

"Something about a phone call. He said you needed to hear about it. I don't really know. He's all over the place."

"Thank you, Hannah."

Roy pressed the button to open the door. The lock buzzed and the door slid open. Roy stepped inside. His father sat at the table in the center of the room. The dimming bulb cast shadows across his face. His sunken eyes like hollow, black pits.

"Dad?" The old man at the table seemed very unlike Roy's father. He looked like him, but something was off. This man was menacing. Dark. A harbinger of terror wearing his father's skin.

The man at the table moved forward into the light. The harsh shadows pulled away from his face.

"Dad." Repeated Roy. This time sure it was him. "What's going on? Why are you here?"

"Roy. I tried to call you. I needed to tell you."

"What did you need to tell me?"

"The voice. That voice. I know that voice. I've heard it before."

"Dad, calm down." Roy sat across from his father and took his hands. His father seemed weary about Roy touching him but he didn't pull away.

"I need you to breath okay," said Roy. "Count with me. One."

His father took a deep shaking breath.

"Two."

Another breath.

"Three."

His father let out one last burst of air.

"Now, Dad," said Roy. "What's going on? What voice?"

"The voice on the phone. He called. He wanted to talk to you. He said he had something for you. Something you needed to see."

"When did this happen?"

"Right before I left the house. I tried to call you. I know his voice."

"You know his voice? He's called you before?"

"Yes. But that's not how I know it. I've met him. I've spoken to him. I know I have."

"You've met him? Who was it?"

"I don't know. I can't remember. I tried. I tried so hard, but I got confused and the next thing I knew- "

Henry's eyes darted around the room. He pulled his hands from Roy's grip and wrapped them around himself. "Where am I?"

Henry's eyes searched his surroundings until he noticed Roy.

"Roy?" said Henry. "Where are we?"

"Were at the station, Dad."

"The station?" Henry studied the room. He realized where he was. "I hope I'm not late again. I have a newborn at home. Keeps me up all night. Sometimes I sleep right through the alarm."

***

Jane's foot tapped the floor of the lobby a hundred times a second. She watched the doors through the metal detectors waiting for Sheriff Hill to return. The echo of her footfalls the only noise in the station.

Most days, Jane considered herself a patient person. Today wasn't one of those days. Every second she spent waiting in reception made her skin itch more and more.

The killer was still out there. Out there walking free while she sat around waiting for him to dispose of Sarah Morris and grab some other helpless girl. If he hadn't already.

Jane pulled her file from her bag and flipped it open. She looked at the list of addresses. One left. Only fifteen minutes away. He could be there. The one they were looking for. She wanted to get in the car and go.

But what if he was there? What if she found herself in the middle of nowhere with no backup and a killer standing in front of her? No. She would wait.

Five minutes passed.

Then ten.

Then fifteen.

She told herself the Sheriff was coming. One more minute and he would walk through the doors. They would drive to the last address and check it off the list.

Twenty minutes.

Twenty-five.

He was getting away. They waited too long, and the killer was slipping through their fingers. Jane looked at the address one last time. The itch made its way into her brain. A tickle at the back of her mind overwhelmed her senses.

"Go", said the itch.

"Go and get him. If you wait, it will be too late."

She tried to ignore the itch. Tell herself she was being paranoid. The itch persisted. Whispering inside her head.

"You're letting him get away. You're letting those girls down."

Jane couldn't explain how, but she knew the itch was right. If she waited any longer, they would never catch him.

Jane stood and walked to the front door of the station. She looked out into the parking lot. Hesitated. Then walked outside and got into her squad car.

***

Roy and Hannah stood in the hallway outside the interview room. They looked in at Roy's father through the window.

"Is he alright?" asked Hannah.

"I think so. He's a little shaken up. Confused."

"Did he say what this was about?"

"He says he got a phone call. Someone was looking for me. Must have really freaked him out."

"A phone call? You don't think it was- "

"I do," said Roy. "The strange thing is, he said he knew the voice. He recognized it. Like he knew the person talking to him."

Hannah's face tightened with a grave expression. "Is he sure?"

"He seemed sure."

"But Roy." Hannah stared at him fixedly. "If he knew the caller, then he knows the person who killed those girls."

Roy and Hannah jumped as something thumped against the door of the interview room. They looked through the window to see Roy's father slapping the glass.

Roy pressed the buzzer and slid the door open.

"What's wrong, Dad?"

"Roy," said Henry. "Thank God, I found you. I remembered what I had to tell you. The one who called me. I remember his name."

When Roy got back to the lobby, Jane was gone.

"Did you see where Officer Barlowe went?" Roy asked the receptionist.

"She left."

"What? When?"

"Just a couple minutes ago. She tore out of the lot like a bat out of hell. Must have gotten a call."

Roy ran back through the labyrinth of the station. Back passed the pointing officers and whispering secretaries. He went into his office and closed the door. He sat at his desk and pulled up the address list on his computer. Roy prayed the feeling he had was wrong.

He scanned the list checking the names of the truck owners. He read through it until he found what he was looking for. His stomach tightened. He found a name he recognized. Benjamin Haverty.

He's dead Roy. You know he's dead.

He'd witnessed the scene himself. Blood-splattered walls. The stink of death. He was dead, all right. His wife blew him to pieces with a shotgun down in Edmonton.

Ben was dead, but someone had his truck.

An image flashed in his head. A young man in a dark suit, standing over his mother's coffin. Hat down, collar up against the cold. Hiding from the world.

Roy checked the list for the truck's last known address: 183 45th St. NE. Stevens, ND. The last address on his and Jane's list.

"That's where Jane is," said a little voice in Roy's head.

Roy grabbed the phone from his desk and dialed Jane's number.

You're already too late.

<u>The House</u>

Jane drove past the address at least a dozen times trying to find it. The property was surrounded by scraggly, unkempt trees. The house sat alone at the end of an unmarked road. When she pulled up, she couldn't help but think the house looked sad. The wood was worn and stained, drained of any color it once had. The windows glazed over with dust and filth. Patches of moss clung haphazardly to the rotted tiles of the roof. The house sat among the overgrown brush, grey and alone. Above the front door she could make out three numbers. A one and an eight tacked up with rusted nails, followed by the vague orange stain of a three that once hung beside them.

This was the place.

Jane stepped out of her squad car and observed the property. The red truck that should have been there was nowhere to be seen. The only vehicle was a tractor of indistinguishable color that sat on blocks in the driveway. The chassis corroded beyond repair. Tires sagged from the rims, dry and cracked.

Besides the main house she could make out several other structures scattered throughout the overgrown lawn. On the far south corner of the property there sat a small wooden structure that might have been a barn. The maybe-barn sagged to the ground beneath the strangling weight of unkempt vines and branches. Beside the barn were four large water storage tanks. Each one spotted with holes where rust had eaten through. The other structure was a small shed, sitting against the tree line at the end of a long dirt path. While not in good condition, the shed clearly saw more upkeep than the rest of the property.

Jane walked to the front door of the house and knocked. Flecks of dried paint stuck to her knuckles. She waited on the porch for several minutes with no response. The idea of someone living here seemed laughable. She stepped down from the porch and started to walk back to her squad car.

The shed drew her eye. Something inside called to her. Her feet moved of their own accord, as if a greater power willed her towards it.

The door of the shed was made of lacquered oak boards banded in rust spotted black iron. The door was sealed shut with a length of chain and a padlock. They looked to be the two newest things on the entire property.

Jane searched the perimeter of the shed. She looked for any vents or split boards she could use to look inside. As she searched, an itch began to tickle the back of her eyes. The feeling of being watched.

"Can I help you, ma'am?"

She almost jumped from her skin when the man spoke. She turned to see him standing in the doorway of the house, hands in his pockets. He looked young, barely over twenty. Tall and sinewy. A course black beard covered his jaw. He wore faded jeans and a loose button up flannel. His eyes appeared flat. Tarnished, like a counter worn down from generations of elbows.

"Hello, sir," said Jane. "I'm Officer Barlowe. I'm with the Ramsey County Sheriff's Office. I'm looking for Benjamin Haverty."

"Benjamin was my father. He's passed." His voice was strange. Vacant and emotionless. "What's this about, officer?"

A familiar taste filled Jane's mouth. Bitter. The same bitter taste she noticed when she sat at Mrs. Mitchells kitchen table. The same feeling that night at the station. The night Margaret's killer called to taunt them. "Nothing in particular, sir. I just have a few questions for you."

"Okay. Not sure what I could know that would help you out, but sure. Ask away."

"Mr. Haverty, do you own a red '91 Chevy Silverado?"

"I did?"

"You don't anymore?"

"Nope. Sold it. About two weeks ago."

"And who did you sell it too?"

"Some girl on Craigslist."

"Do you remember her name."

"Might have been Nancy or Natalie- something like that. Do you want to come in and sit down, officer?"

"No, I'm fine out here, thank you."

"Alright, suit yourself. Anyway, the girl she had, uh- dark hair, brown eyes. Pretty. Matter of fact, she kind of looked like you." He laughed but was soon silenced by the look on Jane's face. "Anyway. She came by with a friend of hers. She had greenish eyes. Red hair, kind of blonde I suppose. Strawberry blonde, I think they call it. Anyway, I think her name was Sarah. I thought they were trying to pull one over on me at first, but they had the money. Paid cash. I didn't ask too many questions."

Sarah. Maybe it was just a coincidence. Maybe it wasn't. The voice itched at her brain, tended towards the latter. She thought she heard the truth in the tone of his voice.

Sarah.

He said her name like a taunt. *I took her. I took her and you'll never find her. I made her hurt. Hurt like you can't even imagine.*

She shook the thought away. She was imagining things. She knew this was the last chance. The last address on her list. The last place she needed to check off.

She wanted so badly to find him. The monster who hurt those girls. But did she? Part of her hoped she would never find him. That she was wrong. Those girls' deaths had been accidents. Tragedies. Their similarities and connections nothing but a series of coincidences.

Deep down- or maybe not so deep at all- she knew that wasn't the case. If she was honest with herself, she was afraid to find the person who did this. If she found him, he existed.

Mr. Haverty leaned heavily against the door frame, scratched at his beard. The skin on the back of his right hand was tight and shiny, as if burned or scared.

His eyes studied her. Insects crawled across her skin as he scanned her from head to toe. His lips parted to reveal a toothy smirk. "Say, don't I know you from somewhere?"

"I don't think so, sir."

"Yeah, I do. Where is it I know you from?" Mr. Haverty leaned back in the door. He clapped his hands in recognition. "I've got it. I saw you in the paper. Terrible business. I was sick to my stomach when I heard about what happened to those girls. They ever catch the one who did that?"

It's him.

The itch in Jane's head gnawed at her. This man was the one they were looking for. The one who called the station. The one who killed Margaret. Except it wasn't just Margaret. It was all of them: Abby, Jackie, Bethany, Jennifer and who knew how many more. He killed them. All of them.

Sarah was probably dead by now as well. She could feel it in the deepest part of her being. The girls' faces were stuck in her head. Burned into her eyes. She sensed them here. Their presence watched over this place. Waiting for someone to set them free.

"Not yet, sir," said Jane. "It's only a matter of time."

"Well, you better find him soon. You'd think the Sheriff would have cared enough to have someone like that behind bars by now. Who knows what kind of twisted stuff someone like that could get up to."

Jane's pulse throbbed in her throat. She balanced herself on the balls of her feet, ready to run if the need arose. He wouldn't attack her, though. He was a coward. He only hurt little girls who couldn't defend themselves.

"I'm not surprised though," said Mr. Haverty. "I hear some mighty funny rumors about the Sheriff. They say he's a drinker. God knows how some of those people act. My father was a drinker too. In the end, it put him in the ground."

She should end it here. Pull out her gun and empty the clip into his chest. Watch as he coughed and wheezed until he suffered through his final breath. The way he watched those girls suffer.

She couldn't. She wasn't a killer, and she wouldn't end a man's life based on a feeling. What if she was wrong?

You're not.

It's him.

You know it's him.

He may have been the man from the police sketch. He was tall and thin. Messy hair and a clean-shaven face replaced by long dark hair and a gnarled beard that covered his most distinct features.

Jane's jaw clenched hard enough to bite through steel. She should have called in the address and waited for backup.

Stupid.

She waited for him to make a mistake: Move the wrong way. Step to close. She wanted a reason. An excuse to get justice for those girls.

Jane jumped when her phone rang. Her heart raced so fast she thought she would collapse. She pulled the phone off her belt and answered. "Hello. Officer Barlowe."

"Jane, it's Roy, I know who he is. His name is Thomas Haverty."

"Affirmative, sir." Her voice strained as her throat tightened. "I'm at my last address now. Headed back to the station ASAP."

"Jane." The Sheriff's voice was entwined with fear. "Is he there?"

"Affirmative, sir. Headed back now."

Jane pretended to hang up the phone holding it at her side with the receiver pointing towards the house. "Mr. Haverty, I'm sorry for bothering you. Someone will call you if we have any further questions."

Jane attempted to stay casual as she moved towards her squad car. Halfway to the car, the gun clicked behind her.

"I'm waiting for you, Sheriff," said Thomas. "You know where to find me."

"I'm sorry, Sheriff," said Jane. She pulled her gun as she spun and fired.

Too late.

The world went black.

<u>Sarah</u>

The room was dark. A cold impenetrable dark. A concrete cell with walls that closed in on her with every passing hour. She'd seen the details of the room only a few times. Baron, except for a small metal drain in the floor and a vent near the ceiling above a rusted-out slop sink. Both of which were far too small to fit through.

He visited a few times, back when he first brought her here. He would pry open the door and let the light spill in. Bring her food and water and ask her about herself. She lied. He asked a hundred questions, and she never told the truth. Except her name.

He never called her by her name. He called her Georgia.

She wasn't sure why, but she couldn't allow that.

He took her freedom. Took her innocence- whatever that meant. He would not take her name.

She would not die as someone else.

"My name is Sarah." That was the only truth she had ever spoken to him.

When she said it, his eyes ignited with fury. She could still feel the sting from where he slapped her. Right after he hit her, the fury melted away, replaced by an unrelenting sadness. He apologized. Swore up and down he would never hurt her. He cared about her more than she could ever know. That was the moment she knew she was never going to leave this place. He hadn't been back since.

She knew the man who took her. She didn't know his name or anything about him, but she'd seen him before. She'd described him to the police, watched as Jenny got into his truck as she waved goodbye to her for the last time.

Her mom had told her about things like this. She heard about it all the time at school and online. Men would see a girl on the street they'd never met and become obsessed. Follow them around until they have the courage to make their move. She never figured this would happen to her. Jenny she could understand, but not her. She wasn't someone to be obsessed with. She wasn't much of anyone at all.

She wasn't naïve about the reality of the situation. She prayed at first. Pleaded with him. "Let me go. Please let me go. I won't tell anyone I swear." It was a useless effort. She knew that now. She might have known all along. Known as soon as she recognized him. But after he slapped her, when he looked into her eyes, she knew for sure.

She didn't know how long she'd been in the room or how long it would be before he came back, but she knew eventually he would kill her, just like he'd done to Jenny.

She sat amidst the darkness. An odd taste coated her mouth, like when you eat something sweet after brushing your teeth. The only indication time was passing was the sliver of light that crept in through a crack in the bottom of the door. She had taken to pressing her face against the cold concrete floor. Pressing her lips into the gap, trying to slurp up any remnants of fresh air. The taste of it gagged her. Dust and damp.

Her hunger had long since left, her body had accepted it wouldn't be getting anything to eat. The thirst is what drove her mad.

Her fingernails were cracked and raw from clawing at the wood and cement. She punched and kicked and scratched at the crack beneath the door. Willing it to budge, but it never did. She pressed herself against the door, fighting with everything she had. If she could get free. If she could make it out into the light. Taste a drop of moisture on the tip of her tongue. Take in a breath of air that didn't taste like her own filth and decay. She found it strange, the things she craved when she knew she was going to die. Light. Water. Air. Things she had every day of her life. Things she had taken for granted because they were always there.

She slept most of the time. Dipping in and out of consciousness. The squealing of rats traveled through the vents. The closest she would ever get to a lullaby.

The sounds of footsteps woke her. A heavy tread on the ceiling above. A door opened somewhere overhead, and she could swear he was talking with someone.

She fought down the urge to call for help. To slam on the ceiling and pray she was heard. What if it wasn't a friend? What if whoever was at the door was even worse than him? Maybe there wasn't anyone else there. Maybe her mind was playing tricks on her. Convincing her the scurrying of rats in the walls was the muffled voice of her savior.

She felt her way through the dark, positioning herself beneath the vent. She climbed onto the sink, the metal groaning under her weight. She balanced on her tiptoes so she could hear what was happening above. Someone was there. A woman. She couldn't make out the words, but she was sure someone else was up there.

Something exploded overhead. She had never heard a gunshot, but that must have been what it was.

The vent erupted with shuffling chatter. The chittering of rats grew closer before the vent door exploded open, smashing into her temple.

She lost balance. Then she was falling. Her head collided with the cold hard floor. For a moment the world was silent, then she slipped away into darkness.

PART III

I live where the grass touches the sky,
Where the rain falls in storms of never-ending tears.
I live among shadows,
They pace in all directions: Aimless, lost, broken.
I live beneath a sky of moving glass,
The world blurs before it reaches my eyes.
I live where ghosts stalk the streets,
A constant reminder of the past I wish to hide from.
I live here,
Not as myself, but as a memory of who I wish to become.

<u>Edmonton</u>

Then

Tommy pulled up to the run-down house on Eighth Avenue. His father's truck wasn't in the driveway.

Tommy hadn't been home in a while. He didn't come back to Edmonton anymore. There was nothing here for him. Everything he needed was down in Clareborne. Along the shore. Standing in the waves waiting for him to come and take her away from this place. The endless expanses of nothing. The town where no one cared about him. Where his father tortured him while his mother looked on.

He could take the beatings. He'd been doing it all his life. What he couldn't take was having a mother who loved that piece of shit more than her own son. Tommy wanted her to leave. To pack up and run. Get out of that house and go somewhere where his father couldn't find her.

She never would.

He didn't blame her. She was scared. Scared of what that man could do to her. Tommy feared him for a long time too, but not anymore.

He opened the car door and stepped onto the curb. He lit a cigarette and took a long drag. He took his time smoking it, standing on the sidewalk, and looking at the house. Peeled yellow paint and a white door with a rusted knob. The patch of shingles on the roof that had been missing since before he could remember. The smell of cheap whiskey and light beer. The driveway where he learned to ride a bike. The bathroom he threw up in the first time he got drunk. The living room where his **father** gave him his first concussion. The medicine cabinet where he stole his mom's Zoloft. The bedroom where he OD'd for the first time. The house he hated. Where his father lived. Where his mother stayed even though her husband was the world's biggest pile of shit.

He dropped his cigarette and stomped it out with his heel. He walked to the trunk and popped the lock.

The shotgun was heavier than he thought it would be. It felt good in his hands. Purposeful. Powerful. He loaded in the shells and walked towards the house.

The front door swung open on crying hinges. He flipped on the kitchen light and watched the roaches scurry into their holes. The stench of stale beer clung to the air. The smell disgusted him. The floors were lined with garbage. Dust and ash clung to every surface. Nothing about the house had changed.

He moved through the house with confidence. Nothing here could hurt him. Not anymore.

"Mom," called Tommy. "Mom, it's me."

His mother didn't answer. He looked in the living room. He expected to find her passed out in the corner. She wasn't there. He checked her usual spots. The bathroom floor. The basement. The bedroom closet.

He left his parents' bedroom and walked into the kitchen. The bible was sitting on the table. He picked it up and blew off the thick layer of dust that clung to the cover. He ran his hands over the worn black leather, the impression of the golden cross pressed into the cover. Smears of dried blood stained the spine. A by-product from years of Tommy's repentance.

The book was heavy. Heavier than any book had a right to be. Words on paper that controlled how millions of people lived their lives, used to humiliate and belittle. A book for people who wanted to know God. But what was God? A protector? An all-powerful being that looked over the world of his children?

Tommy spent the last twenty four years as one of God's children and he never once felt protected. The only thing the word of God ever gave him was bloody knuckles and broken bones.

He dropped the book on the table with a loud *thump.*

A window in the living room looked outside where his mother sat in an old lawn chair on the back porch, looking out over the fields.

He went to the back door and slid it open. "Mom, what are you doing out here? It's freezing."

She ignored him. She didn't move or talk or acknowledge him in any way. She only stared.

"Mom?"

Nothing.

"Mom are you o-"

Tommy's jaw tightened at the sight of his mother's eyes. Blank. Unseeing. Glazed over as she faced towards the sunset. He went to his knees in front of her and held her face in his hands. "Mom?"

Tommy put his hands on his mother's shoulders and tried to shake her awake. "Mom?"

He shook her again. Harder this time.

He looked down to the pill bottle gripped in her cold stiff fingers. A half empty bottle of whiskey on the table beside her.

Tommy's mother was gone. He held her hands in his and looked at her. The woman who welcomed him home from school with a smile, wished him goodnight after his bedtime story. The woman so scared of the man who was supposed to protect her, she made herself numb so she wouldn't need to feel the pain.

Tommy placed his mother's hands gently on her lap. He smiled despite the ache in his chest. His mother was finally free. He sat beside her on the ground. Together they watched the sunset and waited for Tommy's father to come home.

<u>Oneirataxia</u>

It's been eighteen months since I left. Since then, I've seen incredible things. Lights dance across the sky, spilling color onto the world below. Endless waves crashing onto the shore at my feet. So much beauty everywhere I look. But it all feels wrong.

Distant.

Like seeing the world through fogged up glass.

I feel like I'm in pieces. Some of me is off basking in the light. The other piece- the main piece- is still at home. Stuck in that town. Trapped by the lake with no way to free itself.

More and more I find myself lost in my head. Lately, I spend more time dreaming than anything else. My mind is in a constant jumble. A tangle of interwoven thoughts and feelings.

Do you know the feeling when you're drifting off? Caught somewhere between being awake and being asleep. Everything seems so real, but no matter how vivid or vibrant, somewhere deep down you know it's your imagination.

I dream of the shore on a spring day. A fire burning against the cold.

Flowers blossom among the grass. Reaching out in cascades of color across the dull beauty of the never-ending landscape.

I dream of insects in the ground, their homes destroyed by unceasing rain.

A blanket of unmarked snow, thrown over everything; The world turned into a ghost.

I dream so long I can't tell I'm dreaming. No more than dust, carried down the street on the wind. Never resting long enough to call one place home.

I am the clouds in the sky and if I cry long enough, I can wash away the memories of a town that's lived past its time.

I am the sun. Hiding behind the perpetual grey of the winter sky. Never showing my face long enough to make a friend.

I dream of the earth. Of water, fire, and wind. Ribbons of invisible light that connect the world together.

I dream of the lake. The way it keeps rising and taking. The way it took my mother and father. The way people had to watch while everything they knew disappeared under the surface. What else would it have taken from me if I didn't leave?

They don't really seem like dreams when I'm having them. More like hallucinations. Truths that exist somewhere beyond my control.

Sometimes I dream of things so beautiful I want them to stay with me forever. I tell myself it's real. If I convince myself I'm dreaming, the beauty will disappear, and I may never see it again. I dream of Dad getting sober, letting go of all the anger trapped inside. I see him sitting with Grandpa by the fire reminiscing about happier times. Opening his heart and becoming the good man that's been caged inside for so long. I dream of my castle on the water. The way the moonlight glitters on the waves. Cool refreshing water on my toes. Autumn leaves filled with songbirds.

Other times, I dream things so terrible I can't breathe. I dream of blood and pain. I see my dad losing himself. Falling so far down the rabbit hole he can't find his way out.

I see Grandpa forgetting about me. I scream out to him. Tell him I'm here with him. Tell him I'm not really gone. If he looks out over the water, I'll be there with him. He can't hear me, and I fade away. Swallowed up by the lake just like everything else.

No matter how hard I try to wake up, I can't. Even if I did, those pictures would still play behind my eyes. Catch in my chest and drown me. Push me under the surface and hold me there until I'm too weak to try and gasp for air.

All my dreams are like that nowadays.

I used to dream of far-off places. Letting my soul into the wind and landing wherever the world saw fit to put me. Now I dream of home. A reluctant observer without eyes of my own, forced to see whatever the world wants to show me.

Honor Thy Father

It was almost seven o'clock when his father's truck rattled into the driveway. The last whispers of light faded as the sun dipped below the trees.

Tommy pushed himself to his feet. He turned to his mother and closed her eyes. "Goodbye, Mom."

Tommy turned from his mother and went back inside. He stood in the dark of the kitchen with the shotgun aimed at the door.

The keys jingled in the lock.

Tommy's father stepped inside and closed the door behind him. He didn't notice Tommy or the gun until he flipped the lights on. When he did, he stopped in his tracks.

"Thomas?" said his father. "What the hell are you doing? Put that thing down before you hurt someone."

"But that's why I'm here."

"What the hell are you talking about? Put that thing down before- "

"Before what?" Tommy stepped closer to his father; the barrel of the shotgun close enough for him to kiss.

"Listen, Thomas. You don't want to do this. What would your mother think?" His father's eyes searched his face. Looked him over for a sign of weakness. Something to show him Tommy didn't have the balls to kill him. To prove to himself his son was still the scared obedient little boy he could push around.

That boy was dead, and for the first time in his life, Tommy saw fear in his father's eyes.

"Mom's dead," said Tommy.

"What the hell do you mean? What did you do, boy?"

"No. Not me. *You.* She's outside sleeping. She won't be waking up. She's finally found a way to get away from you."

His father's face went slack. He looked disappointed. Not angry or sad. Disappointed. A dog upset his favorite toy was ruined.

"So, what are you gonna do? Kill your father?"

"Sit." Tommy tightened his grip on the gun.

His father moved to the table. He pulled out a chair and sat. The fear on his face switched to terror. He eyes were those of a man who knew they were about to die.

Tommy grabbed the Bible off the table and handed it to his father.

His father stared at it, bewildered. "What do you want me to do?"

"I want you to beg," said Tommy.

"What the fuck are you talking about, boy? This game has gone on long enough. You might as well shoot me cause I ain't gonna beg you for shit."

Tommy racked the shotgun.

His father fell to his knees on the floor. "Please, Thomas. Don't do this. Your mother wouldn't want you to be a killer."

"Don't bring her into this. You don't get to use her to save you. Not after what you did to her. Now, beg."

"Please Thomas. Please don't do this. I'm your father."

"Stop," said Tommy. "'Don't beg me. Beg Him." Tommy gestured to the Bible in his father's hands. "Beg God to forgive you for what you've done."

Tommy's father held the Bible to his chest. He mumbled a prayer beneath his breath.

"Louder," said Tommy. "Make sure He can hear you. He's your last chance. Beg Him and see if He'll come to save you."

Tommy's father began to pray louder. "God, I ask for your forgiveness-"

"Louder."

"God, I ask for your forgiveness and pray that you never forsake us- "

"Louder!" screamed Tommy.

"GOD, I ASK FOR YOUR FORGIVNESS AND PRAY YOU NEVER FORSAKE US. I HAVE FAITH THAT YOU HEAR MY PRAYER AND THAT YOU WILL GUIDE ME OUT OF HARDSHIP." Tommy's father suffocated the Bible with a white-knuckle grip.

Tommy looked at the ceiling. He waited in silence for a few moments. "Well, I guess he's not coming."

He aimed both barrels at his father's chest and pulled the trigger.

***

Tommy was headed south on Route 3 when sirens lit up the horizon. The neighbors must have called when they heard the gun shot.

He pulled over and waited for them to pass. They flew down the road until the blue and red lights turned to specks in the rearview mirror.

Soon, they'd find the mess. His father on the kitchen floor. Crawling towards the phone with a hole through his chest. The blood that stained the carpet and painted the walls. His mother on the back porch, a shotgun across her lap and a belly full of pills. They'd blame her for it. That was okay. She deserved the credit. Nobody would be surprised to find out she finally got sick of being afraid all the time.

Tommy's phone vibrated in his pocket. He pulled it out and flipped it open.

"Hello? Oh, hey Georgia. I was just about to call and wish you a happy birthday."

He looked out the window, thousands of ponds and lakes scattered across the landscape.

"He canceled again?" asked Tommy. "Of course, I can be there. Everything will be fine. I'll be there as soon as I can. Yes, I promise. Have I ever broken a promise? All right. I'll see you real soon."

The road ahead was clear. He left all his problems back home, in pieces on the kitchen floor. He was headed south. Headed to Georgia. Ready to take off and start a new life.

Birthday

The last time I saw my dad was a Sunday. He went to work in the morning and promised he'd be back in time for dinner. We were supposed to go to the movies after, my choice which one because it was my birthday. I hadn't decided yet. Probably would have been something funny. He needed a reason to smile again. We were going to laugh together. Drink too much soda and eat popcorn with greasy, butter-soaked fingers.

I wasn't surprised when he canceled. He had to stay at work. From the way he sounded on the phone it must have been real bad. He said he was sorry. I believed him, but I acted like I didn't. Maybe if he thought I was upset he wouldn't cancel next time. That wasn't fair to him. He didn't really have a choice.

That day had been cold. You could tell winter wasn't far off. I grabbed my jacket and just started walking. I thought about spending the night with Grandpa instead. We could walk to our spot and look out over the lake. Remember when things were simpler. Before everything started to go so wrong. I stopped by his house to see what he was up to. I walked up to the door but couldn't bring myself to knock.

I ended up going by myself. Something inside of me just wanted to be alone. I wish I would've knocked. Said hi and told him I loved him. You never know when it's the last time you're going to talk to somebody.

I knew eventually I'd end up at our spot, but I just wanted to see where my legs took me.

The leaves had started to change. Some stayed green. Others transformed into oranges, yellows, and reds. They were at a strange point in their life. Bright and bold. Showing the world their true colors before they shriveled up and floated to the earth. Dead.

Maybe that's why they did it. They knew the end was coming so they showed the world what they could do before they were gone for good.

Dying wouldn't be so bad if it could happen that way. Floating on the breeze. Quiet. Showing the world how beautiful you could be.

Eventually, I made my way to the lake. To my special spot where the world couldn't hurt me. I looked out over the water. To the sunken houses and faded memories of what the town used to be. To the abandoned world where my heart could run free, fill me with visions of fantasy and delight. Today, I didn't feel that wonder. I felt alone.

I called Tommy to tell him what happened, my dad canceled our plans for the night, and I didn't quite feel like myself. He told me everything would be okay. He'd meet me after he finished up a few things.

While I waited, I wrote a letter and watched the sunset over the water. I addressed the letter to my dad, but it wasn't really for him.

After my mother died, I started seeing a doctor in Grand Forks. She told me that sometimes when we have something to say to someone but can't bring ourselves to, it can help to write a letter to them. You never send the letter. You just write it to get everything off your chest.

There were so many things I wanted to say to my dad. How I understood the pain of losing mom. How I didn't blame him, wished he wouldn't blame himself. I understood what it was like to feel trapped. Trapped in a town intent to judge you when you needed its support. Trapped in a house you couldn't stand. Every tile. Every inch of scratchy blue carpet. Every locked door. Every moment of unbearable silence, a reminder of what you lost.

The night my mother died played out in my head over and over. A looping record, scratchy, yet somehow exceptionally detailed.

A nightmare that didn't go away even when I woke. Every drop of rain and gust of wind forced me to relive that moment.

I needed my dad to understand I wasn't angry with him. I didn't hate him like he thought I did, even if he hated me. I wanted him to make an effort. Try and get better even if he thought he would never be able to. Try and get back to himself. To the person he was before.

I don't know if my letter got any of that across. I guess it doesn't matter. He would never read it. That was the whole point.

<u>Leaving</u>

Gravel crunched as the truck pulled down the path. Tommy packed the bare minimum. A couple changes of clothes and a few hundred bucks his father kept tucked between the pages of his bible (His reading bible, not his beating bible.) They could get whatever else they needed on the way.

Georgia sat on a rock by the shore. Her golden hair danced in the autumn breeze. Her poetry notebook in her hands. She scribbled away, focused on everything and nothing, the way she did when she wrote, letting the words come to her, not forcing herself to find them.

He turned off the engine and climbed down to join her.

"Hey, Georgia."

"Hey, Tommy. Thanks for coming." She flipped the notebook closed as he walked towards her.

"Are you ready?" Tommy sat beside her on the rock and breathed in the clean, floral scent of her hair.

"Ready for what?"

"To go."

"Go where?"

"Away." Tommy placed his hand under her chin and turned her face towards his. "We're getting out of here. Like we said we would. I've got the truck. I saved up some money. We can finally get out of here. Be the people we're meant to be."

Something shone behind Georgia's eyes. A light of hope. A sense of freedom she longed for for so many years.

"I can't go, Tommy. Not right now, anyway."

"Why not? There's nothing here for us. There's nothing here for anyone."

"My Dad's here. He needs my help."

"He doesn't want help. Hasn't he made that clear. What else does he have to do before you figure out he doesn't care about you."

"My dad loves me."

"Your dad doesn't give a shit about you. He never has and he never will. Can't you see that. Don't you feel it in the way he looks at you. The way he can't look you in the eye. Every promise he breaks."

Georgia stood and stepped away from Tommy. "He's lost right now but he'll find his way. I know he will."

"He won't," said Tommy. His tone softer, as though he spoke to a child. "Not when he's here. Not when he's stuck in this town. That's why we have to leave. Get the fuck out of here before we end up like our parents. Miserable and alone, waiting for life to suck the last bit of happiness out of us. It's too late for them, but it's not too late for us. We can go. We can leave right now, and all of this will be behind us. We won't have to worry about any of it anymore."

Georgia turned from him. She didn't shake her head or tell him no. She didn't give the impression she was sad or angry. She was silent in a way only she could be silent. A silence that tore at Tommy's chest, spoke of a thousand unsaid feelings. Silence was easier than talking. Easier than disagreeing. Easier than having to tell someone the way you really feel.

Georgia placed her notebook on the rocks beside her and waded out into the lake.

"Georgia," said Tommy. "I'm sorry. I know it's hard to hear. My father doesn't give a shit about me either. That's what fathers do. They let us down." Tommy moved closer to Georgia.

She stepped out further into the water. Her silence tore at him.

"Georgia, look at me. Georgia, please. I can't stay here. I can't spend another night in another nothing town."

Georgia looked out over the water, her back still turned to him. "I can't go right now, Tommy. I'm sorry."

The feeling took him over before he knew it was coming. The rage. The hatred. The feeling of abandonment. Everything that had gone away when he watched his father gasping for air on the floor. Anger boiled inside of him. If he didn't release it, the pressure would make him explode.

He thought that rage was gone for good. Now that his father was out of the picture, what did he have to be angry about?

Tommy's mind went blank. He blacked out, his brain and hands disconnected. He didn't remember picking up the rock. He remembered the crunch as it collided with Georgia's skull. The way the blood swirled with the water. More blood than one body could possibly hold. He remembered the way she floated. Face down. Pushed around by the tide as it came to rest on the shore.

Blood rushed from his face. His skin turned to ice. The only thing faster than his pulse was the shaking of his hands. The edges of his vision blurred, and his head seemed oddly light as every thought and memory drained out his ears.

The cough brought him back to reality. The spluttering, choking cough of someone fighting to stay alive. Georgia puked up lungfuls of water as she crawled her way to the shore. She collapsed in the dirt as she tried to suck in all the air in the world with every breath.

Her eyes darted in a thousand directions as she tried to understand where she was, how she got there. Her eyes rested on Tommy and the realization set in.

"Georgia?" asked Tommy. "Are you okay?"

She nodded weakly; her eyes never looked away from him.

"I'm so sorry, Georgia. Are you okay?" He pleaded with her. She would understand. She had to understand. She knew him better than anyone. Understood him when no one else ever could. Loved him when no one else was capable. "I don't know what happened. It just came over me. You understand, right? You know I'd never do anything to hurt you."

"I understand, Tommy." Her voice was hoarse and strained. "I know you'd never hurt me."

Georgia's arms shook as she pushed herself off the ground. Tommy ran to help her to her feet. When he reached for her, she pulled away.

"Georgia, I'm so sorry."

"I know. I just- I just need a minute."

Tommy wanted to believe her. Trust that she could forgive him, and they could move on. Forget each other's faults and start a new life as far from Devil's Lake as possible. He wanted to, but he couldn't.

He knew it was over the second he looked at her. The brightness that used to shine behind her eyes was gone. The vibrant light of adventure and dreams that fueled her every step had burnt out. Replaced by revulsion and fear. Fear of him.

Nothing would be the same after this.

Tommy's mind went blank, his thoughts replaced by a dense fog. Before he knew what he was going to do, he was on top of Georgia. She thrashed in the water, clawing at Tommy's hands to get them away from her neck. He squeezed tighter, forcing her head under the surface. Her arms flailed. Fists and nails punched and tore at Tommy's face. Bubbles erupted from Georgia's mouth and nose.

Georgia gave up on trying to stop him. She was too weak to keep fighting. Her arms dropped into the water. The bubbles stopped. The last of the air in her lungs replaced by cold stinging water. Her eyes bulged, staring at Tommy from beneath the surface.

The fog in his head cleared. He looked down into the water to see Georgia. Floating lifeless under the glass surface of the lake. He jumped to his feet and pulled her onto shore. He searched desperately for a pulse. He ripped off Georgia's shirt and pressed his palms to her clammy goose-fleshed skin. He pressed down on her chest with everything he had, touched his lips to hers and forced air into her lungs.

It didn't matter how hard he tried to bring her back.

She was gone.

He was almost back to the truck when he noticed Georgia's notebook clutched in his hands. The pages heavy with water, a bystander of the horror that had occurred here.

He flipped through until he found the last entry. The thing she hid when he walked up. A letter. A message to her father about why she needed to leave. His heart sank. Maybe he could have convinced her to go. She clearly wanted to. But it was too late now. Now that she was-

Tommy looked back to the shore. The lake lapped at the sprawl of Georgia's golden hair. She slept amid the rocks, unblinking eyes beholding the vastness of the sky.

His heart was at war with itself, bursting with contradicting emotions. A euphoric sense of sorrow. A panicked bliss. Belligerent melancholy. Adrenaline flooded his veins, throbbed in his neck and numbed the tips of his fingers.

How could he do this? How could he watch her wither away and do nothing to stop it? Stand by while the greatest woman in the world suffered? Watch until it was too late to save her? Georgia was gone and no matter how long he waited she would never come back.

He grabbed the pages and tore the letter from the notebook.

Georgia's father would pay for this, and it would be as painful for him as it was for Tommy.

Into Darkness

Now

Jane woke in a haze. The air was heavy. The scent of rust and ash. Pain tore at her shoulder, too loud for her to focus on anything else. Her tongue was thick inside her mouth, coated in a harsh metallic film.

A strange rushing sound came from somewhere she couldn't see. Above her, patches of black mold sprouted across a white popcorn ceiling. A semi-transparent curtain hung by her feet. She looked side to side to find herself surrounded by walls of dirty white porcelain.

She closed her eyes and forced herself to breathe.

One. Two. Three.

When she opened her eyes, the haze at the edge of her vision had lessened. She was able to focus long enough to piece together where she was. She was in a bathtub. A bathtub that was quickly filling. She moved her hands to the pain in her shoulder. They came back red and sticky with blood. She searched until she found the source of the bleeding. Something entered her right shoulder just above her vest. Birdshot- based on the way the wounds were grouped.

Somewhere in the room, a man grunted. She reached for her gun. It was gone. She looked around to find the source of the noise. Thomas Haverty stood in front of the sink on the far side of the bathroom. The faucet on full blast. His shirt was pulled up onto his shoulder as he pressed a clump of blood-soaked rags against his ribcage. Her gun was tucked into the back of his pants. Her theory about her wound was confirmed by the shotgun, leaned against the wall beside the sink.

Thomas stared into the mirror. His face burned with unmatched anger. His bloodshot eyes flicked towards her.

She forced her eyes closed and laid as still as possible, like a little kid playing hide and seek. The more she focused on quieting her breathing the more she was sure everyone in the house could hear it.

Jane listened to Thomas. She attempted to piece together his actions based on sound alone. The soft squeak of hinges. Rummaging in the medicine cabinet. The shake of an almost empty pill bottle.

The knob squealed as Thomas shut off the sink. Her heart skipped a beat as footsteps made their way towards her. She could hear the pain he was in from the way he walked. Slow heavy footfalls favored one leg to the other.

Thomas limped out into the hallway, slammed the bathroom door behind himself.

Jane forced herself to stand despite the pain. Her clothes suctioned to her skin, heavy and cold. Her vest was soaked through, pressing down on her shoulder like a demon digging in its claws. She looked down into the tub. How much blood had she lost? The sight made her dizzy, but she pushed through. She wouldn't die here.

Jane moved towards the sink, her eyes on the door the entire time. She grabbed the shotgun and checked to see if it was loaded. Three shells. She held the shotgun up with one hand, reached for the doorknob with the other. The rusted hinges screamed. She cringed away and held her breathe as she waited for the shot that would kill her.

The shot didn't come. She peeked out into the hallway, checking both directions for any sign of Thomas. She moved left, hoping it took her outside instead of further into the house.

She turned the corner. The world exploded. She shuttered as the force of the bullet smashed into her vest. She caught a quick glimpse of Thomas and pulled the trigger on the shotgun. Across the room a TV exploded in a shower of glass and sparks. The gun bucked back into her shoulder. The pain blinded her. She forced herself not to black out.

Thomas ran down the hallway, firing blindly behind him as he went.

Jane moved towards the remains of the TV. Blood soaked into the carpet where Thomas had been. She followed the trail down the hall. The shotgun leveled in front of her.

Adrenaline coursed through her, thrummed to the rhythmic pain of her wounds. She half squeezed the trigger, ready to decimate anything that jumped out at her.

The blood led her to a staircase, slopping down into what she assumed was the basement. The light through the window illuminated the first two steps before being consumed by the shadows of whatever waited down below.

She looked down into the darkness. Nothing stirred. Stagnant. Waiting.

She flipped the light switch at the top of the steps. Nothing. Blackness stared at her from the depths of the basement.

She should wait for backup. But what if there was a way out down there? A back door or a bulkhead.

If Thomas got away, they may never find him. He would move to a different town with a different name. Find more girls, turn them into his victims. The cycle would start all over again.

No.

She wouldn't allow it.

She stared into the shadows of the staircase. The gaping black throat of some terrible beast.

End this now.

She turned on her flashlight, directed the beam down the black throat of the stairwell. She fought against every instinct she had and descended into the darkness.

The stairs screamed in protest as she made her way down. She knew he was down there. Gun aimed, waiting for her to poke her head around the corner before he took it off. That didn't stop her from taking the final step into the basement.

She leveled the shotgun, scanning every shadow with the utmost attention to detail. Any movement. Any color or shape that seemed even a bit out of place and she would have him. She would end it, here and now. No more questions. No more doubts. This was the man she had been searching for and she would give him what he deserved.

The sound was almost inaudible. A breath. The weak wounded sound of an animal on its last leg. She turned and without a second thought, pulled the trigger.

<u>Wounded Animal</u>

Tommy waited inside the laundry room, gun in hand. He pressed his ear to the door and listened to the creak of the basement stairs. The officer was coming down. She was caught in his trap. The bottom step gave one final cry as she stepped down onto the cold concrete floor.

Footsteps echoed as the officer moved closer to Tommy. Closer to her death.

He imagined her terror. Alone in the dark, knowing these could be her last moments. The dread that lurked under the surface. A fear he was familiar with. The way it gleamed in a person's eyes when they knew the end was coming. He saw it in Georgia's eyes when he held her under the water. The same fear she wore every day. The fear of being stuck. Trapped in the same place forever.

He could still feel his hands around her throat. Her pulse fading to an arhythmic stutter as her heart fought to beat one last time. He couldn't save her. No matter how many times he tried.

He found Georgia wherever he went. He found her in Abby. In the pain behind her smile. In the way she longed for a father who was never there for her. In the way she needed him to save her.

He found her in the others as well. Over and over and over again. But he could never save her.

Tommy gripped the gun and aimed. He heard the softest of noises. The barest scrape of a boot against cement.

He pulled the trigger.

An explosion ripped through the silence. The door between Tommy and the officer burst into splinters.

Tommy's vision blurred, growing darker at the edges with every heartbeat. For a moment he didn't understand where he was. His tongue tasted like seawater. Briny and acrid. A dull ache settled into every muscle.

He looked through the jagged hole where the laundry room door used to be. The officer was sprawled on the floor. Unmoving in a pool of vivid red. He got her. But why was he on the ground?

The adrenaline that pumped through him faded out. The dull ache turned to agonizing pain.

The pellets from the shotgun were lodged deep in Tommy's flesh. Burning balls of lead freckled his cheek and neck. His shoulder took the brunt of the shot. The wound was raw and bloody, closer to hamburger meat than human flesh.

The air was thick and hot. A sour scent bombarded his nose. The same thing he smelled on his father after he shot him. The smell of death.

Pain froze him in place when he tried to move. He couldn't die now. Not before he showed the Sheriff.

The Sheriff was on his way. Everything Tommy had done; he did for him. To remind him of the pain he caused. He would come and see the truth. All the lives lost because of him. All the ones he couldn't save. Their faces burned into his eyes. Their names looping inside his head.

Tommy pressed his hand to his neck as he looked for something to stop the bleeding. His shirt and pants were soaked in thick dark blood. It coated his hands, slick and warm between his fingers. He pulled himself across the floor towards a pile of rags in the far corner. Agony tore through his body with every movement. He flickered in and out of darkness, his head too light for his body. He pulled himself inch by inch towards the corner. His arm stretched as far as he could manage. A wave of torture burned through his body.

The old rags smelled of ammonia and grease. He pressed them to his neck and tied them in place. He tied another, tight around his torso, putting pressure on the hole in his ribcage.

He forced himself to his feet. It took everything he had not to black out.

He couldn't stop now. Not when he was so close.

Tommy limped across the basement towards the bulkhead. Every step left a bloody boot print on the floor. His eyesight started to wobble. His legs fought with his brain, begging him to collapse.

He wouldn't. He couldn't. He needed him to see. He needed to show the Sheriff what he took from the world. Tommy pulled himself up the steps. He undid the latch and used all his strength to lift the bulkhead door. The effort almost killed him. Blood gushed from his ribs soaking the rags.

He lifted himself out of the basement and collapsed in the backyard. The bulkhead slammed shut behind him. He clawed at the dirt, dragging himself across the yard towards the shed.

His vision fuzzed. The blur around the edges of his eyes pressed in towards the middle. He pulled himself through the dirt. He wanted to stop. He knew he wouldn't make it. But the shed was so close now. What if he died here? Died in the dirt bleeding like a stuck pig. Died before he showed the Sheriff what he did.

He could feel himself growing heavier. The blur in his eyes closed in. The world reduced to a smudge. No edges, no intricacies, just messy patches of color mixed into sludge before they reached his eyes. He was going to die. If he did, they'd search the shed. They'd find what was in there and show it to the sheriff. They'd say, *"Look at what you did. How can you live with yourself?"*

But what if they didn't search? What if finding him dead was enough? He had to be sure.

He had to show the Sheriff. Had to show him what he'd done. Make him live with the pain of knowing. The same pain Tommy felt every day.

<u>All is Lost</u>

Roy raced down the center of the highway. He pressed the gas pedal so hard he thought it might break through the floor. The world outside the window shot by in an indistinguishable blur of color. The sirens roared like the thunder of the coming storm.

The sky was dark. The sun cloaked in a shroud of black. Heavy clouds swelled with rain and lightning. Wind tore across the grass. Treetops swayed and bent. Branches tore free from their trunks and plummeted to the earth with no one around to hear them. The clouds swirled and boiled. A dark mass looming over everything. Watching. Waiting.

Roy remembered Ben Haverty's funeral. Normally, he wouldn't have gone. He didn't know those people. He'd only be intruding. He had only seen Mr. And Mrs. Haverty once. Mr. Haverty sprawled on the kitchen floor in a lake of blood. Mrs. Haverty on the back porch in a self-induced eternal sleep. He had seen them both in a moment so personal, he felt connected with them. He owed it to them to be present for their last moments above the ground.

There was a young man at the funeral. One of the very few people who had attended. The boy was young, seventeen or eighteen. Clean shaven with pale skin and messy black hair, tucked beneath a baseball cap.

After the pastor gave the eulogy- A harrowing speech about the role of God in Ben and Helen's lives- the boy walked up to the coffin. His mother's coffin, not his father's. The boy's hands were red and swollen when he placed them on his mother's casket and cried. Cried for the woman who killed his father.

Had she?

The case was simple. Open and shut. Or maybe it just seemed simple through the fog of grief and bottom-shelf vodka. Maybe it wasn't simple at all. Maybe Roy wanted it to be over so he could go back to being alone and miserable. Maybe he neglected to do his job and a scorned young man walked free to kill again.

***

Roy found the turn at the last second. A rusted mailbox hidden inside a tangle of overgrown ivy. 183 peeked from below the leaves on faded peeling stickers.

Roy slammed on the brakes and skidded into the turn, almost rolling the truck into a roadside ditch.

Jane's squad car sat empty at the end of the driveway. Roy pulled up beside it and jumped out of his truck. He drew his gun. The storm cast a grim shadow over the house. He moved towards the front door, quick and cautious.

A dark smear ran across the ground from the driveway into the house. Blood.

He's here.

Backup was coming. In ten minutes, the house would be surrounded by police. But Jane was inside, and she might not have ten minutes.

Roy kicked in the front door. His stomach flipped as he took in the carnage. Fresh holes littered the walls and furniture. Souvenirs of the bullets that had ripped across the room. The TV in the corner was blown to splinters. The dark smear continued across the carpet. Roy followed the trail of crimson drops across the living room and down the hallway.

The blood led to the bathroom. The contents of the tub overflowed into the hallway.

Too much blood in the house. It coated the floors, soaked the rags and gauze that filled the sink to the brim. Ran through the trenches between tiles. A dozen red rivers flowed to the lake of pale pink bathwater that spilled from the tub.

Roy went back to the living room. He walked through the wreckage, looking for some clue as to what happened. He used his foot to move the remnants of the TV. Beneath the broken fragments was a bloody boot print. The tread pressed into the carpet like rows of crooked red teeth. The same tread as his boots, only smaller.

The footprints ran down a long stretch of patchwork green linoleum into the kitchen. Roy followed them to the end of their path. A staircase plunged down into the dark of the basement.

"Jane," Roy called down the stairs. "Jane, are you down there?"

The silence tightened his chest. Roy pulled his flashlight and clicked it on. A perfect circle of light illuminated a cement floor far below. Halfway down the steps the light blinked out.

The smell hit him. Metallic and bitter. Blood. Death.

He reached the bottom of the stairs and paused, letting his eyes adjust to the dark. He stood like a statue listening for a sign of life.

Something moved in the darkness. A vague figure masked in shadow. Roy gripped his gun tighter. The figure shifted against the wall as Roy stepped towards it. He stepped on something slick and wet. More blood.

"Sheriff?" said the figure.

The voice was so weak, Roy thought he imagined it.

The figure spoke again, "Sheriff?"

"Jane?"

Jane slumped against the basement wall. She pressed one hand against the wound in her shoulder. The other kept pressure on her stomach.

Overhead sirens squealed. Tires crunched on the driveway. Thirty pairs of feet thudded across the floor upstairs.

Jane was barely able to speak, "I'm sorry, Sheriff."

"There's nothing to be sorry for."

Roy turned and screamed up the stairs, "Medic."

"I let him get away," said Jane.

"Don't worry about that. Just breathe, okay?" Roy pressed his hands against Jane's, trying to stop the bleeding.

"Medic," screamed Roy. "We're down here. Officer down."

Three officers stormed down the steps, guns drawn. The EMT's followed close behind. There flashlights cut through the darkness.

When the light hit Jane, Roy saw how much she was bleeding.

"Don't worry, Sheriff," said Jane. "It's not all mine."

Jane lifted her flashlight with a trembling hand, flicked it on. She pointed it across the basement at a bulkhead that must have led to the backyard. "Go get him, Sheriff."

Jane's eyes closed as Roy was pulled off her by the medics. They rolled her onto a stretcher and started pumping air into her lungs. They cut away her blood-soaked clothes and pressed fresh bandages onto her wounds. Jane's chest heaved as she fought to stay conscious.

Missing Pieces

Roy stepped out of the basement into the fresh air of the backyard. He tasted the storm that loomed overhead; sweet and pungent. Beneath the fresh, cool scent, Roy smelled something different. Something inorganic. Chlorine and burning wire.

A light trickle of rain bounced off the dirt. Small, clear drops beaded on the dry packed earth. The beads connected into puddles and soaked into the thirsty ground. Thunder rumbled through the sky, but the clouds still held back the best part of the storm.

Roy heard something in the rain. A sick, wet gurgle, like a clogged sink trying to slurp down water. He followed the sound around the front of the house to a small, tin roofed shed. Police cruisers lined the driveway. Red and blue strobe lights painted the house.

A chain hung from the shed's door handle. The end of the chain was adorned with a large steel lock with the key still stuck inside. Roy opened the door and found the source of the noise.

A young man sat against the back wall. Roy recognized him. He was a little older now, his face no longer clean shaven. His eyes were dark, dilated pupils drowned any color.

"Hello, Thomas," said Roy.

Thomas' messy black hair and unkempt beard were caked with thick, dark blood. He shook as he forced down air with wet, rattling breaths. This wasn't the same boy who cried over his mother's coffin. This was a monster, clinging to its last scraps of life.

Roy looked to his right. An ambulance sat in the driveway surrounded by EMT's. Roy could have called them. Maybe they could save this boy's life. He wasn't going to take that chance.

Roy stepped inside the shed and closed the door behind him. He looked into Thomas's eyes. Fear. The same fear in the eyes of all those girls. Fear, blame, and judgment.

A small cardboard box sat on Thomas' lap. He lifted it ever so slightly towards Roy. Thomas tried to speak. Blood bubbled from his lips and the box fell to the floor.

Roy took the box and placed it on a work bench in the corner. He pulled out a small, travel sized notebook with a red vinyl cover. A young woman with dark blond hair stared up at Roy from the first page of the notebook. She had blue eyes and a soft smile.

Another photo was pasted below the first. A road closed sign on a short stretch of gravel road that led down into a lake. Warped rotted branches sprouted from the lake, their trunks hidden beneath the surface.

Beneath the photos was a small block of text written in bold capital letters.

ABIGAIL MITCHELL - 16
STUMP LAKE

Every page was the same. Thomas had reduced every girl to a picture, a place, and a name. Roy flipped through the books. He recognized the faces: Abby, Jackie, Bethany, Margaret, Jennifer. He flipped to the last page, Sarah Morris stared up at him. Thomas didn't even bother writing where he left her.

Six girls. One of them yet to be found. Her body was probably still in the water. Cold and alone. Still frozen with unimaginable fear. He would search the shed and the house, look for some sign of where Sarah might be, but without evidence she may never be found.

For the rest, at least there would be closure. Roy wasn't sure what closure was worth. Maybe it would bring peace to their families. Peace was a small reward in the grand scheme of things, but at least knowing was something. They wouldn't have to worry about what their girls might be going through. They could start to grieve. One day they may be able to accept what happened and move on.

Roy looked down at Thomas's pathetic gasping form. "Where's Sarah?"

Thomas didn't move, he only looked at Roy and then looked at the box.

Roy placed the notebook on the table and reached back into the box. There was only one thing left inside. Another book, significantly larger than the first. Bound in faded blue leather. The book was in rough shape. The spine twisted, pages swollen as if dropped in water. He opened the book. The handwriting was thin and slanted. Roy began to read.

Nothing lives here.
Not even me.
I am beneath the waves,
Observing but never knowing.
Wishing but never doing.
Searching but never finding.

Nothing lives here.
I see the light overhead.
I see the trees scraping the sky,
Begging to be set free.
I see the people doing the same.

Nothing lives here.
Except for dreams.
Except for hope,
That we'll find what we're looking for.
In time even that will leave.
Nothing lives here.
Not even me.

The clouds reached their limit and the sky opened. Rain slammed into the shed's tin roof. Roy knew what he was holding, but his brain wouldn't let him admit it. He flipped through the pages of the notebook until he found the last passage.

The pages were missing except for several fragmented words in the bottom left corner. Someone had torn the rest of the words out.

He reached into his pocket and pulled out a worn envelope. He thought of the letter inside. The pieces would fit perfectly in the notebook. He knew the details of that tear. Every pit and valley. He wondered at those missing words for so long. Wondered if they contained some hint as to where Georgia had gone. Now he had them and wished to God he didn't.

Guilt washed over him. An overpowering feeling only a parent could understand. A parent who lost their child.

Roy turned to Thomas and crouched down to meet his eyes. Roy held the poetry book in front of Thomas' face, open to the pages where the letter had been torn out. "Where did you get this?"

His only response was a weak shaking breath.

"Where did you get this?" repeated Roy. "You shouldn't have this. Why do you have this?"

Thomas' eyelids fluttered as he prepared himself to die.

Sheriff Hill grabbed him by the front of his shirt and shook him awake. "No. You don't get to die yet. First, you tell me why you have this."

Thomas lifted a hand towards the book. Blood smeared the pages as he began to flip through. Tremors racked his body. He stopped on a hand-drawn picture of a house and pointed to the page. The house sat in the middle of a lake, run down and decrepit. Overrun with moss and mud and twisted through with ivy.

"What is this?" asked Roy. "Did you do something?" Roy shook Thomas with such force his head thudded against the wall of the shed. "Did you hurt Georgia?"

Thomas looked Roy in the eyes and shook his head. He pointed a trembling hand at Roy and forced out one last word. "You."

For a moment, Roy wasn't sure if he was breathing. His chest had grown heavy, like someone had replaced his heart with a lead weight. He made a mistake. He should have called the medics over. Maybe they could have kept Thomas alive long enough to get answers from him. But he was selfish. Too caught up in his hatred to think rationally. He swallowed the tears that burned at the back of his throat and forced himself to breathe. This wasn't over yet, and it wasn't about him anymore. "Where's Sarah Morris?" The words barely escaped his trembling lips.

Thomas's eyes fluttered closed.

Roy slapped him with all his strength. "Where's Sarah?"

A smile curled the corners of Thomas' lips. A final choking cough escaped his throat.

The monster was slain.

Roy placed Georgia's poetry book on the work bench. He walked outside into the rain. His body lurched forward as he emptied his insides onto the ground.

Thunder roared like an animal free of its cage. Roy fell to his knees with his palms to the sky. Lightning struck the house's chimney with a deafening crash. Bricks rained down from the sky, denting hoods, and shattering windshields. Roy sat on his knees in shocked silence as the world around him crumbled.

The rain pounded the world with unrelenting brutality, and through it all, he could swear he heard a scream.

<u>Trapped</u>

She woke to a storm. A rampant pounding somewhere in the darkness. She opened her eyes. Blood pooled beneath her throbbing head, fell off her cheeks in huge flecks were it had dried.
Overhead, the pounding continued, like a herd of elephants marching across the floor, raining ancient dust from the ceiling.

She pressed her hand to the wound on her head. Her hair was slick with dark viscous blood. Her thoughts were heavy, weak, her brain suspended in thick amber syrup. The kind her mom used to put on her pancakes.

Her heart wrenched at the thought of her mother, of her little sister. She would never see them again.

She thought of Jenny too. About how she would never get to apologize for the way she treated her.

She would die. Bleed out on the cold grey concrete while the crashing chaos above shrouded her existence.

She looked at the crack beneath the door. Her salvation from the pressing darkness. Small, jagged circles glowed on the floor. Dust floated in streams, swirled through the air like beams of solid light.

Light. Her mind must be playing tricks on her.

But no. There was light. Swinging beams of pale blue cut back and forth through the solid black wall she was so accustomed to. She pulled herself across the floor. Every bit of effort a hammer to her skull. The chaos outside continued as she forced herself to her knees.

The door was freckled with holes. A cluster of small, splintered dots from which the phantom light shone through. She put her eye to the hole and peered out at the chaos. There were people outside. She took in the look of them. Bright orange coats and pants striped with high visibility tape glowed in the beams of a dozen frantic flashlights. A single word sprawled across their backs. Paramedic.

They were here. Someone had come to save her. Someone to pull her out of this never-ending darkness. She pounded on the door with her fist, but she was too weak, the commotion outside too frantic. She tried to scream but her throat was cracked and raw. The only sound that escaped was a sad puff of tepid air.

The medics were circled around someone. A woman. Her clothes soaked with blood. They loaded her onto a stretcher, spoke words of assurance. "Stay with me, officer. Stay with me."

They lifted the stretcher with practiced precision and rushed up the stairs, leaving her alone in the dark once again.

She couldn't let it end like this. Not when help was so close. Not when she could get out of here. See her mother again. Her little sister. See their smiling faces and promise them she would try harder. She would be better. She promised to God she would be better. If He could save her. If He could get her out of this prison, let her breathe fresh air and feel light on her face, she would be better than she'd ever been.

Somewhere overhead a storm crawled through the clouds. Something shook the room. A deafening crash tore through the world. She fell to the floor and with everything she had, she screamed, loud enough for God himself to hear.

Absolution

Jane remembered the basement. Descending into inky darkness. The sound behind the door, pulling the trigger, the unbearable pain.

The darkness of the basement slipped away and became a different darkness- an eternal, more peaceful kind. She wasn't herself anymore. She wasn't anything. A profound presence floating somewhere in the deepest depths of oblivion.

The girls stared down at her from impossibly far away. A line of faces. Margaret, Abby, Jennifer, Jackie, Bethany. At the end of the line was Sarah. The guilt of the realization twisted her gut. She was too late.

Jane observed the faces, found the look of blame they always cast had dissipated, replaced with a pulsing sense of thankfulness. A thankfulness she couldn't accept.

She had a duty to those girls. She needed the world to remember their names. They would remember Thomas. His name would be splashed across every paper in the country. He would have books written about the inner workings of his troubled mind.

The girls' names would fade away. Compared to Thomas they would be footnotes, statistics. The monster always outshined his victims.

She would remember the girls. Their pain, their fear. But what use was remembrance if she wasn't alive to tell their stories.

A light appeared in the dark. A pinprick of warmth radiated through the blackness. The light grew and grew until it erupted with impossible beauty. A tunnel pulled her in like a tractor beam. A welcome abduction.

Someone stood at the end of the tunnel. A vague form silhouetted against the blinding light. The form spoke in words she couldn't understand. The warmth pulled her closer and closer. She reached out for the form, stretched her very being towards his grasp and just before their fingers brushed- she was pushed away. Back to earth. Back to the creeping, biting agony of the world.

The blackness lifted. She found herself in a strange place. A bed she didn't recognize, the smell of antiseptic and sickness. Half a hundred tubes and machines pumped and beeped.

She didn't know how long she'd been in the hospital. Time passed in a strange way. Slipping between dreams and reality, not quite awake, not quite asleep.

Now it was reality's turn. She fought to open her eyes despite their insistence to remain closed. Last night's dinner sat beside her bed, cold and untouched.

"Jane?" She turned her head towards the voice.

It took her eyes a moment to come into focus. "Hey, Sheriff." Jane's voice sounded foreign to her, weak and muffled.

The Sheriff sat beside her bed in a hard plastic chair. "How are you?"

"I'm not sure. What day is it?"

"Sunday."

Jane nodded absently as if what day it was had any effect on her. She stared at the ceiling with burning eyes. "How long have I been here?"

"Two weeks."

"So, this isn't a dream?"

The Sheriff hesitated for a moment. "Honestly, I find myself asking the same question. But no. I don't think so."

"Did we get him?"

"Yes."

"And is he?"

"Dead? Yes."

"And-" the name stuck in her throat. "Sarah?"

"She's alive. They found her in the basement, she was boarded up in an old storage closet. She's shaken up but she's gonna be okay. Thanks to you."

Gratitude bloomed in Jane's chest. There was so much she wanted to share but her mind couldn't make sense of her jumbled thoughts. She only managed to say a few words. "Good. That's good."

Jane's eyes wandered around the room, aimless. She held her breath until her lungs threatened to burst, but no matter how hard she tried to stop it, tears began to well in the corners of her eyes. "Was my mom here? I think I remember my mom being here."

"Yes. The doctors aren't sure what happened, but it seemed like her being here was upsetting you. They asked her to leave. She's down in the lobby, she's been there every day as far as I can tell."

Jane pressed her knuckles into her eyes, but the tears wouldn't stop. "She hates me."

"No. She doesn't."

"You don't know what she did to me. The things she said to me. The things I said to her."

The Sheriff hesitated, swallowing the lump in his throat. "I don't. But I do know what it's like to be a parent. And I know people- especially parents- do things they regret. I also know what it's like to hurt someone you care about. I know the feeling eats at you when you can't make the pain go away. I know how hard it is to want to apologize for things words will never heal. And I know sometimes we don't try to fix things until it's too late. Much, much too late."

Jane's throat began to close as tears streamed down her face.

"Why am I alive?" sobbed Jane. "Why am I still here?"

The outburst left the Sheriff speechless, concern and heartache etched in every line of his face.

"I thought it was over." Jane forced the words from her burning throat. "I died. I know I did. I felt myself slip away. I *let* myself slip away. I was at peace. No pain. No resentment. Every fuckup and regret, it was all just- gone. So why am I here?"

The Sheriff leaned back in his chair. He threw his head back with a sharp aching sigh. "I don't know. I don't know why any of us are here. If there's a purpose to any of it. Are we just here to collect tragedies? Absorb all the fucked up shit the world throws at as us until we give up and shut down? Maybe. But maybe the pain is good. Feeling pain is the only way to know you care about something. So, maybe in a way the pain is there to remind us of everything that went right, instead of the few things that went wrong."

Jane laid back in bed. She managed to breathe through the tears, her face hot and swollen. "I saw my father. There was this light. A beautiful light. I couldn't see his face, but I knew it was him. I could feel him there, you know? He was waiting there for me. Waiting for me to join him."

"He still is. And he'll keep waiting for as long as he needs to. I told you the people we love never really leave us."

The Sheriff stood and started towards the hall. "You need some rest. I'll see you soon."

"Sheriff?"

"Yes."

"Could you ask my mom to come in?"

The Policeman

She woke in slow motion. A vague sense of presence followed by a flutter of heavy eyelids. Every blink revealed a sliver of blinding white. She squinted against the light before forcing her eyes open and taking in her surroundings.

Bleach white tiles and blinking lights filled her peripherals. Her vision blurred at the edges smudging the details.

She took in the light. The sweet, serene light that enveloped her like a blanket. She breathed deep. Disinfectant mixed with the faint plastic smell of the hospital's heater.

This wasn't the first time she woke. She had been in and out since they pulled her from the basement. The past few days came back to her in images. Flash frames of light and noise screamed from her subconscious. Gunshots, paramedics, the full body fuzziness as she fought to stay conscious. Trying to scream for the police, for anyone. Using all her strength to make the slightest noise, to give the outside world any indication of where she was. The frantic scramble of footsteps. The voice that called to the others asking if they heard the scream.

She woke for the first time to the sound of snapping boards. The deep blue glow of the flashlight burned her eyes. She was afraid. Afraid he'd finally come back. Help was gone. She had missed her chance and now he was back again to finish what he'd started.

His hand reached for her.

She tried to pull away, but she was empty. She couldn't run or scream or fight. The only thing left to do was give in.

His skin was hard and rough against hers, but she didn't sense any malice. She looked at him through the haze and the blinding light. Her fear disappeared when she looked into the officer's eyes. The emotion in them. Their pulsing warmth shouted above all the chaos.

I'm here to help you. You're going to be okay.

She had seen the officer after. When she managed to emerge from bouts of drug induced unconsciousness. He was always there. Speaking with the doctors or just standing by the door checking in to see if she was okay.

He was there again now. His badge pinned to his chest.

Some of the fogginess cleared and she managed to speak. "Hello."

"Hello, Sarah. My name is Roy Hill."

"I recognize you," said Sarah. "I remember your eyes."

Her mother was asleep in a chair in the corner of the room. Her little sister curled up beside her as she hugged her teddy bear with all her might.

She looked at the ceiling, a checkerboard of sterile white squares and too bright lights. She closed her eyes, thought of Jenny. How she'd lied to her.

She'd convinced herself she wanted nothing to do with Jennifer. That she'd outgrown their friendship. That being liked by Ashley and the other girls was more important than their friendship.

She'd pushed her friend away when what she really wanted was to pull herself closer. Pushed her away into the arms of that monster.

Hot tears streamed down her cheeks. She wiped them away, but new ones took their place. "Do you think she'll forgive me?"

The policeman glanced towards her mother and then back to her. "You haven't done anything wrong."

"Yes, I have. I told her I hated her. That I never wanted to see her again." She dug her nails into her palms, slammed her fists into the too stiff mattress. 'Now's she gone. She's gone and I'll never be able to tell her how much she meant to me."

The policeman walked towards her, sat beside her bed. He was silent for a moment as he looked out the window. "We all say things we regret. Things we wish we never said. Things we wish we could take back. We can never unsay them. Never take away the hurt we caused. You may have said some things to her you didn't mean, but the good thing is it's never too late to apologize, as long as you really mean it."

"But she's gone. She's gone and I'll never see her again."

"Yes, you will. I know it doesn't feel that way, but you will. She'll always be with you. The people we love never leave us."

He still stared out the window, eyes unfocused as if looking at something immeasurably far away. Past the hospital doors. Past the cars in the parking lot. Past the streetlights and the bus stops and the trees. Past the fields and mountains and sky to somewhere he knew he'd never reach. "You know. You remind me of someone. Someone very special that I used to know. I owe her an apology. I have for a very long time."

"But it's not too late, right? As long as you really mean it?"

He turned from the window and looked at her. His warm eyes flooded with tears. He nodded as he wiped them away. "That's right. As long as you really mean it."

Brighter Days

My funeral was on a Sunday. The clouds managed to shed their usual grey, drifting free against the clear blue sky. The trees shook off the last of the winter frost, bloomed anew in a thousand shades of green. The wind blew, warm and strong as it weaved through the endless fields on its way to nowhere in particular.

Most of the town showed up to the funeral. Faces I'd never seen kneeled in front of a closed casket. They said their prayers and asked God why such a terrible thing could happen. They still didn't understand God had nothing to do with it.

I was dead and still didn't know if God existed or not. If he does exist, then I don't think he has any say in how we live our lives. I still wonder why He put us here. Why he puts us through so much hardship. I don't think anyone will ever have the answer to those questions.

Dad wore a suit to the funeral. I hadn't seen him in a suit since mom's funeral all those years ago. Hannah's with him. She holds his hand tight, so he knows he's not alone. People point and whisper, but neither of them care. I'm happy she's there for him. He needs someone to watch over him. Help him through the rough patches.

She stands beside him as people step up one by one to tell him how sorry they are for his loss. As though they could imagine the pain he endured. You can't know the pain of lose until you've suffered it, and you can't suffer it until you've felt the greatest pain you'll ever know. Dad doesn't hold back the tears. Each one runs down his cheeks and leaves a small black blotch on his suit.

Grandpa gave my eulogy. He stepped up to the podium as tears streamed down his face. He had my poetry book. He squeezed it with all his might, as though I wouldn't truly be gone if he didn't loosen his grip.

"Georgia was a beautiful soul," said Grandpa. "She wasn't only my granddaughter; she was my best friend. I don't know what I did in this life to deserve her, but I know I'm better for having known her." His body shuttered as he let out a heart-wrenching sob. Dad stood to help him, but Grandpa put up his hand to let him know he was all right. He wiped his eyes and took a deep shaking breath. "When Roy told me about Georgia, suffice to say I didn't take it well. I didn't believe him. I didn't want to believe him. I wanted to forget. That's something I'm pretty good at." Grandpa laughed to himself. "Roy reminded me of something that many of us often forget when faced with hard times. We often think of loss as the end. A tunnel with no light. But that's not the case. Georgia is not gone. She lives in the hearts of everyone who knew her. Everyone she touched. Everyone whose day she brightened with a smile. She lives on in our memories of her. Every time she made us laugh, and every time she made us smile."

Grandpa opened my poetry book and began to read.

"Yesterday, I dreamed of tomorrow,
The wind beneath me,
Carrying me to a place I've never seen.
Yesterday, I dreamed of a new beginning,
The road below me and the sky overhead,
My eyes set on the sunrise,
Headed into that infinite horizon.
Yesterday, I dreamed of something new,
Far from the whispers at my back,
Free from the chains that bind me to myself.
Today, I dreamed of yesterday.
Of the sunlight painting the water with brush strokes of infinite color.

IAN MATHIEU   259

It's a strange feeling when someone else speaks the words you wrote. An echo of yourself left for the world long after your last breath.

I learned a lot since I left. Figured out some things I'd only ever guessed at. What it means to be a family. What it means to love no matter what obstacles try to stop us. The importance of forgiveness- that's one I wished I learned before it was too late.

I used to have so many regrets. Now, the only regret I have is my dad will never really know what happened to me.

They found my body, out in my castle on the water. A place my mind used to take me to keep me safe. I was asleep in a bedroom upstairs. My flesh long gone from my bones. My soul hovering above, never able to escape the town my body longed to leave.

My dad knew it was me the moment he saw me. A small gold ring still around my neck. A remnant of the love that had been taken from him time and time again. He didn't scream or cry, didn't beg God to bring me back or tell him it wasn't really me. Not because he didn't hurt, but because the pain was beyond tears. Beyond denial and anger.

I suppose in a way he'd already grieved for me. He can stop worrying about me now. He still will, that kind of loss leaves scars that will never heal. My only hope is one day he'll forgive himself, stop believing everything that goes wrong is his fault. I hope he can see the poetry in the falling of autumn leaves, the song of the water over rocks and the wind through the grass. I hope he can see that despite it all, the world is a beautiful place.

The town hasn't changed much, but the people have- or maybe I'm just being optimistic. The world seems warmer. Brighter. Like the sun had risen in the morning and shone new life into a world that spent so long shrouded in darkness.

The water's still rising, but there's beauty in that. Maybe one day the lake will swallow up everything and we can all start over. Live together under the waves. No tears, no screams. Just peace, quiet, and lights that dance on every surface. The world Abby dreamed of.

Dad started smiling more. He went back to the doctor in Grand Forks. He's working on forgiving himself. He moved back to Clareborne with Hannah. They seem to really care about each other.

They visit grandpa on Saturdays for dinner. Grandpa finally convinced Dad to redo the barn. They spent three months on it in the summer. They scraped away old paint and replaced rusted nails and rotted boards. They talk and laugh and enjoy each other's company.

Jane drove out west until she reached Montana. She found where the Missouri river started and followed it all the way to Mississippi. She stopped at Fort Berthold on the way. Her father's grave was on a hillside by the old house, overlooking the river. Purple and yellow wildflowers bloomed around him.

She sat among the flowers and listened as the river rushed by. She sensed him there, sitting beside her looking out over the mountains. She spoke with him for a while; asked him questions she knew she'd never have an answer to. She told him she forgave him. Part of her sensed he already knew.

She reached Mississippi in mid-summer. She thought about staying but found herself missing Devil's Lake. She finally had a place she could call home. A place where people cared about her, despite her past and her flaws.

For the most part, everyone seems to be doing a bit better. They still have bad days. They wake up and remember all the reasons they should be sad. All the reasons they should give up. But they don't give up. They focus on the good times. Winter nights reading bedtime stories. Spring days on the porch watching their mother paint. Moments spent with the ones who are still with them, knowing somewhere, the ones who are gone are waiting to see them again.

They allow themselves peace. For a few minutes or a few hours, every trauma, every horror, every painful memory, fades into the background. They choose to live. To remember the good things. To continue through the fog despite what life has thrown at them. To remain afloat in a world so focused on pulling them beneath the surface.

Turn the page for a sneak peek at
Ian Mathieu's next novel:
Secrets Buried Deep

Sixteen years ago, Tara's best friend went missing. Now she is plagued with dreams that seem to be drawing her back to her hometown and the truth that has been buried for far too long.

"The woods are lovely, dark and deep,

But I have promises to keep,

And miles to go before I sleep,

And miles to go before I sleep."

-ROBERT FROST,
Stopping by Woods on a Snowy Evening

Aldridge, Vermont – Tuesday, July 10th, 2008, 1:35am

Her body shuttered with every stride, feet swollen and bleeding, cut to pieces by rocks and broken beer bottles that littered the path. Her fingernails were cracked and bloody from scraping her way free, burning wounds caked with gritty black dirt. She ran full speed towards town never stopping to rest or look over her shoulder.

Her heart pounded in her throat. Blood pulsed behind her eyes. The only light came from a sliver of moon that silhouetted the trees. Each branch was long and twisted; Mangled hands that reached out to grab her. Choke her. Take her and drag her back to her prison. But they were just trees. They weren't any danger to her. The danger was behind her.

She felt his eyes on the back of her neck, tasted his thick scent. Dusty and sick. The taste of mud and maggots and corpses. Those terrible eyes. Wicked and seething. The smell of rotting teeth and unclean flesh.

She'd heard about them her entire life. The Gods who roamed the forest. Stalked the mountains. Singing sweet songs of wind and rain to lure in their prey. She'd never believed the tales. Nothing more than scary stories to tell around the campfire. Folklore. Made up so a nowhere town hidden in the forest seemed a little less boring.

She knew better now.

A pin prick of light pierced the dark. She ran into the blackness between the trees. A gaping maw ready to swallow her whole. A stitch ripped at her side. Her lungs were about to burst. She was ready to quit and accept her fate.

She wasn't sure if any of this was real. The moon, the trees, the smell, the light. She wasn't sure how long she'd been gone. The last thing she remembered was the lights. Two beams of blinding white light, like the eyes of some folkloric creature shrouded in mist.

How long had it been since then? Hours? Days? Weeks?

She wanted to collapse but she was close now. The light. The street that would take her home. Would she wake before she got there? Wake up back in her cell? Four cracked concrete walls with no windows and no lights. Trapped in the dark, caught somewhere between reality and a living nightmare.

She saw awful things in the dark. Visions of torture and death. Deformed children with bloated grotesque faces. Eyes like a starless midnight. She felt the pain as they were torn apart. So young, so innocent, so...*beautiful.*

The children were sprawled across the ground, blood soaked, unbreathing. She felt the sting as the knife cut into them. The tearing of flesh and the splash of blood. The hot sickly aroma.

Darkness surrounded her. Surrounded everything. Not a simple absence of light, but something deeper. The rotted obsidian viscera beneath the surface of the earth.

She burst from the tree line at full speed, scrambled up the embankment onto the Englund Street bridge. She ran down the center of the road beneath the faint yellow glow of the streetlights. Each light pierced the blackness, a pool of safety in the dark. She ran from light to light, somehow finding extra speed to span the darkness between them.

Fear tightened her throat. She wanted to scream. Cry for help at the top of her lungs. *I'm here. I'm here. Please help me.*

No sound came.

Her heart seized mid-beat, forcing her to stop.

He stood in the center of the road, illuminated by the pale blue light of the waning moon. The deer. A massive buck. The largest she'd ever seen. Another of the forest Gods she'd come to know while trapped in her prison.

Colossal antlers stretched towards the sky, just as beautiful as they were terrifying. His muzzle was coated in blood, the same way it always was, steaming in the cool night air. He stared at her with small, wet eyes, soulless and black. Eyes with no bottom. No boundaries. Eyes deep enough and dark enough to swallow up the world.

Her vision blurred, black pressed in from the edges of her consciousness. Before she faded, she saw the light. Brilliant and bright as it sliced through the darkness of the storm.

The buck approached, silhouetted against the light, ready to bring her back. Back to the old growth where she would lie forever among the moss. Entangled in ancient roots until she was one with the earth. Back home, to the place she was meant to be.

PART I:
DREAMS

"Sweet dreams 'til sunbeams find you.

Sweet dreams that leave all worries behind you.

But in your dreams, whatever they be

Dream a little dream of me."

-ELLA FITZGERALD,
Dream A Little Dream of Me

ONE

Tara – Now

Stale air, stagnant, dry despite the vents pumping in the high corners of the room. Sick coats my tongue, the bitter taste that fills your mouth after a sneeze. The office is dull, muted dark tones and muddy grays. No life. No vibrance.

The man seated across from me is bloated and saggy, puffed red nose of an alcoholic. Stuffed into a grey three-piece suit, two sizes too small for his ample mass. His jowls droop like the dog from those old cartoons- the short white one who was depressed all the time. Fitting.

His name is Doctor Randon. A therapist. Not a psychologist, meaning he knew all the bullshit terms but was unable to write prescriptions. If I'd known that I never would have started seeing him.

I never liked shrinks. Randon was the latest in a long line of therapists and psychoanalysts that stretched back as far as I could remember. I suffer from a variety of ailments. A list of psychological problems that make War and Peace seem like a grocery list. I've been diagnosed with a lot of things over the past sixteen years: Paranoia, depression, substance use disorder, schizoaffective disorder, etcetera, etcetera. All the things that come with your best friend going missing when your seventeen.

My psychoanalytic profile was being written long before I had a real need for a therapist. When I was a teenager, my best friend's stepdad (the same best friend who went missing) was a shrink, a child psychologist. He'd always analyze our behavior. Tell us why we acted the way we did. When we argued with our parents it wasn't because we were teenage girls, it was because, *"our need for independence and control caused us to lash out at authority figures so we could establish our own identity."*

You'd think someone who understood the depths and intricacies of the developing brain would have realized something was off with his stepdaughter. Would have known her behavior wasn't *normal.* Whatever that meant.

I'm sure I do have a few things wrong with me. Olivia's disappearance did a thorough job of fucking me up.

Dr. Randon's lips move, quivering the sacks of skin that hang from his face. I can't make out the words, find myself focusing on the clock. The steady tick overpowers my senses, muffles the rest of the world. My range of hearing reduced to the whining ring of tinnitus.

My ears pop. The world comes back into focus. I feel my eyes realign. The office seems peculiar, familiar in an uncanny way, like waking from a dream and finding yourself in the place you were dreaming about.

"Tara, last we spoke, you mentioned you'd been thinking of an old friend. One from your childhood." His voice is naturally condescending, the pretentious self-importance of higher education.

"Yes," I say.

"Have you still been thinking of her?"

Stupid fucking question. Of course I'd still been thinking of her. I'd thought about Olivia every day for the last sixteen years. "Yes."

"You mentioned she passed away."

"I did."

"Was this recent?"

"No. Sixteen years ago."

"Does her passing still effect you?"

Another stupid question. I couldn't figure out why I was shoveling money to this guy. *Because you need help.* The thought invaded my brain, intrusive, unwanted. "Yes."

Doctor Randon nods. His Jeffrey Dahmer glasses slide down the bridge of his nose. He pushes them back into place with his middle finger. "How do you feel when you think of her?"

I root through my brain for an answer. Thousands of thoughts, memories, and feelings coalesce into an ever-shifting picture of my childhood best friend. "I feel profound sadness."

"Why do you think that is?"

"Shouldn't I be sad my friend is dead?"

"I can't tell you how you should or shouldn't feel. I only wonder why you use that word, *profound*."

"Seems the right word. Sounds convincing."

"Who are you trying to convince?"

"Myself, I suppose."

He nods again, notes something down with his stub of a pencil. Even the simple up and down of his chins is patronizing.

"I've been dreaming about her." I blurt it out before I can stop myself, like maybe if I tell him enough secrets he'll like me. Some ingrained need to please everyone I meet.

"What happens in these dreams?" He readies his pencil, prepared to jot down his diagnosis, *crazy bitch*.

I dream of Olivia's smile, candy red lips twisted into a deranged scream. All alone in the woods, the night sky full of stars. The darkness between the trees where ancient eyes watched, bore into your brain, unfurled your secrets like spilling intestines. "My hometown. Where we grew up. The time we used to spend together."

"You were close?"

"Best friends."

"Have you ever visited?"

"She's dead."

"I mean your hometown. The place where you share all those memories with her."

"Those memories aren't all good. To be honest I have a hard time remembering things from back then, especially around the time she died."

He nods, as if any of the shit I'm spewing makes any sense. "These dreams. Are they about things that really happened? Things you experienced?"

"Sometimes." A headache starts to form at the base of my skull. "Sometimes we'll be at school or in my room. The park, the drive-in, places like that. Other times were in the woods. Not woods I recognize. There more like- scary woods. Like woods from a horror movie, dark and quiet. It's always so quiet, like everyone else in the world is gone and it's just me and her." My eyes go glossy, the stinging wetness that precedes tears. "But she never talks. I hear her voice, but I never actually see her speak, like, her lips don't move, but I know it's her voice, and it's playing in my head. I haven't heard her speak in sixteen years, but I know it's her and- and the things she's saying don't make any sense and I can tell she's in pain, and I want to run to her and tell her it's going to be okay, but I can never reach her."

A soft pressure fills my chest, and I realize I'm afraid. Not a normal kind of afraid. The kind of afraid you feel when you're in your bed at night, reading by the lamp light. You hear a bump in the night. You turn off the lamp, bunch up under the covers- Everyone knows the monsters can't hurt you if you're under the covers- You hope it's in your head and you know it probably is but that doesn't stop the feeling. The burning in your throat. Your stomach sinking into a pit. But the fear I feel when Olivia visits me in my dreams doesn't feel like an imaginary intruder in the night. It feels like when you come out from under the safety of your covers, convinced everything is fine. You look out into the shadows of the hall, and someone is standing there, and it wasn't in your head after all. The screaming inside you you're too terrified to let out. The numbness in the tips of your fingers. The smell of bile in your throat wafting into your nose.

I realize I'm crying. I wipe my eyes, avoid Dr. Randon's gaze.

"I can see this makes you very emotional. There's nothing wrong with that." He places his pencil on his desk and leans towards me. "Do you want to understand these dreams?"

"You really think there's something to understand? You don't think I'm just crazy?"

Dr. Randon shakes his head disapprovingly. "Crazy is not a word I like to use. But no. I don't think you're crazy. Dreams can be powerful things. Perhaps these dreams about your friend are trying to tell you something."

"Like my dead best friend is speaking to me from the grave?"

"Probably not. I was speaking more along the lines of self-reflection. Maybe there's something you're trying to tell yourself. Clearly this friend of yours-" He pauses in the way people pause when they're waiting for information.

"Olivia."

"Clearly Olivia meant a great deal to you. She's been gone sixteen years, and you still refer to her as your best friend."

"Do you think that's strange?"

He steeples his fingers, leans back in his chair, contemplative. "Do *you* think it's strange?"

"I guess I never real thought about it like that?"

"Perhaps you should think about why Olivia still occupies so much of your mind."

The clock strikes noon. Our time runs out.

I leave Dr. Randon's office and head to the stairs. I don't take the elevator. I have a thing about enclosed spaces. It's not so much the confinement as it is knowing that if something was to go wrong there's nowhere for me to go. No escape.

I have a lot of time to think as I descend eight floors to reach the parking garage. I think about Dr. Randon's suggestion that a visit back home may help me come to terms with Olivia's death. Visiting the places we used to go together. Places with positive memories. Remember the good stuff to block out the bad. Maybe being in the place where all my trauma was born would knock something loose, send me spiraling down a rabbit hole of self-discovery or some overpriced shrink bullshit like that.

I tell him I'll think about it, but I won't. This kind of thing isn't new to me. I've had dreams like this before. Recurring nightmares. I don't tell him that. I also don't tell him the last time I had nightmares like this, the girl I had them about ended up dead. That's not the kind of thing you tell people if you don't want them to think you're an absolute nutjob. That wouldn't matter anyway. Not his time. Olivia was already dead.

"There is something beautiful about the dark. Twisted through with invisible lights. Colors that only show when the truth has been revealed."

TWO

Tara - Wednesday, June 11th, 2008, 11:59pm

Tara woke in the dark. Not the cool, damp dark of early morning. The hot, heavy, humid dark of a summer night.

A film of sweat clung to her skin. Her mouth felt like it was stuffed with cotton. She grabbed the glass of water from my nightstand, gulped it down.

She jumped at a sharp squeal from the corner of her room. An ancient fan oscillated. A burst of air struck her. The air was warm, but it sent a chill down her spine as it brushed over goosefleshed skin.

She'd had the dream again. The same dream she'd been having for weeks. A nightmare really. Vivid and horrible. The details etched into her mind even when she was awake.

In the dream, she stands in the middle of the road, trees on both sides. The sun begins to dip behind the mountains, bathing the forest in golden light.

She recognizes the place. She recognizes it because it's the same place she ends up every time she falls asleep.

Her feet are bare. Caked in dirt and blood. Ankles swollen, ringed in a gash of deepest red. Her toes are branched out at odd angles, twisted and bent, more like antlers than feet.

She sensed there was something in front of her. Something down the road that every instinct she had told her to look towards. She didn't want to look. Even though she couldn't stand the sight of how she'd been maimed.

If she looked up, she knew what she'd see, and the sight was far worse than the carnage of her feet. But this was a dream, and in the end, she knew she had no choice.

She looked up and sure enough she saw her. Ahead of her in the road, straddling the yellow line as she stumbles forward. Black hair flows down her back, brushes against her pale skin. The girl is naked. Nothing to guard her from the elements, from the cold that begins to seep in from all sides. Nothing to hide the wounds that cover her body.

Bruises blossom around valleys of burning red. Blood and filth cover her from head to toe. Her feet were black and swollen as she fought to stay standing.

Tara caught up to her without even trying, suddenly upon her, traveling through space without moving, the way you do in a dream. She reached out to touch her, knowing her skin would be cold and dead.

She turned her so she could see her face. The eyes that look back were dull and lifeless, devoid of any warmth or life they may have once had.

Tara's fingers brushed the girl's cheek. Her skin rippled against the touch. Her features became muddled as though Tara was mixing wet paint.

A whisper drifted on the breeze. A horrible breathy clicking reminiscent of chattering insects. The sound came from the forest. From the monster that lived among the shadows.

He waited inside, just like he always did. Nested between the trees. Pale faced and bloody lipped. He smiled. An ear-to-ear toothy smile soaked in vibrant red.

The dream is always the same. The sunset, the trees, the painless mutilation of her feet, the girl, and *him*. She didn't know him; didn't even think he was a real person. How could he be? Real people don't look like that. Glossy black eyes and a mouth of razor-sharp teeth, more animal than man, more monster than anything.

Tara picked up her phone and typed out a text to Olivia. The only person she felt comfortable enough to talk to about things like this.

Olivia was a big believer in dream analysis. She thought if you looked deep enough into the details of someone's dream you could find meaning behind it, traumas so deep in your subconscious you didn't even realize you had them.

Before Tara sent the message, she realized something. The dream was not the same as it always had been. Something was different this time. The girl. Until now she'd never recognized her.

Her face was always blurred, smooth, devoid of detail. A lump of clay only half sculpted.

This time she saw her. The curve of her nose and the blush of her cheeks. Green eyes and dark painted lips. Rebecca.

Rebecca was Olivia's neighbor. Neighbor is a strange word for it because in Aldridge your nearest neighbor could be a few miles down the road. Rebecca was a year behind Tara in school. A junior while she and Olivia were seniors.

Rebecca would have graduated the year before, but she'd been held back a couple times for her truancy record.

What did it mean that after weeks of these dreams she'd seen Rebecca? Had it been Rebecca the entire time? Had she always seen her face and just not realized until now? Had she-

She shook herself. She was overreacting. It was just a nightmare. Seeing Rebecca didn't mean anything. Her subconscious filling in the blanks with a familiar face.

Tara looked at the clock. 12:01. It was late and she was so tired. She didn't feel like getting into what the dream may mean or what feeling it was trying to make her realize. At the moment the only feeling she sensed was fear. A low rumble deep in her gut. A pulsing sense that something was very wrong.
She laid her head on her pillow and tried to fall back asleep, hoping the dream had shown itself for the last time.

THREE

Tara – Now

I come home to an empty apartment. Not empty in the sense that there's nothing inside, empty in the way that no one else is living there. Living alone is a recent development in life. Brought on by my own actions- or so I'm told.

Sam moved out three weeks ago. Right around the time the nightmares started up again.

I wasn't sleeping. When I tried, I'd wake up screaming.

Sam tried to talk to me about it. Tried to get me to confide in them. Tried to get me to spill every part of me so they could pick me apart and make a diagnosis. The same thing the doctors and shrinks had been doing to me since I was a teenager.

Not talking about the nightmares turned into not talking about anything. Every time we did talk it would loop back to me needing to see someone. Me needing to be examined. Prodded. Poked with a stick like roadkill to see if there was any life left in me.

I refused to talk to anyone about it. I told Sam it would get better. It was just stress. The nightmares would stop sooner or later.

I knew they wouldn't. They didn't. They got worse. Now I live alone.

I open the fridge to find it empty- a door full of long expired condiments and a single beer from a six pack with the ring still attached to the top. I have a bag of chips, the beer, and two cigarettes for lunch. A third cigarette for dessert.

My head is pounding, an out of nowhere migraine presses against the back of my eyes. I draw the curtains, shroud the room in dark. I lay down in bed and grab Sam's pillow. Their scent still clings to it. I squeeze it to my chest, breathing them in as I drift off to sleep.

The wind is cold, storm clouds bruise the sky, a seething black mass blotting out the sun. I'm sitting in the middle of the road, pavement cold against my skin. No one around. Trees and silence on all sides. The forest doesn't speak, birdsong and the humming of insects a distant memory.

I'm surrounded by dark. No streetlights this far outside town, no anything. I can smell the storm in the air. An electric scent. Burning wire mixed with the harsh smell of damp earth.

Down the road someone's light flicks on. A lone square of warmth shining against the night. Someone is standing in the window, a silhouette framed in night.

I hear a voice, a whisper from the far edge of the universe, calling, beckoning.

I stand outside the window. Gravel crunches beneath my feet as I try to see inside. My breath fogs the glass. I wipe it away and I see her. Olivia, as beautiful as the day she died. My heart stops, equal parts fear and excitement. She's on the couch in the living room. She stares at the TV. The picture nothing but static.

Overhead I hear footsteps. The familiar tread of someone descending the stairs. The subtle groan of floorboards. He's behind her now, hands on her shoulders. His fingers start to move, kneading her flesh. His hands dig beneath her skin, mend to bone and muscle. They become one, a horrid ballet of meat. She remains still. Not a twitch, not a sound.

The TV flickers. Static replaced by color. Olivia as a little girl, staring into the camera. Her eyes are black, unmoving and devoid of light. Static. The picture changes. Olivia in her backyard, staring into the woods. Her mother calls her, she doesn't hear. Olivia nods to the trees, agrees to some unspoken command. Static. Olivia walks down the street, two other girls walk beside her, one on each side. Best friends. Inseparable. They shared every secret. Even those they wish they hadn't. Even those that would tear them apart.

The images begin to flicker, burn away. A hole opens in Olivia's chest, smolders towards the edge of the frame. The air is strong with the scent of burning plastic, something deeper, rust and spoiled meat.

The man is gone now. His presence still lingers, hangs over the house. Smothers the light, poisons the air. I close my eyes, breathe through the tightness in my chest. None of this is real. It can't be. But it is. As real now as it has always been.

Olivia stands in the living room doorway when I look back. She stares at me through the glass. Her eyes go black. Her hand shoots towards me, finger raised. Blaming. Accusing. Her head rolls back. She screams but no sound leaves her lips.

I feel my pulse in my fingertips, numbness in my heaving chest.

Olivia starts to rise, heels lifting until she balances on her toes like a ballerina.

The living room is gone. Tall, dark trees stand in place of the furniture.

She keeps climbing, feet leaving the floor until she's floating. Her hand drops, body going slack. She unravels. Agony etched on her face as she is deconstructed. Skin peels away to reveal deep red muscle, dark and twitching. Muscle pulls from bone, organs turn to mush, her brain a puddle in her skull, leaking from burst eyes.

I slam my fist against the window. I scream at the top of my lungs, but no sound escapes I am helpless, forced to watch as she is stripped away, bit by bit until not even her skeleton remains.

I turn away. I don't want to see Olivia's unmaking. I don't need a reminder of what I've lost. A reminder of the fear and pain she must have felt.

I hug my legs to my chest, rock back and forth on the ground as I do my best to breath. I am a child again, terrified of the monsters that hide in the dark. I feel a hand on my shoulder, a calm caring touch. I look up into the eyes of my mother.

She wears a freshly laundered police uniform. *Aldridge Police* embroidered on a patch on her shoulder.

Her bright blue eyes look into my own.

The tremble in my hands begins to lessen

My mother smiles at me. Her presence brings me warmth.

I reach for her. Throw myself into her arms and squeeze her so tight I think I might be suffocating her.

She rests her chin on top of my head, strokes my hair with a gentle hand. "It's up to you now."

The statement confuses me. After all this time, is that really all he she had to say? What did she even mean?

I want to look at her. Ask her what she meant. Berate her for-for what? Because that's how I respond when I don't understand something. When I get overwhelmed. I resort to anger.

I can't look at my mother. Can't ask her any questions or scream my disappointment. She is gone. Disappeared as quickly as she arrived.

I look out to the trees. A familiar silence envelops me. A shroud of uncanny calm shrouds the forest.

He is there. I haven't seen him in over a decade, since the summer all those years ago when my life collapsed in on itself. He stands among the trees. A vile grin stretched from ear to ear. A ghostly pale face with a seething red smile.

-

I wake up screaming, coated in sweat despite the cold. My eyes search the dark around me, scan every corner, every shadow knowing that I'll see that face. A pale orb floating in the darkness. Black eyes piercing my skin, worming their way through my body until they reach down to my very soul.

I open the drawer of my nightstand, pull out a picture. The same one from the dream. Olivia walking down the street, hand in hand with Alicia and myself. Three girls who promised to be friends forever. Three girls who got in way over their heads.

My phone vibrates on my nightstand. My heart almost leaps from my chest at the sudden sound. The screen shows an 802 are code. Vermont. Someone from home.

I answer the phone, my voice quivering. "Hello?"

"Hello? Is this Tara? Tara Hale?"

The voice seems familiar. Someone I've met. Someone whose voice I've heard thousands of times, but I couldn't place them. Couldn't match the voice to a name or a face.

"Yes. This is Tara. Who's this?"

"Hi Tara. I'm not sure if you remember me. It's been a long time since we've seen each other. My name is Spencer Morris. I'm the Chief of Police in Aldridge, Vermont."

"Uncle Spencer?" My pulse is arhythmic. My heart simultaneously stopping and beating out of control.

"Hey, Kiddo."

"Hi. Why are you calling? Sorry, I don't mean to be rude but- It's just been so long."

"I know it has. And I'm sorry to have to call you under these circumstances-"

Everything snaps into place. The dream. A late-night call from my mom's old partner. "Did something happen to mom?"

"I'm afraid so. I found her this morning. I would have called sooner but I had a hard time tracking you down."

"Found her? You mean she's-"

"Yes, Tara. I'm sorry to have to tell you this, but your mother has passed."

I hang up the phone. The world goes quiet. A buzzing fills my ears, crescendos into a high-pitched whine. My skin prickles. I stare into the shadows of my room, overcome with the sense of being watched. I press myself into the corner, pull the blanket up to my chin. I stay that way until morning.

*"I feel time passing by, pulling humanity through its paces, inching us ever
closer to desolation. I feel him watching. Waiting. Drool dripping from ruby
red lips as he anticipates our inevitable end."*

FOUR

Tara - Now

I remember Aldridge in snapshots. Faded polaroids, desaturated
and overexposed. Blurred imperfect edges.

I have a hard time making sense of the pictures as I drive the
105 towards town. Some flame had burned holes through the
delicate cellophane, scorch marks on my memories of the place.

I didn't know how long I'd been driving. Miles and minutes
disappeared out here, insignificant when viewed against the
massive scale of the forest.

Aldridge had always been this way. No matter which way you
looked, trees blocked the horizon. The town was trapped. An
imperceptible speck among endless acres of pine.

The sign flashes by, dented and scratched, WELCOME TO
ALDRIDGE, VERMONT. It reads like a threat, a warning, pass
this sign and there's no turning back.

I drive on. Clouds begin the shift in my mind. I'm shown
glimpses, fragments of a whole I can't yet comprehend. I tell myself
I want to remember, but I can't convince myself I mean it. Still,
something stirs. A memory of my mother. A farm in the back end
of nowhere where some unspeakable thing occurred.

Fear swelled in my chest, squeezed, pins and needles spreading to
my fingertips. I keep driving. Turn after turn, taking me farther
into my past. The remains of a town I never really left. Decades
old regrets. Words and actions I wished I could take back. A girl's
regrets, so far removed from the woman I was now.

I broke through the tree line onto Main Street. The same as it
was fifteen years ago. A town stuck in time, left behind by a world
with no place and no sympathy for it.

If you didn't know any better, you might have thought Aldridge
was pulled straight off a postcard (One of the overpriced ones you
could buy at the rest stops along the interstate.) Cars bumbled

through the streets on their way to work. Cozy houses nestled between the trees. A big white church in the center, crowned with a golden cross.

Main street sang with life. A haven. An oasis among the trees. Happy people, good neighbors, smiling kids. A ruse. A mask to cover up reality.

I drove straight through until town proper faded into the outskirts. The real Aldridge. Shining store fronts and smiling commuters replaced by empty fields of broken liquor bottles and cow shit. Rust eaten trailers with peeled paint. Stores and farmstands boarded up and collapsed.

Hidden among the trees across town was the old lumber mill, silhouetted against the melted sherbet sky. A sad structure. Eerie streaks of rust-red smeared down corrugated metal. Triple smokestacks shot above the tree line. 'Aldridge Lumber' ran down the length of the tallest tower in faded white paint. You could read the tower from anywhere in town. A constant reminder to everyone of what they no longer had.

The mill went belly up in April of '97. Open one day, closed the next. The state passed some bill to regulate heavy timber cutting. Smaller mills like the one in Aldridge turned defunct. A thousand people out of a job. Between 1997 and 1999, the town's population shrunk from nine thousand to just shy of five. People who had spent their lives in Aldridge, given forty years to the mill, dropped in the gutter, no severance, no thank you for your time, no nothing. Still the mill sat up on its ridge. Silent. Observing.

The people left in town fell into two categories. The mansion dwellers down on main street, old money and powerful connections, and normal people, too old or too afraid to move away. Retirees and veterans, living of social security checks. Parents and families, too poor to do anything but pull themselves up by their bootstraps and get over it.

Olivia moved to town in the summer of '04.

I was going into freshman year, all bones, loose-jointed and gangly, no real curves to speak of. Not like the senior girls, plump pouting lips and rounded hips, swaying back and forth as they walked like a greyhound with hip dysplasia.

Olivia lived in the outskirts with her mom and stepdad. A double wide trailer, powder blue with a red door.

Olivia's mom was from town, way back in its heyday. When the mill still ran. People coming instead of going.

My mom and Olivia's mom were friends in high school. They both took separate paths in life.

Olivia's mom moved away after she got married. Things didn't work out. She met her current husband on a summer trip to Cape Cod. His name was Curtis, everyone called him Dr. Drescher. They bought a cabin on Lake Champlain, about two hours west of town.

My mother moved to New York when she was eighteen, searching for a place as far removed from Aldridge as possible. She found a shitty apartment in Brooklyn. She met my father at a party. I was born nine months later.

Given the paths our mothers took in life, Olivia and I never should have met. In any other world we would have grown up hundreds of miles apart, unaware the other existed. But as fate would have it, both of our families ended up back in Aldridge. A black hole no one ever really escapes.

Olivia was the first girl I ever saw with a nose ring. She had a hard time, like all kids moving to a small town. She was different from the other kids. Not in a cliche teen romcom kind of way where she, 'wasn't like other girls.' She *was* like other girls. She wanted to be treated with kindness and respect, but for some reason no one ever did that for her.

I pulled off to a gas station. The only structure still standing on this stretch of road. The pumps were too old to take a credit card. I gathered some crumpled bills from my center console and headed across the cracked parking lot.

The bell over the door clanged as I stepped inside, no one at the counter. I peruse the shelves, scoff at the miniature snow globes, a bright red barn trapped in a cheap plastic dome, I heart Aldridge written proudly on the base.

I grabbed a bottle of Advil, walked to the counter.

The cashier entered through the back door, a skeleton in a living man's skin, surprised to find someone had entered his store. "Hello there Miss. Anything, I can help you with."

I slid the pills onto the counter, "Twenty on pump two and a pack of cancer sticks."

He turned to grab the cigarettes from the shelf. I swipe two nips of Jack Daniels from the counter, slip them in my purse.

He turns back, places a pack of Newport's on the counter. "Driver's license."

"Excuse me?"

"For the cigarettes. Store policy."

I reluctantly pull my license from my purse, hand it to him. Figures, in town less than ten minutes and people will already know I'm back.

"Tara Hale." He reads my name off the license like it's a question, studies the picture, compares it to my face. "You wouldn't have any relation to Beth Hale, would you?"

"She's my mother."

"No kiddin'. So, your little Tara all grown up. Your mother was a good woman. I was sorry to hear about her passing."

"Me too."

<u>FIVE</u>

Beth Hale - Thursday, June 12th, 2008, 7:00am

Mud sucked at Beth's tires as she navigated the lonesome stretch of road that led to the Baumann farm.

Ray Baumann was a volatile man with a love for self-medication and hatred for people. He'd had the police called on him before, many times, but this was the first time she could remember a call concerning his well-being.

The farm came into view as they broke through the tree line. Farm wasn't the right word for it. A run-down ranch home and a dilapidated barn. A screened in porch had turned into a collection place for broken furniture and appliances. The screen hung off the frame in the corners where the staples had crumbled away, taken by rust. The rest of the house was no better. Patches of shingles were missing from the roof. Any trace of paint had long since worn away, leaving the wooden siding grey and weathered.

Her eyes scanned the house before moving across the property. The property was big. A couple of acres of field that hadn't been planted since God knows when. The grass was sad and discolored, a grey to match the storm that lurked on the horizon.

The only color left in this place was the green of the forest, but here, even the vibrance of neverending pines was dull and washed out.

Beneath the trees the river flowed, weaving through the woods on its way to wherever it was headed.
"That him?"

Spencer's question snapped Beth back to reality. She followed his gaze to the front porch were a man sat alone in a rocking chair. "Looks like it."

They pulled up in front of the house and stepped out of the truck.

Ray was barefoot, nothing but a ragged grey bathrobe barely tied in the front. He looked tired, hollow cheeks and grey skin.

Grey like all the things that surrounded him. A grey man in grey house on a grey field under a grey sky.

He sat with his eyes closed and his head back, he mumbled to himself, words to quiet to hear.

"Everything alright Ray?" asked Spencer.

His eyes eased open. He tilted his head forward and looked at Beth and Spencer, a look of puzzled wonderment in his eye, as if seeing other people for the first time. "I knew you'd come. Saw you in my dream."

"We got a call," said Beth. "Neighbors said they hadn't seen you in a few days. Asked us to check on you."

"In my dream you were a messenger. A horseman come to announce the beginning of the end." Ray's eyes flicked beneath half closed lids. "Horrible, horrible dreams."

"You been drinking, Ray?"

Ray's gaze slithered like a serpent, like *the* serpent. The snake in the garden who tempted Eve into the original sin. There was something about those eyes, a dark, otherworldly light somewhere deep in their center. "They watch me. Stare at me from the trees through my windows. But something about them ain't right. It's their eyes. Huge black eyes. Eyes with dying stars inside 'em. I used to think they were just dreams. But I know the truth now."

"And what's the truth?" asked Spencer.

"I heard the screams of those dying stars." Ray seemed on the edge of a breakdown. Whether he was laughing or crying was impossible to say. "They spoke, and I heard their song."

Beth scanned Ray from head to toe. His body hung loose in his chair. His pupils two black saucers that swallowed up all the light. Whatever Ray had gotten himself into this time, it was something a hell of a lot stronger than his usual diet of bottom shelf whiskey.

"I took her. I didn't want too, but they made me."

Beth tried to swallow, but all of the moisture had been sapped from her mouth. The unease in her gut descended towards panic. "What do you mean you took her? Did you do something Ray?"

"What we do means nothing. There is no free will. There is no consequence."

"Enough with the fucking riddles, Ray," said Spencer. "You said you took her. What do you mean by that?"

"She's out in the barn. All torn apart. I didn't even know until I woke up."

Beth looked to Spencer. A shared sense of dread enveloped them.

She clicked on her radio and called the station. 'This is car two-three-seven requesting additional units at sixty-five River Street North. We have a possible crime scene. Over"

"*Affirmative two-three-seven sending additional units your way. Over.*"

"Stay with him," said Beth, drawing her gun. "I'm gonna look around."

"Alright. Be careful."

Beth nodded her confirmation and started towards the backyard.

Before she could round the corner, Ray's head lolled around on his neck. The blackholes of his eyes were on her. She waited him for him to speak. Babble some cryptic riddle or speak a new nightmare into existence. But he remained silent, and that was somehow worse, the bottomless depths of his eyes gazing at something deep within her soul.

She made her way down the side of the house forcing her way past the heft of overgrown grass. She rounded the back porch into the yard.

The stretch of land between the back porch and the barn was littered with chewed dog toys and piles of rotted wood. Describing the yard as unkempt was a massive understatement. Everything rusted and decayed.

A tractor sat on blocks behind the barn, a crusted orange shell of its former self, tires long since disintegrated. A set of lawn chairs rested against a fence, tied to the chain-link by the overgrown bushes that weaved through the cheap plastic.

The state of the yard made Beth think of the old zombie movies Tara and her used to watch- when she was still at an age when she enjoyed spending time with her mother.

On the edge of the property the Missisquoi River flowed beneath the summer trees. Her eye was drawn to the sky over the water. Only it wasn't really the sky, more like a patch. A patch of air over that water unlike everything else around it. A faint glimmer of light, waves of rainbow color like shimmering oil. Reds and blues and greens. Other colors as well. Colors she must have known but couldn't identify. The open air over the water danced. Undulating ripples of distortion like heat haze off a parking lot. Those colors permeated the waves, dripping upwards towards the sky in long gossamer strands.

What was this? A trick of the light? Some kind of rainbow she hadn't heard of? The weather around here was known to do strange things, especially before a storm.

She continued across the yard, stepped around rotted boards and rusted nails until she came to the barn. Her foot sunk into a patch of mud on the ground. She examined it to find the mud had an oil like sheen, not dissimilar to the strange rainbow she'd observed over the river.

She pulled her foot from the mud and swung open the barn down. She swung her flashlight around the barn, checking the shadows for- she wasn't sure. Why had she come back here? Because Ray said he'd taken a girl. said he'd done something to her. But Ray was so high he could barely move. What he said meant nothing. More nonsense about dreams and dying stars.

She wanted to stop. Turn off her light and walk away. Nothing to see here. Everything in order. The call was for a welfare check on Ray. They'd checked him, and while he wasn't exactly well, he was alive, if only barely. Yet, something inside her told her she needed to look around, screamed louder than the voice of protest she tried so hard to comply with.

She entered the barn. A sharp, sour smell filled her nose. She gagged on the thickness of the air. She knew that smell, and her stomach dropped into her feet.

She's out in the barn. All torn apart. Ray's words echoed in her mind.

He'd done something. Something unspeakable. Something she had to set her eyes upon because that was her job.

She searched the barn, shining her flashlight in slow wide arcs until she found the source of the smell. For a moment she couldn't tell what she was looking at. Some colorful mass: orange and pink and red and grey. The shapes and formations of the mass shined with a thick wetness as if smothered in Vaseline. Her stomach boiled and she doubled over, regurgitating her breakfast into the dirt.

www.ingramcontent.com/pod-product-compliance
Lightning Source LLC
Chambersburg PA
CBHW032354310726

48973CB00007B/2002